SCREWBALL

A sports romantic comedy

EVA HAINING

Cardinal Knights Publishing LLC

Copyright

Also by Eva Haining

MANHATTAN KNIGHTS SERIES

FLAWLESS

RELENTLESS

ENDLESS

COMPLETE MANHATTAN KNIGHTS SERIES BOX SET

MUSTANG RANCH SERIES

MUSTANG DADDY

MUSTANG BUCK

MUSTANG HOLLYWOOD

MUSTANG RANCH BOOKS 1-3 BOX SET

MUSTANG CHRISTMAS

MUSTANG BELLE

HALL OF FAME SERIES

FUMBLE

A VERY FUMBLING MERRY CHRISTMAS

INTERCEPTION

SCREWBALL

STRIKE ZONE

STANDALONES

WILD RUGGED DADDY

A CHRISTMAS TO REMEMBER

THE CARDINAL BROTHERHOOD (EVA HAINING WRITING AS E.L.HAINING)

THE CARDINAL BROTHERHOOD BOOKS 1&2 BOX SET

LUXURE

KADEDUS

GIER

About the Author

I'm happiest when wandering through the uncharted territory of my imagination. You'll find me curled up with my laptop, browsing the books at the local library or enjoying the smell of a new book, taking great delight in cracking the spine and writing in the margins!

Eva is a native Scot but lives in Texas with her husband, two kids, and a whizzy little fur baby with the most ridiculous ears. She first fell in love with British literature while majoring in Linguistics, 17th Century Poetry, and Shakespeare at University. She is an avid reader and lifelong notebook hoarder. In 2014, she finally put her extensive collection to good use and started writing her first novel. Previously published with Prism Heart Press under a pen name, Eva decided to branch out on her own and lend her name to her full back catalog! She is currently working on some exciting new projects.

Prologue

WE'RE GOING to the World Series. I can't believe it! The stadium is jam-packed and lost in the moment. Their cheers are deafening as they celebrate with thunderous applause. I've been waiting my whole career for this moment, and the fact that it came down to the final inning and that one last pitch—the most important of my career to date—is mind-blowing.

My teammates tackle me to the ground, shouting my name.

"Wrong sport, guys, you're not supposed to take me down like a star quarterback." I'm not going to lie, it's an ego boost to hear everyone shouting my name, but these guys are dangerously close to tackling my tackle, and if there's one thing I love more than base-ball, it's my cock.

This is the moment, the one I've been dreaming about my whole life. My mom always tells anyone who'll listen that I came out of the womb with a baseball and glove. It's not that farfetched— I think I was six months old when she bought me my first mitt.

I came to the Yankees at the beginning of this season, and what a debut. The endorsement offers will be coming in left and right after tonight's performance. As a pitcher, you dream of throwing the ball that ends the game in your team's favor, but that idea pales in comparison to the real deal. Tonight, I'm going to celebrate in style —with wine, women, and song, as the saying goes. A more apt summation of my evening is booze, breasts, and banging—the three B's of any major league baseball player.

Chapter One

ANDERS

"DID I miss the memo that you became Santa-fucking-Claus?" I thought Coach would give me some kudos this week for helping get the team to the World Series, but with game one looming and my stock going up, he's pissed about something. It's never a good sign when you get pulled into his office. I've learned this in the short time I've been here.

"What?"

"Apparently, all the mail that goes to the North Pole came here instead with your name on it. Fucking fangirls."

"Is fan mail even a thing?" Women hit me up all the time, telling me I can bed them if I want. Who the hell does that shit? They could be a stalker or a black widow.

I prefer to do it the old-fashioned way—go to a bar and hit on a woman who gets my junk stiff.

Coach dumps a ton of letters in my lap. "What the fuck do you want me to do with these?"

"Get them out of my damn office."

"Sure thing, Coach." I gather the odd-smelling letters into a pile and head out the door. Why the fuck does this shit smell like perfume? And cheap perfume at that. There's no way I'm reading all these, so the second I get into the locker room, I throw them in the trash.

"What've we got here?" My teammate and wingman, Linc, reaches in and pulls out an envelope covered with lipstick kisses. For fuck's sake—it's like Valentine's Day in the third grade all over again.

I swipe the letter from his hand and put it back in the trash can. "Nothing."

"I beg to differ. Looky here, boys, Anders has got himself a fan club." Now, all eyes are on me. He tears it open.

"Give it here. You aren't reading that shit."

"These ladies put their heart and soul into the most archaic booty call in history, and you won't even hear them out? That's cold, bro. Those carrier pigeons have been getting a workout on your behalf."

"Yeah, yeah. I'm all for getting down at a club or in a hotel, but this is just weird."

"Yep. So, let's see just how freaky these girls are willing to get. If there's anything kinky, I might have to use their number myself. Sure, I'd be sloppy seconds to the man of the hour, the indomitable Anders Verbeck, but baseball cock is baseball cock."

"Have at them. I'm not interested." Just as I say it, his eyes go wide as saucers, and he descends into a fit of laughter.

"Holy shit! This girl added a photo." He holds it up, looking at it upside down before shoving it in my face. "What body part is this? I can't even tell. If they're going to include a picture, it should be of the standard stuff. Easily identified fun sacks."

"I think they call it vajazzling. And the only thing more disturbing to me is that you said the words *fun sacks*. Also, you clearly need some pointers on the female anatomy. If you can't tell this is a blinged-out pussy, I worry for the women you're sleeping with."

He grabs it back, taking another look. "I'm phenomenal with the anatomy of a woman, so there's no cause for concern, but Jesus Christ, why would she want fucking rhinestones on there? It would shred my dick."

"It's not your junk she's looking to shred." He tosses the snapshot into the trash and starts reading the letter, faking a disturbing female voice.

"Dear Anders, you're so hot. I want to suck on your big, hard…" I grab it out of his hand as the rest of the guys in the locker room start laughing.

"And we've heard enough of that. You guys shower with me all the time, so you already know I'm blessed in the…"

"Small dick department." Linc thinks he's hilarious, as does everyone else in here, apparently.

"Jealousy is a terrible thing, my friend. Just because my dick and I are a hot commodity doesn't mean you need to be hating on the D. Are you insecure about your little wiener?"

He rolls his eyes and drops his towel, letting the entire locker room get an eyeful of his junk. "Come on now, I defy any one of you to say your dick is bigger than mine. It's spectacular."

Coach appears from his office with his head in his hands. "Put it away, Linc. It ain't that special. I don't need to be watching you wave that thing in the breeze. They don't pay me enough for the therapy I require now. So, get out of here. We've got a World Series to win. No partying, no booze, and no orgies. I feel the need to point out that last one with you guys. That alone is disturbing."

Linc is standing, cupping his junk as we get told off like teenage horndogs, and the second Coach disappears out the door, he reaches for his towel.

"Did your cock just shrivel and die?" I can't help but laugh. "This is what happens when you give me shit, bro. Karma is a beautiful bitch."

"All right, golden boy, but you're under the same restrictions as the rest of us. It doesn't matter that you're getting snail mail from desperate women. No sex for you."

"You don't actually adhere to that, do you? If I'm horny, I'll have sex. It's relaxing."

"*If* you're horny? That implies there are moments in your day when you're *not* horny."

"True. What is it they say? Men think about sex at least nineteen times a day. I think it's bullshit, and I think about it way more than that."

"I'm pretty sure if you look up horndog gigolo in the encyclopedia, there's a picture of you right there next to the definition."

"Fuck yeah!" he says as he heads for his locker. "Was that supposed to be a burn? I take it as a compliment."

"Of course, you do."

"Are you seriously not going to read some of those letters?"

"Why would I? It's not like I'm going to hook up with a woman who sends me a picture of her vagina. It's fucking weird. I think I'll stick to my tried and tested moves."

"And what are they?"

"I walk into a club or a bar, and I'm just Anders Verbeck. That's enough! I'm the starting pitcher for the Yankees, for God's sake, and I'm blessed with this face." I'm winding him up now, but it's so easy.

"Fuck me. Do you give yourself blow jobs? You seem to be in love with yourself, oh mighty one."

"I just threw up in my mouth a little."

"Better than a mouthful of jizz."

"What the fuck? Why would you say that shit to me? The only thing I want a mouthful of is a great rack. You up for a little bar action tonight?"

"If Coach sees us tearing up the town, we'll never hear the end of it."

"I know just the place. The owner is discreet, and there are no pictures allowed, especially in the VIP section. Come on. We're about to give our all to win this thing, and one night isn't going to ruin our chances."

"I like the way you think, Beck."

"Cool. I'll pick you up tonight."

"I'm not your date for prom, bro. Just tell me where to meet you."

"You're such a douche sometimes," I say while trying to stifle a laugh. "Viper. Eight o'clock."

THIS PLACE IS BANGING. IT'S ONE OF MY FAVORITE HAUNTS SINCE I moved to New York and the Yankees. I love everything about Manhattan. It's just a really cool place to live and work. I've been to Viper once or twice before, so I knew it would be perfect for an incognito night of drinking and debauchery before we have to double down on training.

I called ahead and arranged to have the VIP lounge ready and waiting for us. The owner, Carter, said they have another party in tonight, but he didn't think it would be a problem. When he told me why, I just about jumped for joy. The women's USA baseball team is the other party. Some of those girls are hot as hell, and when a woman can talk baseball—forget about dirty talk, that shit gets me hard as a rock.

Linc is already in the thick of it when I arrive. He's got at least three women ready to drop to their knees for him, but one woman is sitting at the far end of the bar, and I'm pretty sure I recognize her. She's cute, but if memory serves, she's a real ballbuster.

I tap Linc on the shoulder, letting him know I'm here. He doesn't take his eyes off this one little blonde who's hanging on his every word. I head toward the end of the bar and the sassy brunette.

I take a seat on the barstool next to her. "Brooke, right?"

She turns and stares at me like I've sprouted a second head. "Not interested." She doesn't even lift her gaze to look at me.

I signal to the bartender. "I'll have a glass of your best whiskey on the rocks and whatever the lady is drinking."

Now I have her attention. "I said I'm not int…" Her words trail off as she turns to face me.

"One drink. If I drink alone, I won't enjoy it as much."

"Anders Verbeck."

"The one and only. I suppose that's not strictly true. My dad and grandfather have the same name." Why did I just say that?

"Wow. Does that usually work on the ladies? Announcing that you're Anders Verbeck the third." She plays with her straw, stirring whatever fruity drink she's been nursing alone.

"When you say it like that, I sound like a douchebag."

"When it walks like a duck and quacks like a duck."

"You like to fuck? That's where you were going with that sentence." I give her my best, panty-melting smile.

"Not even close." She just sounds pissed off. I'm not used to this reaction.

"Have I done something to offend you in the past that I'm not aware of?"

"That would be difficult. You haven't met me before."

"I know who you are. We run in the same circles. We must've been at an event together at some point in the past year."

"Are you that much of a manwhore? You think knowing my name means you've slept with me before and didn't remember, don't you? Trust me, if you'd had sex with me, you'd remember it."

"I bet I would, but that's not what I meant."

"Of course, you did. You're Anders Verbeck. I bet you flash that smile of yours, and women fall over themselves to have a tumble in the sheets with you. Am I wrong?" I don't think there's a good answer to that question. Avoidance is the best option.

"Brooke Lexington, shortstop and top batter for the USA women's team."

"Bingo. Give the man a prize. He knows my name."

"Of course, I know your name. You've been crushing it this season. Your stats are seriously impressive."

"I know."

"So, confidence isn't an issue for you, I see."

"I'm good, and I am not going to hide it because guys find it intimidating. You clearly don't hide your light under a bushel. Why should I?" Shit, this girl is fierce.

"I dig it. You're shit-hot. Own it."

"Thanks for your permission."

"Fuck me, what's got your panties in a wad tonight?" She rolls her eyes.

"Look, Anders. I'm sure you're a good time in the sack, and under normal circumstances, I'd be on you like white on rice, but I'm not in the mood tonight. I just want to have a few drinks and stay here long enough that the girls don't give me shit for ducking out on them."

"Message received loud and clear. I'd still like to buy you that drink. Maybe even have a few laughs."

"There's no way you're out on the town and planning to go home alone. You don't have to waste your time talking to me when I'm PMS-ing. I'm sure any one of my teammates would be more than happy to warm your bed for the night."

When the bartender sets our drinks down, I push Brooke's in front of her. "I can hang with you for a while if you don't mind?"

"Sure, but just know that you're not getting lucky. So, if that's your goal for the evening, keep on moving, pitcher."

"I'm good, thanks. You don't need to worry about my junk. You're so warm and inviting, why wouldn't I want to forfeit some hot and dirty sex for your sparkling conversation?" She cracks a smile, finally.

"Women just lap you up, right?"

"Why would you say that?"

"Don't do the modesty thing. It doesn't suit you."

"Fine. Yes, any other woman in here would already be finding a dark corner to have her wicked way with me. You, though, seem to be impervious to my charms." Unfortunately, my cock didn't get the memo. I'm rocking a semi just watching the way she wraps that sassy mouth of hers around her straw. That's one lucky straw.

"I hate to bruise your ego, but… actually, I don't hate it. I'm sure your ego is just fine without me stroking it for you. You're hot. You know it. I don't need to point it out."

"Well, okay then."

"I'm sorry. You're catching me on an off day. Apparently, I'm channeling my inner bitch tonight."

"Want to talk about it?"

"Not really."

"Want to drink about it?" I signal the bartender for another round.

"Now, that's a plan I can get behind. But you have to promise me that if I get stupid drunk, you won't let me take you home."

"Fuck, that's a big ask. I'm good with you shooting me down, but then if you start giving me the bedroom eyes and grinding on me, I'm not sure I'll be able to resist. You're hot if you hadn't noticed."

"I know. And you're ridiculously gorgeous, so if I get drunk, I'm going to stop caring about the bad decisions." I don't understand this woman at all.

"I feel like you might be well on the road to drunk already. Why would I be a bad decision? Maybe it would be a great decision to ride all this hotness."

"I'll tell you, but only if you promise not to come home with me." She grabs her drink and starts chugging it.

"I promise. Scout's honor, but let it be on the record that I'm all for the questionable decisions of hot women."

"Guys don't like dating an accomplished female athlete."

"Really? I don't believe that." She clutches my chin and leans in as if she's about to tell me the biggest secret.

"It's intimidating. They like it at first because I keep in shape, and I don't have an ugly face. But when they realize I'm their equal, or shock horror… more successful than they are in their given profession, they flip out and do stupid shit." Her words are getting a little slurred now.

"How many drinks did you have before I came in?" She's definitely tipsy at this point.

"A few."

"Okay, so here's my two cents. Any guy who's intimidated by the fact that you're amazing at what you do doesn't deserve a second thought. You're kickass. I've been following the USA team this year. You're the fucking star player. If the guys you date don't see that, then you're dating the wrong guys."

I'm not prepared when she grabs my face and pulls me in for a kiss. As much as I'd like to show her a good time, my brotherly instinct kicks in. If my little sister were in this drunken state, I'd want someone to make sure she's okay and doesn't get taken advantage of.

Fuck.

I force myself to pull away, a single kiss causing a visceral reaction throughout every cell in my body. "You just made me promise not to go home with you. You can't kiss me like that."

"But you're so pretty."

"I'm a guy, I am not pretty. I'm manly and rugged."

"I think if you have to say you're rugged, it's probably not true." She giggles to herself, and then her expression changes on a dime. Her eyes go wide, and I realize what's about to happen just a fraction too late.

If only I could side-step the projectile vomit as fast as I can pitch a curveball. I suppose I should be grateful she didn't blow chunks when her lips were locked with mine only seconds ago. I fucking hate puke. I'm the guy who can see all kinds of blood and gore and bone breaks on the field that would make a grown man weep, but when it comes to vomit, I'm the biggest pussy on the planet.

Linc walks up behind me as I attempt to help Brooke while trying to keep my nose as far away from my now-ruined shirt. "Holy shit, bro. You really know how to pick a winner. I'd say *winner, winner, chicken dinner,* but from the look of your shirt, she had some kind of meatballs for dinner."

"Can you stop the one-liners for a second and fucking help me?"

"I'm not getting anywhere near some random girl's puke. No thanks. Nope. Nada. No Bueno. I'll ask the bartender for a blowtorch for your clothes. That's the best you're getting out of me."

"You're a shitty best friend." Brooke is now limp in my arms, and I've resigned myself to the fact that I'm taking her home for all the wrong reasons. I was supposed to be getting laid tonight. That ship has well and truly sailed.

"I bet that vajazzled woman seems pretty appealing right about now."

"Just shut up and order an Uber. I need to take her home."

"Are you serious? You don't even know this girl, and she just covered you in vomit."

"Well, I'm not getting laid smelling like the janky toilets at a gas station. She's not in any fit state to get herself home."

"You're a bigger man than me, bro." He takes out his phone and does as I ask.

"Tell me something I don't know."

"And yet, here I am, about to take home that pretty blonde over there while you escort Lady Pukes A Lot home."

"She's not a stranger, Linc. She's Brooke Lexington."

"Fuck." He takes a look at her face as she rests her head on my shoulder. "She's hot when she's not a hot mess. You should totally hit that after you both shower."

"Sleeping with her is literally the furthest thing from my mind right now. I just want to make sure she gets home safely."

"Good man. Your Uber will be outside in five. I'll say goodbye now because I honestly can't stand the smell of you two for another second."

"Thanks, bro. You're a real gentleman."

He flips me the bird over his shoulder as he heads back to his catch of the evening, leaving me to get Brooke out of here. She's unsteady on her feet, so I scoop her up into my arms. In for a penny, in for a pound. I'm already gross as fuck, so a little extra isn't going to matter now.

The second the Uber driver catches a whiff of us, he's ready to leave, so I give him a hundred bucks not to. I manage to rouse Brooke long enough to get her address before she groans against my chest and apologizes for ruining my night.

"I can't believe I threw up on Anders Verbeck."

"Funny that. I can't believe Brooke Lexington just puked all over me." She gives a half-hearted laugh that obviously pains her.

"Don't make me laugh. My head hurts."

"Relax, girl. I've seen worse. I haven't *smelled* worse, but I've definitely *seen* worse."

Chapter Two

BROOKE

I FEEL like my head is being clobbered with a sledgehammer. My mouth is so dry that my lips are stuck to my teeth and reeks of alcohol and barf. What the fuck did I do last night? I don't even remember getting home.

I'm in my own bed, but the sheets feel different, and it's not until I pry my eyes open that I realize I'm lying on a towel. At least I was cognizant enough to stop myself from ruining the bedding. Catching a whiff of dried-in vomit, I leap from the bed and stumble into the bathroom. Hugging the toilet bowl is such a wonderful way to start the day.

There's nothing worse than retching on an empty stomach. Not that it's particularly pleasant either way, but the dry heaves are agony. It takes me twenty minutes to pick myself up off the floor and put the shower on. I take a look at myself in the mirror, and I'm horrified. Last night's mascara is streaked down the sides of my face, my lipstick is smudged, and my clothes—God, my clothes are nasty. There's no saving these. I peel them off, gagging the entire time, and shove them in the trash rather than the laundry hamper.

I'm never drinking again.

My stomach muscles ache from contracting so much, and my

legs are weak. I step into the shower and feel a fresh wave of nausea, so I sit on the floor and let the warm water do its thing. Washing away the stench of last night, I remember moments—snippets.

Oh shit!

His face is clear as a bell as well as the moment I threw myself at him. Damn, damn, damn. I kissed Anders Verbeck. Thank God I didn't do anything else. At least, I don't think I did. He's the most popular man in baseball right now. If I weren't so drunk, I would've grilled him like any good fangirl and asked him a million questions about his rise to the top of major league baseball.

When I've washed away the grime of last night, I go in search of my favorite sweats. Whenever I'm hungover or overtired, I like this one specific pair of sweats and my team USA jersey. I find the jersey and pull it on, enjoying the comforting smell of my laundry detergent. My sweats are nowhere to be found, so I pad down the hallway to the laundry room.

Even the fabric of my jersey rubbing against my skin is painful right now. Stopping in the kitchen, I grab a bottle of water from the refrigerator and go in search of the aspirin. I accidentally slam one of the cupboard doors, and it reverberates in my brain.

"Can you keep it down to a dull roar?"

What the fuck? I scream at the sound of a deep, booming voice coming from my couch. I reach for a knife in one of the drawers and hold it so tight, my knuckles turn white. My heart is pounding. "I've got a knife! You better get out of here before I call the cops."

I don't have my phone on me, so my best bet is to reach the front door before the intruder.

"It's me, Anders. Verbeck." He pushes himself up off the couch and into my line of sight, half-naked.

"What the hell?" Suddenly, I'm very aware of my lack of pants.

"Can you stop waving that knife in my direction?" His voice has that delicious morning rasp, but my hand is shaking at the shock of him in my living room.

"Why are you here? Why are you half-naked? Did we have sex last night?"

"I brought you home… after you puked on my shirt. Hence, the shirtless thing. And no, we didn't have sex."

"Then why are you still here?"

"A thank you for bringing you home and not letting some douchebag take advantage of you would be nice."

"Thank you." My pulse is racing as I set the knife down on the countertop. "Why didn't you leave?"

"Because I was worried you might choke on your own vomit. I put my shirt in your washing machine because the smell was making me want to barf. It's in the dryer right now, and as soon as it's ready, I'll get out of your way." He shoves his hands in his pockets, his gaze dropping to the floor.

"I'm so sorry. I didn't mean to ruin your night or your shirt."

"No harm, no foul, as long as you don't stab me."

"Sure. Just let me go and put some pants on, and I'll buy you breakfast." The second I say it, my stomach protests. "Maybe we can start with coffee. I may never eat again… or drink."

His eyes rake the length of me, and my stomach somersaults for an entirely different reason. Damn, he's hot—and his abs—come to mama.

"Are you going to stand there and stare at me, or are you going to put some pants on? I'm fine either way." He flashes me a wicked grin, and I contemplate just leaving my pants off. If I wasn't utterly mortified by last night, I'd mount him right here, right now.

I scurry off to grab my sweats from the pile of fresh laundry and get Anders' shirt out of the dryer. When my ass is no longer hanging in the breeze, I return to the living room and reluctantly hand over his shirt.

"Can I get you some coffee? I promise I won't spill it on you or projectile vomit all over you."

"Yeah. Black, one sugar." He shrugs his shirt on, and I'm practically salivating at the sight of him. What is it about an open shirt that's so damn sexy?

I busy myself with the coffee maker and avoid eye contact.

"So, why were you so drunk last night?"

"Do I need a reason?"

"No, but in the club, you said I caught you on an off day. It seemed like you were drowning your sorrows. Guy trouble?"

"God, no. It's been a while since I've had that issue." That doesn't sound right. "I'm not like a dried-up old spinster or anything. I have sex. Lots of it. I just meant that I haven't done the boyfriend thing for a while."

"Okay."

"Well, shit. Now I've gone and made myself sound like a whore. Can I go back to puking on you instead of this verbal diarrhea?"

He scrapes his hand over the stubble on his jaw and disarms me with a panty-melting grin. "There's no judgment here. Just because you enjoy sex doesn't make you a whore. If it does, I'm a total manwhore."

"Good to know."

"Don't get me wrong, I respect women, and I'm always safe. Our lifestyle just doesn't exactly lend itself to relationships, right? Now, who has verbal diarrhea?"

I hand him a cup of coffee and lean back against the counter.

"It's cute."

"This might be the first time anyone's ever called me cute."

"Let me guess. You usually get handsome, rugged, athletic, gorgeous, jaw-dropping, hot, totally fuckable. Am I close?"

Holy crap, Anders Verbeck is blushing. "You're in the ballpark."

"Then why would you leave a club with the only girl who wasn't going to put out for you? Even if I hadn't puked on you, you knew I wasn't going to take you home."

"Tell me the irony of that statement isn't lost on you. I knew I was going home with a woman, I just didn't expect it to be in a high-school-sober-ride type capacity."

"Do you ever get tired of it all? The hook-ups, the constant questions about if and when you're going to settle down? Or is that just a chick thing? Maybe it's just a 'my mom' thing."

He eyes me warily. "The hooking up with hot women doesn't get old. I'm in my prime. It's all about the wild oats right now. And sadly, I think women get a harsher judgment on that stuff. My mom gave up asking me about relationships a long time ago."

"Lucky you. My family is incessant. If there's a family event, I'm always the topic of conversation and disappointment. They don't care that I'm at the top of my game right now or that I'm paving the way for future female athletes."

"That's insane. I don't get that. For guys, everything about us is measured by our career success. Am I right that you're now the highest-paid woman in baseball?"

"Wow, you really do keep track of our league." I'm surprised that someone like him would bother keeping tabs on women's baseball.

"I love baseball in all its forms. I don't care if you're a guy or a girl, major league or minor. If you're crushing it, then I'm interested."

"So, you're an advocate for women in sports?"

"I've never thought of it like that. I advocate sports."

"Well, aren't you a unicorn?"

"How so?"

"You helped this damsel in distress last night. You stayed on my couch without making a move of any kind. You're into women in sports. What's your deal? Are you a secret axe murderer?"

"By their very nature, aren't all axe murderers secret?" He gives me a wicked grin.

"You know what I mean. You have a reputation in the press."

"Yeah, and you know as well as I do they see what they want to see. The truth doesn't really matter."

"True."

"And I didn't take advantage of you because I'm not a total douche-nozzle. Consent is my top priority with any woman. Also, you made it really easy for me not to want sex. The stench of vomit isn't exactly a turn-on."

I'm mortified. "Sorry about that. How can I repay you for your chivalry and all the puking?"

As he buttons his shirt, I can think of many different ways I'd like to repay him.

"Just don't blow chunks on me the next time we hang out."

"Deal. Besides, when are we going to be in each other's

company again? It's highly unlikely I'll get the chance to over-drink in your vicinity."

"I can think of one way you could pay your pukey debt."

"O-kay."

"I have a charity dinner to go to next weekend. Coach has us on zero drinks, zero women until the World Series is finished, and we'll only be a few games in by then. I'm not exactly good at staying away from either. Come with me. Be my date."

"I..."

"Not an actual date. Friends. You can be like my sponsor for booze and women." I'm not sure if I should be happy or sad about this. One of the greatest pitchers in baseball history wants to be my friend. That's amazing. But he's also wicked hot, and I'd love to round all the bases with him.

"Way to make a girl feel ugly. I'm all showered and fresh-smelling now."

"Yeah, you look hot as hell, and the jersey without pants was a true high point in my week."

"And yet you want me to be your chief eunuch?"

"Not the way I phrased it at all. You're easy to talk to, and as much as I love the guys on the team, I'd like to have someone new to hang with at this charity thing. If you don't want to, it's fine." He runs his hand through his deliciously messy hair, and I find myself clenching my thighs together. He's a special kind of hot.

"Sure. Why not. I'll be your cockblocker." He laughs out loud, deep and breathy.

"You're going to get on really well with Linc. He says shit like that all the time."

"Lincoln Nash?"

"The one and only."

"Oh my God. He's having his best season to date. His batting average is through the roof."

"So, now you're planning to make me *your* wingman when it comes to seducing *my* wingman?"

"You're the one who's abstaining right now. I'm free to have all the sex I want." I give him a wicked grin.

"And he's under orders from our coach as well. Sorry to be the bearer of bad news."

"He doesn't strike me as a rule follower."

"He's not. Do you have a pen and paper? I'll give you my number."

"Are you sure you don't want an address book? A pen and paper? I'll just tell you my number, and you can drop me a text or call to make sure I have yours. What are you, ninety? Would you like high-tea and scones with your pen and paper?"

I love his smile. "You're a funny woman. I see the sass isn't contained to just when you've been drinking. You're a minx. I can tell."

"Yep. I'm sassy, and I hit a mean screwball."

"Then we're going to get along just fine."

I type my number into his phone and make a quick call, so I have his. We sit for another hour or so chatting about baseball before he leaves. I must have thanked him a million times for being a gentleman last night. I think I'll be laying off the drinking for a while. As a woman, it's something I worry about—being too drunk to fend off a potential asshole. If it hadn't been Anders who brought me home, last night could've ended really badly.

"I'll message you with the details of this charity thing."

"Cool." As he heads for the door, I can't help but appreciate his lean and toned physique. "And thanks again for last night."

Of course, my neighbor is at her front door right now. "Your cock was a-mazing."

He turns to look at me and spies my nosey neighbor. "The anal was my favorite part!"

I burst out laughing and spill now cold coffee down the front of my t-shirt. I think my poor old neighbor just had a heart attack. Her eyebrows would've shot up if her forehead wasn't so full of Botox. I can hear Anders chuckle as he heads for the elevator.

"Morning, Mrs. Rayburn." She shakes her head in disapproval, tutting and clucking like a hen. I give her a wave and retreat inside.

What a strange twenty-four hours. I've gone from drowning my sorrows to having a non-date with Anders Verbeck. I guess we'll see if he actually calls me this week.

———————

I'VE BEEN GLUED TO THE TELEVISION WATCHING THE WORLD SERIES this week. The first two games were in LA, and the Yankees lost the first game and won the second. Tonight is game three, and they're in New York.

I've text with Anders a few times since the night he saved me from ending up on the bar floor in a drunken stupor. I'm nervous for him tonight. He really brought his A-game to the win in LA, and I'm hoping they pull out front with these next two games in their home stadium. It's always advantageous to play on your own turf with fans screaming and clapping for every hit.

They clinch the win in the ninth inning, and Anders is on fire. Although he won't see it for hours, I can't help sending him a quick message.

Me: *Incredible game! You were seriously amazing tonight. You're going to win the World Series!*

I busy myself with other things, and when my mom calls, I go against my better judgment and answer.

"Hey, Mom."

"Do you have a date yet?" My mom is more concerned about me having a date for her and Dad's vow renewal in a few weeks than she is about the fact that I just set the record for home runs in a season.

"Not yet."

"Are you seeing anyone?"

"Not right now. I'm busy with the team. I have no time for a boyfriend."

I can almost hear her rolling her eyes. "Are you at least having sex? It's beneficial to your health, you know. You don't want to be keeping all that tension in your body."

"Mom! I'm not talking about my sex life with you. What the hell?"

"I'm a woman with needs, Brooke. Just because I am your mom doesn't mean I'm not a sensual, sexual being."

"Put Daddy on the phone." Why the hell would she say that to me? I've been a good daughter, and she goes and says crap that I'll never be able to unhear.

"You're a grown woman. Surely you don't think the stork brought you. Sex is a big part of a healthy relationship. How do you think I've kept your dad happy all these years?"

"*Mom!* For the love of God, please stop talking about it and put Daddy on the phone."

"Ugh. Don't be such a prude, Brooke. Here's your dad but remember to let me know when you have a date. I want to make sure the place cards have all the right names on them. I refuse to put *Brooke's Plus One* on it."

"Why don't you just put one less seat at my table and save me the trouble of inviting someone?"

"Because it's a wedding. You bring a date to a wedding, Brooke."

"It's a vow renewal."

"Just find a date."

"Fine." She hands the phone to my dad, and he's already grumbling about my mom losing her shit over this party. I don't understand why they're doing this—they are already married, and it's been thirty-five years. It seems like a stupid reason to spend tens of thousands of dollars and inconvenience everyone you know.

"Hey, Brooke."

"Hi, Daddy. Were you watching the game?"

"Sure was. Verbeck is killing it with the Yankees this season. Best decision they ever made bringing him into the team."

"Right? His curveball is wicked. I really think they're going to win."

"Me too. More importantly, how is your training going?"

"Why can't Mom be as enthused about my career? She only cares about me getting a boyfriend."

"She means well. She doesn't talk to you about baseball because she's never understood why we love the game so much. I like to think that's something special that you and I share. Your mom just wants you to find happiness, no matter how graphic her ways of communicating it are." I can't help but laugh. My dad never has a bad word to say about my mom. It's awesome to have such a solid gold standard for marital bliss, but at this point, I don't think I'm going to find what they have.

"In answer to your question, training is going great. My stats are the best they've ever been. I just wish women in baseball could get the same kind of notoriety as their counterparts."

"Keep the faith, Brooke. You're a trailblazer. I knew that from the moment you picked up your first bat. The world hasn't caught up to you yet. I know that probably doesn't make you feel any better about it, but someday when women in sports are considered equal, those players will be smashing that glass ceiling from being able to stand on your shoulders. You've always been destined for greatness, baby."

"Thanks, Daddy."

"But please, for the love of God, bring a dumbass date to this shindig. Your mom will chew my ear off about it, and I don't want to pay all this money to tell her I still want to be married after decades and then have to divorce her ass for incessantly chirping that you need to bring a plus one." If it were anyone else, I'd be livid, but my dad just has a way of making me laugh.

"Only because you asked, Daddy. I'll figure it out. I have how many weeks until Mom completely disowns me?"

It sounds like he put his hand over the phone as if that would mute his yell in my mom's direction. "What date are we getting married again?"

"On our wedding anniversary, John."

"And that specific date would be?" Oh shit! Mom is going to kill him for that one.

"November 28. I think the diamonds in my new eternity ring are going to be bigger for that."

"Did you hear that? You just cost me multiple carats."

"And on that note, I'm going to hang up now. Sorry! I'll find a date, so tell Mom to stop stressing."

"She's incapable of any kind of Zen at this point."

"Love you."

"Love you, too, Brooke. Will we see you this weekend?"

"No. I've got some charity thing I said I'd attend. Next weekend for sure."

"Okay. Have fun."

When I hang up the call, I have a text from Anders, and my heart stutters to a standstill.

Shit!

Chapter Three

BROOKE

I WASN'T EXPECTING to hear from Anders tonight. I thought for sure he'd be out celebrating with the team. I suppose they can't exactly go on a drinking spree right now. Wine, women, and song will have to wait until after they lift the trophy.

Anders: *You were watching? Shucks. I'm flattered.*

Me: *Don't be. I always watch the World Series. Some hotshot pitcher caught my attention this year.*

Anders: *Way to knock a guy down.*

Me: *I'm sure the throng of adoring female fans will make the blow sting a little less.*

Anders: *Where are these females you speak of? I'm in a locker room full of sweaty, exhausted men right now.*

Me: *Can you repeat that? Or better yet, FaceTime me. Send some pics at least ;o)*

Anders: *No chance.*

Me: *Ugh, I thought we were friends. Do a girl who hasn't had a date in months a solid.*

Anders: *I can DO YOU SOLID, but I'm not DOING YOU A SOLID. There's a big difference.*

Me: *I bet there is… and I'm sure it's big.*

Anders: *You know it.*

God, my stomach is doing somersaults as a torrent of desire washes over me. I don't want to get giddy over this guy. It smacks every relationship blunder I've ever made. The knight in shining armor rides into my life, and I mistake a grand gesture and sexual chemistry for love and a happily ever after that's never going to come.

He's Anders Verbeck, for God's sake.

There's no scenario where he isn't a complete player. The baseball groupies must drop their panties if he even looks in their direction. I've been around guys like him my entire life, and I've been the girl dropping her panties more than I should have.

Anders: *No witty comeback?*

How do I answer that?

Anders: *We still on for this weekend?*

Me: *Yes, although I've been expecting you to cancel in favor of whatever groupie is warming your bed right now.*

Anders: *My bed is cold.*

Me: *Is this how you talk to all your friends?*

Anders: *My friends don't usually ask about the temperature of my bed sheets.*

Me: *Fair point.*

I want to probe him further, but I fear I may not want to know the answers.

Me: *I'll see you on Saturday night. Eight o'clock, right?*

Anders: *Yep. I'll pick you up around seven thirty.*

Me: *Don't you need my address for that?*

Anders: *You weren't exactly lucid the last time I navigated my way to your place, but I know where you live.*

I start to reply, but I can see he's typing again.

Anders: *That sounded chivalrous in my head but turned out super stalker.*

I can't help laughing until my phone starts ringing—he's calling me. After a momentary brain fart, my smart mouth kicks into gear. "You realize calling doesn't help your stalker vibes, right?"

"I knew you were going to say that." God, his voice is like

molten lava cake—a blend of sultry with a heavy dose of sex dripping from it.

"Again, stalkerish."

His laugh is delicious. "Are you my kryptonite or something? Most women in New York would be happy to get a call from me."

"And bigheaded too. You're the total package of red flags right now, buddy."

"Admit it, you're happy to hear from me."

"I admit nothing." *I'm one hundred percent happy.*

"Throw me a bone here."

"I'm sure you have plenty of *bone* without me."

"You're a pun girl. I like it. Well-timed puns are underrated if you ask me."

"Right!" I can hear voices in the background. "Where are you?"

"I told you. In the locker room. Sorry about the noise level. I'm just about to head to my car. Hold on." He doesn't say anything for what feels like forever, but I can hear him saying goodbye to people before a door slams, and the background noise fades away. "You still there?"

"Yeah. Should I have hung up?" I'm asking a genuine question.

"I'm glad you didn't."

I can hear him throwing his bag in the trunk of his car before getting in and switching on the ignition. Whatever he's driving, it's powerful and has a lot of horsepower from the sound of that first almighty roar.

"What kind of sports car do you have?"

"How do you know it's a sports car? I could be driving a minivan for all you know."

"There isn't a minivan on the planet that roars to life like that."

"You know your cars?"

"I can't tell you much else about it from one rev of the engine, but yeah, I like cars. My dad taught me to rebuild an engine when I was fourteen. He said I had to be able to handle myself before he would let me loose with a driver's license. I don't call AAA when I get a flat. I get out and change the tire."

"Corvette. Stingray."

"Holy shit. I love that car. It's a beast."

"You can't be this perfect."

"What?"

"You like cars, baseball, and you're hot. Triple threat. Why haven't you been snapped up already?"

I can't help but laugh. "My mom was just asking me the same questions a half-hour ago. I guess the guys I've dated didn't appreciate my specific talents."

"Idiots."

"The guys or my mom?"

"What answer will win me brownie points? If I say both, will you hang up on me?"

Why does he care?

"I have to give my mom credit. She's not an idiot, but she is way too obsessed with my biological clock and the idea that I'm going to end up a shriveled old spinster because I dare to focus on my career."

"Okay, I'll adjust my answer. The exes are idiots, and your mom is misguided."

"I'll take it." There's an awkward pause. "I…"

"Are you home?"

"Yes."

"Can I swing by?" My heart is hammering in my chest all of a sudden. Why would he want to come over? "I only live about ten minutes from you."

"What for?" It comes out harsh and not in any way that I intended.

"I'll take that as a no."

"Sorry, I'm just surprised. I don't really get why you'd want to come over here."

"I thought we could hang out. I'm still amped up on adrenaline from tonight, but it's cool. I'll just see you on Saturday."

"No. Come over. I need to be added to the idiot list. I warn you, though, I look like ass right now."

"Are you covered in puke?"

"No."

"Then we're good. I'm sure you look…" he hesitates for a moment, "… fine."

"How far away are you?"

"I'll be there in five."

"Okay, see you then." I hang up the phone and start rushing around the living room like the Tasmanian Devil, trying to clean up the mess. Grabbing armfuls of unfolded laundry off the kitchen island, I run to my bedroom, throwing the pile of clothes on the floor before running into the bathroom to attempt to fix my hair and at least put on some lip gloss and mascara.

I don't bother changing out of my oversized tee and shorts. They're my favorite, and as Anders said, he's seen me looking worse. I'm going for seemingly effortless beauty—not something I pull off very easily. Messy bun, glossy lips, glasses, and legs that go on for days, it'll have to do.

When I hear the buzzer, butterflies take flight in the pit of my stomach. Steadying my breath, I wrap my hand around the handle and wait for him to knock. When he does, I don't play it cool and wait a minute, but instead, I fling open the door while his hand is still balled in a fist. I'm floored at the sight of him. An hour ago, he was on my television, pitching in the World Series. Now, he's standing outside my apartment looking good enough to eat.

"Hey, Lexington. You going to let me in?" He has a wicked grin, and I know my poker face is non-existent at this moment.

"Sure. Sorry. Come in." Suddenly, I wish I'd changed into some-thing more apt for company. His eyes rake the length of me, and I feel laid bare.

"Thanks." Having him here feels different than the last time he was in my living room.

"So you caught the game?"

"Everyone in New York *caught the game*. That last inning was a nail-biter."

"You don't have to tell me. I was ready to shit a brick."

"Well, you looked confident on television. Cocky even." I head straight for the refrigerator. "Can I get you a beer?"

"No alcohol. Coach's orders."

"Water? Or I have some cran-raspberry if you'd like?"

"Water is fine, thanks." I hold out a bottle, my fingertips brushing his as he takes it from me, sending a jolt of electricity straight to my core.

I twist the cap off my drink and extend it to meet his. "Cheers to your win tonight." I *cheer* with a little too much gusto and manage to drench myself in water. It's official, I look like I'm about to enter a wet t-shirt contest.

"Fuck. Sorry." I don't know why he's apologizing. It was completely my fault. He grabs a dishcloth from the counter and starts wiping my shirt.

"Do you realize you're essentially just rubbing my boobs right now?" I was going for funny, but he drops the cloth like it's on fire and backs away from me.

"Shit. I'm so sorry. I didn't come here to grope you."

"Relax. I was just kidding."

"Maybe I should go." I don't know why, but I grab his hand to keep him anchored to the spot.

"No! I'm glad you came over. I seem to have a talent for covering my clothes in liquids when you're around. Just give me two seconds to go and change my shirt, and I'll be right back. Are you hungry?"

"Starving."

"Help yourself to anything in the refrigerator. Don't just up and leave while I'm changing, okay?"

"Sure. You basically told me to make myself at home, so if your refrigerator is empty by the time you get back, it's on you."

"I'll take my chances. A guy deserves some food after a productive day at work. Have at it." As I scurry down the hallway to my room, I'm kicking myself for sounding like a fifties' infomercial for the perfect housewife. My mom would be so proud.

I take a moment to change into not only a dry outfit but a cuter one. A quick once-over in the mirror, and I head back to the living room. Anders wasn't kidding when he said he was going to make himself at home. He's lounging on my couch with a plate piled high with leftovers and the television on sports.

"Are you seriously watching your replays?"

He turns to me with a mouthful of food. "Don't you?"

"Say it, don't spray it, dude." I sit down next to him, grabbing a chicken wing off his plate.

"Did you just call me *dude?*"

"When you say it, it sounds ridiculous. When I say it, it's cute?"

"Oh really?" He's got that wry smile again, and it does things to my insides.

"Yes. Admit it, you find me adorable."

"I like your confidence, Lexington. Not sure about the cute thing. More like, *sexy Lexi.*" Before I get a chance to pass judgment, he does it himself. "That was the lamest line in the history of the world."

I shove his shoulder. "Thank God, you said it. I wasn't sure how to break it to you."

He gives me a little nudge back, and for some reason, I feel shy. What the hell?

"Let's just forget the last twenty seconds ever happened and concentrate on the handsome devil onscreen." Of course, it's a close-up of his winning pitch. I can't really argue. He looks so damn handsome on the mound, and we all know winners are sexy.

"If we could play that game, I'd erase our first encounter and start over."

"Geez, woman. Go easy on yourself. It wasn't as bad as you think, and unfortunately, you're not the first woman I've ridden the vomit comet with."

"Way to make a girl feel special."

"I'm here, aren't I?" I want to jump his bones, but something is holding me back. It could be the dollop of barbecue sauce on his lip.

"Yeah, and covered in hot sauce, eating me out of house and home."

"I'll restock the refrigerator the next time I'm over." He gives me a sly wink, and I feel like my flirt-o-meter is on the fritz. He wants to hang out again—that's a good thing. He's talking to me like I'm one of his buddies—not so good.

"Who says I'll invite you back? Heck, I didn't invite you tonight."

"And yet, you're already giddy at the thought of spending more time with me" He wipes the sauce from his lip and licks it off his thumb. *Fuck me!* Literally and figuratively.

"How about we have this conversation after I spend the evening as your human chastity belt. We're still on for Saturday, right?"

"Yep."

"And what's the dress code?"

"Fancy. Don't go buying a new dress or anything. You'll look hot in whatever you wear." He furrows his brow and thinks better of his comment. "You're hot in a t-shirt and shorts, so I'm certain you'll be the perfect chastity belt."

"You really know how to make a girl feel sensual and sexy. I can honestly say you're the first guy to compliment me for being a cock-blocker."

"Then you haven't been hanging with the right guys." He scrubs his hand over the stubble on his jaw and suddenly becomes laser-focused on the television. "I'm going to shut up now before I say anything else that makes me cringe like a nut sack in an ice bath."

I choke on a gulp of water. "You're killing me here. If I have to change clothes again, I'm going to be pissed."

"You've cottoned on to my devious plan. Make you laugh so hard you soak all of your clothes and end up having to hang out with me topless." He wiggles his eyebrows, which only makes me laugh harder.

"There are easier methods for getting a girl naked."

"True. Usually, this ruggedly handsome face is enough."

"I'm sure it is." There's a tension in the air, and me being me, I need to fill the silence. "Want to play Mario Kart?"

"You're quickly becoming one of my favorite people, Lexington. Fire up the Switch and get ready to lose."

A few hours later, and way past midnight, Anders says goodbye, giving me a chaste kiss on the cheek at the door. Either I'm sending out the wrong signals, or he really isn't into me, despite his constant little hints that he's attracted to me.

With a plan for Saturday, I watch as the elevator doors slide closed.

I can feel this isn't going to end well for me.

WHEN ANDERS SAID A CHARITY EVENT, I WASN'T THINKING ABOUT the biggest baseball charity fundraiser of the year. We're talking ballgowns and tuxedos. The women's teams don't usually attend these things, so the fact he asked me to come is cool. Maybe I can do some much-needed networking.

My closet doesn't house more than a handful of dresses, and none of them would be appropriate for such a grand event. Yesterday after practice, I had my best friend, Lacey, come shopping with me. She likes all the girly stuff that I can't be bothered with. She made sure I had the dress, the hair, the clutch purse, and a ton of makeup I'll never use again.

Tonight, standing in front of the mirror in my hallway, I barely recognize myself. I'm like Cinderella, except I have no desire to find Prince Charming. Lacey is standing behind me, her grin so wide it freaks me out.

"Can you not stare at me?"

"I can't believe how good you scrub up, girl. I'm a miracle worker."

"Am I that much of a mess on a normal day?"

"Can I plead the fifth? You're gorgeous in that effortless athlete way. When it comes to style, you don't exactly go out of your way to dress up. I've turned you into a freaking princess for tonight."

"Ugh. Why did I agree to this?"

"Because turning down Anders Verbeck would result in me bludgeoning you to death. He's hot as fuck. Plus, you puked all over him. You owe him for that."

"Yeah. He's hot, all right, but he wants a cockblocker for the evening. He finds me about as sexually attractive as a lamp. When he came over the other night, I thought I was giving off the come-hither vibes, and all I got was a peck on the cheek."

"His loss. He'll be jealous when you start flirting with Lincoln Nash. He's a player for sure, and when he catches sight of you in this dress, he'll be desperate to show you a good time."

"I wouldn't say no," I say with a devious smile. Anders might not want to tangle in the sheets with me, but there will be plenty of eligible bachelors at this shindig for me to corrupt. The concierge calls to tell me Anders is on his way up, and as I open the door, I see Anders stepping out of the elevator in a tux. God, he's stunning.

"Jesus, if you don't mount him, I will. Damn." It shouldn't irk me, but it does.

When he sees me standing in the doorway, his face lights up.

"Wow!" His eyes are smoldering as he looks me up and down, biting his bottom lip. "Just… wow."

Lacey is quick to shove past me and hold her hand out to shake his. "Anders Verbeck, in the flesh. The very hot, sexy flesh. I'm Lacey. You can thank me for the knockout appearance of my best friend. *Wow* doesn't even come close, am I right?"

He takes her proffered hand but doesn't take his eyes off me. "Right." When Lacey is done drooling all over him, he offers his arm, which I happily take. I'm scared I am going to trip over this dress. Floor-length gowns and heels aren't really my thing, but I'm enjoying the way Anders is staring at me. Having a slit up to my thigh makes it marginally easier to walk, so fingers crossed I don't fall on my ass.

"You two hot people have fun." I turn and glare at Lacey. "What? I'm just stating facts. You're hot when you're not drunk or vomitous, and holy mother of God, Mr. Verbeck here is just mouth-watering."

"I'll deal with you later. Lock up before you leave. And Lacey… thanks for the makeover."

"All the thanks I need is knowing that dress will be on a baseball player's floor tonight." What the hell is she doing?

"Lacey!"

"I didn't say it would be *his* bedroom floor. There are plenty of hot guys on his team who will be on you like a rash."

"It was nice to meet you." I may not know him very well, but the disdain dripping from his voice right now as he speaks to my best friend is unmistakable.

As we step into the elevator, Anders has a firm grip on me, and thank God, I manage to get down to the lobby and into the car without incident. He opens the door like a gentleman before striding round to the driver's side. I'm surprised he doesn't have a town car. He brought the Corvette.

"You look amazing," he says as the engine roars to life. "Blue is most definitely your color."

"Let's face it, anything that wasn't crusty and caked with puke is going to be a showstopper."

"Are you always this self-deprecating?" He levels me with his gaze, and I ignore the butterflies taking flight in my stomach at his cool blue stare.

"You don't mince your words, do you, Anders?"

"Can you just call me Beck already? We're friends, so you can stop using the somewhat pretentious name my parents lumped me with."

"You don't like it? I think it's hot." I think everything about him is hot.

"Then you can call me anything you like. Now, answer my question. Are you always this down on yourself?"

"No." I take a deep breath before blowing out my nerves. "I just made such a bad first impression on you, and I'm beyond embarrassed that you saw me like that. Compound that with the water-spraying incident the other night, and I'm about as sexy as a librarian attempting to work a stripper pole."

"It couldn't have been all bad, right? I asked you to come out with me tonight. Aside from the obvious issue of our first meeting, I enjoyed talking to you the morning after, and we had a blast when I came over after the game. You're easygoing… I think. Basically, the entire dating process is boring as hell. Watching some chick pretend she's full after eating one solitary fry. The morning after is usually awkward as fuck, but we didn't have that problem."

"Yeah, because that happens after you've had sex with someone. That didn't happen, so we missed out on the fun part."

Chapter Four

ANDERS

"ARE you saying I can't be fun unless I'm between the sheets?" I give her my best wry smile.

"Not at all. I'm just saying that I'm a hundred percent certain that you have bedroom skills. As do I." This girl doesn't hold back.

"Now we're talking. I like confidence in a woman."

"Can I ask you something?" I'm not sure if I want to answer her questions, but I can't exactly say no.

"Fire away."

"Two things, actually. First, why are you driving? I had you pegged for being chauffeur-driven." Not the question I was antici-pating. And why would she think I'm *that* guy?

"I love driving. Cars are an extravagance I indulge in. I've worked my ass off to get where I am, and I want to enjoy it. I don't have any desire to sit in the back of a car like some self-important asshole. Plus, you told me you dig cars and that you like the Corvette. I figured you'd enjoy going for a ride. Next question."

"Why did you ask me to come with you? You can get a date with a click of your fingers. You can't say it's my fun-loving personality or my Mario Kart skills because you asked me to come before game night. Why ask the pukey girl to come?" There's the question I was expecting.

"I figure we went straight past the possibility of sex and landed in the friendzone." I don't want to say that I'd have boned her that night if things had gone differently. And to be honest, I don't know why I asked her to come to this event with me. I'm drawn to her. Hanging out after the game just reiterated the fact that she's cool to be around.

"Sure. Totally. Now it would just be weird, right?"

"Yeah." I just well and truly fucked myself over in a single sentence. I guess I'm introducing her to Linc tonight, and he'll be enjoying the—I can't even finish the thought. It makes me grip the steering wheel so tight my knuckles are white.

After a moment of discomfort, I figure I may as well lean into the whole friend vibe.

"Is it weird that I asked you to come to this thing?"

"If you were a random guy, then yes, but we play the same sport. You know who I am, and I know who you are. I'd have to be dead not to have heard about the magical arm of Anders Verbeck this year." She's unfazed and unimpressed by my sporting prowess.

"Yeah, yeah. Seems I'm the one who was stalking your career. That doesn't make me creepy as fuck."

"It's only creepy if you're ugly." I'm not sure how to take that comment, and she picks up on it. "That was a joke. All creepy behavior sucks. Sexy or not."

"I've usually got more game than this."

"I imagine the women you date or hook up with are a lot different than me."

"Why would you say that?"

"For starters, I'm a tomboy. I have a mouth like a sailor. I attract the bad boys every time."

"I'm not a bad boy?" I mock a wounded ego.

"No. You're a player. A player and a bad boy are two very different species."

"If you know you go for bad boys, then why not stop hooking up with them?"

"Do you stop yourself from getting laid by the screaming fangirls? You know they're not going to last, but I bet you enjoy every minute of it."

"Fair point."

"So you basically want me to be your sober sponsor tonight? To make sure you don't go home with some random woman and incur the wrath of your coach?"

"Yep."

"Well, okay, then. I can do that."

"Clearly, I'm going to spend my night taking a Louisville Slugger to all the guys who are going to be hitting you up in that dress."

"You told me this thing was fancy. I didn't want to look shabby on your arm, even if it's not a real date. Besides, I'm not under any no-sex orders. My coach is fine and dandy with me getting my freak on. I hit better when I'm relaxed."

"Can I come play on your team?" Her eyes light up, and she reflexively grabs my knee, only inches away from my cock.

"Oh my God, can we do that? Not the team, but I'd love to see how my hitting measures up to your pitching."

"Okay, you're either my new best friend or the love of my life." She throws her head back and laughs so hard I think she's going to barf… again.

"I'll take the best-friend slot."

"You'll have to fight Linc for it."

"I'd happily wrestle him to the ground… naked. All in the name of becoming your bestie, of course."

"I don't need the visual of Linc naked. I see enough of that in the locker room. The guy just loves walking around with his schlong flapping in the breeze."

"And what about you? Do you let it all hang out in there?" Her smile is killer when she's having some devious thought.

"I can't. It would drag on the floor or spear someone in the chest depending on my state of arousal at the time."

"You naked in a room full of hot athletes with a hard-on… I'd pay money to see that."

"You couldn't afford me."

"Don't underestimate my willingness to bankrupt myself for ten minutes in the Yankees locker room."

"Can we stop talking about my teammates' junk?"

"Sure. If you just want to talk exclusively about your cock, I'm totally down for that."

"You're a minx. You know that, right?"

"I do indeed. Get used to it." I just might take her up on that. We haven't even reached the venue yet, and I'm already having more fun with her than any of the women I've dated in the past two years, at least.

"Shit, bro, you brought barfing Brooke?"

"If you say that in front of her, I'll knock your front teeth out." Linc has zero filters. It doesn't matter what company he's in or who he's ripping.

"Dude, are you into her? I didn't think you'd hook up with the girl after the mess she made on you last weekend."

"I didn't. We didn't. I hung out with her after the game the other night. We're just friends."

"Fuck off!" His voice is about forty decibels too loud, and everyone in the vicinity turns to stare at us. As usual, he doesn't give a crap.

"Can you say that a little louder? I don't think the valet heard you."

"There's no way you're friends with that girl. Look at her. She's too hot for the friends-only vibe."

"I'm capable of being friends with a woman and not sleeping with her." I can't make that sound convincing.

"Shit, she turned you down. You think with your dick just as much as I do. If you don't want to bone her, I do. She's a fucking knockout in that dress."

"I have eyes."

"And a flaccid dick? Seriously, what angle are you playing with her?"

"I don't have an angle. Coach has us on fucking World Series cockdown lockdown. She's easy to talk to and funny. You can't blame me for wanting to have someone other than you to hang out with. I love you, bro, but I'm not taking to the dance floor with you."

"I'm a great dancer." He fakes some moves like he's auditioning for *Dancing with the Stars*.

"Yeah, I just don't want to deal with your raging hard-on if I let you slow dance with me."

"Well, you're a heartthrob. If you won't dance with me, I'll ask your lady friend to do me the honor. That okay with you?"

"I'm not her keeper." As I say the words, she appears at my side.

"You scrub up pretty good, Brooke. Care to dance?" Linc gives her that smile I've seen him give out a thousand times. The one that says he's set his sights on her.

"I'd love to, but I have two left feet."

"I'm sure I can handle you," he says with a glint in his eye, taking her hand and spinning her as they head for the dance floor.

"Why is my date dancing with yours?" Linc's arm candy for the evening is beautiful, I'll give her that, but she has that resting bitch face thing going on. He won't care. I doubt he'll do much staring at her face.

"Your guess is as good as mine."

"Why don't we dance? They shouldn't get to have all the fun." She grabs my hand and drags me onto the dance floor. Dancing isn't high on my list of fun ways to spend an evening.

She gropes me in the name of finding the right dance hold, but I doubt she's going to find it cupping my ass. I take her hands and politely move them up to my shoulders. Her perfume is sickly sweet as if she took a bath in the damn stuff.

Linc doesn't even notice we're on the floor, but Brooke's eyes are fixed on mine. I mouth an apology and my best *help me* face. She quickly shifts direction and finds her way over to me.

"Time for a switch." She's actually sort of graceful as she slides out of Linc's arms and into mine.

"You've got some moves, Lexington." Her hands slink around

my neck with her body pushed tight to mine. Sliding my arms around her waist, we sway to the music.

"Someone needs to teach that girl about moderation when it comes to perfume. What the hell?"

"I was just thinking the same thing. No offense, but you now reek of perfume, which sucks because you're wearing my favorite cologne."

"Anyone with a nose must be thinking the same. Holy shit. Good to know you like my cologne. No word of a lie, I've been wearing the same one for ten years."

"It suits you. All rugged and yet somehow refined."

"So, you met the infamous Linc. Is he all the hotness you thought he would be?" Apparently, I like to torture myself.

"He's hotter in real life. And sexy as hell. Perfume girl is in for a treat tonight."

"I'm sure he'd let you join them if you're into that kind of thing."

"I couldn't stand her perfume for longer than four seconds. And something tells me she's a bit of a bitch."

"Otherwise, you'd be up for it? Or have you done it before?" My cock is twitching at the mere idea of it, and I'm praying she's not feeling it against her leg.

"Wouldn't you like to know?"

"Yeah. We're friends. Friends tell each other stuff… hot, horny, dirty stuff."

"Like the fact that my high school best friend was the person who taught me to kiss?"

"Tell me your high school bestie was a girl. Otherwise, this story is just lame."

"*She* let me practice with her. Still one of the best kissers."

"Fuck. Excuse me while I recite baseball stats to calm down after that revelation."

She throws her head back and laughs. I'm not sure if she thinks I'm kidding or that she's just ignoring the fact that I just became a dancing tripod.

"What about you? Are threesomes something you indulge in?"

"I don't even know your favorite drink or childhood teddy bear's name. You're going straight for the jugular."

"Me telling you about Binky isn't my idea of a fun night out. And yes, before you say it, I did, in fact, call my binky, Binky. Imagination isn't exactly my strong suit. Fess up."

"I can neither confirm nor deny my willingness or previous participation in a threesome." Her eyes go wide as saucers.

"You totally have. If you hadn't, I'd have gotten a simple *no*."

"It makes me sound like a total jackass." I hold her gaze, searching for the judgment I suspect is coming. I should've just said no. What's a little white lie between friends?

"Yeah, but a sexy jackass."

"Nice." This was a bad idea.

"I'm just pulling your leg."

"Is this what I have to look forward to as your newest friend?"

"Probably. Are you okay with that?"

"Sure. Now let me spin you around this floor in a way that's deserving of this dress of yours. Seriously hot, by the way."

"Why, thank you. You're pretty dapper yourself."

"Then hold on, and for the love of all that's pure, let me lead."

"How did you know?"

"You're a ballbuster with no dance skills. Of course, you want to lead."

I find myself laughing at the sound of her chuckle. We spend the next few songs tearing it up until they announce this one is for all the lovers in the room and start playing a slow dance. That's my cue for a sharp exit.

When we find our way back to the table, Linc is bragging about his batting average this season, and I can't help myself. He makes it too easy.

"You realize Lexington's stats are better than yours? You're not the top dog at this table." I love winding him up, and he plays right into my hands.

"There's no comparison. Could you imagine what my average would be if I were hitting the balls she's getting? No offense, Brooke." She's not amused by him.

"Keep talking, pretty boy. Your friend here has agreed to go toe-to-toe with me. You should come. I'd love to embarrass you at your own game."

"Them's fighting words." Linc has that mischievous look in his eye. "Name the day, and I'll be there. I feel sorry for you already."

"It's on." She turns to me. "When can we do this?"

"Are you serious?"

"As a heart attack. Your friend here needs to be taken down a peg or two. You already said you'd pitch for me. Let's do it."

"As soon as we seal the deal and win the World Series."

"Perfect. But bragging rights aren't enough. Let's make it more interesting." She considers it for a second before leveling her gaze at Linc. "If I win, I want a public declaration that I beat your ass."

"Deal. It's never going to happen."

"Shake on it." She holds out her hand, but Linc isn't finished.

"Wait a minute. I haven't decided what my prize is going to be." He doesn't have any kind of poker face. I can read him like a book, and he's about to piss me off. "If I win, you go on a date with me."

"What?" Brooke is surprised, but I'm not.

"A date. Dinner, drinks, dancing. If I win, I want you to go on a date with me."

"Deal." She shakes on it, and I'm aware I have no right to be annoyed, but I am.

Linc's date looks like she's chewing a wasp, and I don't blame her. He basically just asked Brooke on a date. He knows everything about the way I pitch, which immediately gives him an advantage.

"You're so not getting lucky tonight, Lincoln Nash." She folds her arms over her ample chest.

"We both know that's not true, baby. You want me, and you know exactly what you'd be missing out on." He leans in, whispering something only she can hear, but I can take an educated guess. Her pupils dilate, and her breath quickens. Whatever he says, it does the trick because she's out of her chair and dragging him toward the exit in two seconds flat.

"I'm assuming this wasn't their first date?" Brooke laughs as she says it, watching them disappear out the door.

"No. She surfaces every now and then. Nothing serious. I'm not sure he has the capacity for serious."

"Do you?" She catches me off guard.

"I think so… with the right woman. Contrary to popular belief, I don't want to be an eternal bachelor."

"Say it like you mean it."

"What?" I can't help but smile.

"Don't try to bullshit a bullshitter." I want to steer clear of anything she might have heard about me.

"So, you really think you can beat Linc? Or is it a win-win for you? If you win, you get bragging rights. If he wins, you get a date with him."

"I can beat him. And don't go easy on me, I want to win fair and square."

"Not in my nature, Lexington."

"Good. I want Linc's humiliation to be authentic."

"Then you better watch some games of me pitching. He knows every move in my arsenal. He'll see me coming a mile away."

"I'm going to enjoy this win. You've already written me off, and we haven't even started."

"Not true. I'm rooting for you. If I weren't, I wouldn't tell you to go and study my curveball."

"I'll do my due diligence. How soon can we burn this disco out?"

"You want to start right now? I was thinking we could do some more dancing. I'm in this penguin suit, and you're rocking that dress. I doubt either of us will be up for wearing this garb again any time soon."

"True. You're a hot penguin. Let's dance the night away, friend. Tomorrow I'm going to study every move you've got."

"That sounds dirtier than it really is."

"Maybe I'm going to study more than your curveball. I might take a look at your fastball or maybe your *screw*-ball."

"You're killing me, woman. Let's dance." Leading her onto the dance floor, I take her hand in mine, and electricity sparks. I can't tell if it's a two-way street, so I ignore it for now. If she loses this bet with Linc, he's going to take her out on a date. She agreed to it, and I know he's going to win. I'm pretty sure she knows it too.

True to my word, we dance the night away, and with every glass of champagne she indulges in, her hands roam my body as we sway in time to the music. I'm sober as a judge and fighting back the urge to kiss her.

My life's complicated enough. I'm not about to start something with a woman who's more interested in going out with my best friend. That's a headache I don't want.

When she's ready to kick off her heels, I drive her home and make sure she gets inside safely. She's a little tipsy but nothing like the first time I took her home—the vomitorium. She invites me in for a beer and some video gaming, which I politely decline. There's a difference between wanting to hook up with a girl when she's sober or being in the friendzone, and then there's asking for the number of her OBGYN to get my uterus checked. I'm planning on the first scenario. There's something I enjoy about hanging out with this girl, but I'm not sure if it's because she doesn't seem all that interested in me romantically or because she and I could actually be friends.

The last time I was friends with a woman, I was in college, and I was madly in love with her. She was dating my roommate, and I never told her. Instead, I fucked everything that moved.

If Brooke wins the bet with Linc, I'll make a move. If she loses, I'll hang back and let her figure out what she wants—if anything—with Linc.

Chapter Five

BROOKE

TONIGHT'S THE NIGHT. I'm going head-to-head with Lincoln Nash. I've been studying Anders' pitching style for weeks. It's easy to get pulled down the rabbit hole with him—he's impossibly handsome and oozes confidence. I've been grilling him for days with texts and calls, asking about various games and pitches from his highlight reel.

He's probably sick of talking to me by now, but I figure if he's around after our disaster of a meet-cute, he's not going to be scared off by my efforts to best him on the field. In fact, it's a nice change of pace to be around a guy who isn't intimidated by me.

The Yankees won the World Series four games to three, and Anders pitched his heart out—better than anyone I've ever seen, and I grew up watching old game tapes of all the greats. If I'm honest, I thought Anders would forget about me in the hoopla of New Yorkers celebrating their win. The local news has been all about the World Series. Anders and Linc have been on every radio and talk show you can think of. If he was on my mind before, now he's taken up residence.

They've been out partying night after night, and Anders has drunk-dialed me a couple of times, asking me to go meet them at a bar or club, but this is his time in the spotlight. From all the pictures of the team on social media, they've been enjoying the spoils of victory—women hanging off of their arms in every shot, and Linc with his tongue down every fangirl's throat. I'm sure Anders had his fair share of action, but I didn't see it, and we're just friends. That's what I keep telling myself. Don't go looking for it, don't get upset. He deserves all the happiness and attention he's getting, and I have no claim or right to be jealous.

When I pull into the parking lot of Yankee Stadium, I'm excited to batter up with Anders on the pitcher's mound. He's the best there is. And to be hitting alongside Linc will be an honor, even though I won't tell him that. He already thinks the sun shines out his ass, and I can't fault him for it. He's amazing.

I grab my favorite bat from the trunk of my car and head for the side entrance that Anders told me would be open. As I round the corner, Linc is standing at the door with his bat slung over his shoulder.

"You showed. I'm impressed, Brooke. I half-expected you to ghost us tonight, scared of a crushing defeat. We are champions, after all. No one would blame you for crying out on us."

"I'm scared of how sweet it's going to be when you eat your words, Nash." He throws his head back and lets out a hearty chuckle.

"I like you already. So, where do you want to go on our first date?" His grin is wicked and sexy as hell.

"Wherever it is, you'll need a warm jacket because hell will have frozen over by then."

He holds open the door and ushers me inside. "I'm really going to enjoy beating you, and when you can't resist my charms, it'll be all the sweeter."

"Dream on, gorgeous." I sashay down the hallway, pretending to keep my cool as the field comes into view. I'll never tire of emerging onto the vibrant green—the sights, the sounds, and the smell of freshly cut grass. The floodlights are on, and the stands are empty, but it's still awe-inspiring and magical in its own way.

Anders is standing on the mound, his glove in hand as he sends ball after ball spinning into the night. Butterflies take flight in the pit of my stomach as I watch them soar. I'm giddy with excitement.

Linc drapes his arm over my shoulder, letting his bat swing at my side. "It's a thing of beauty, Brooke. A thing of beauty."

"It sure is."

"You're going to have to do better than that, Beck!" Linc shouts to get his attention. With his ball cap on, I can't see his eyes as he turns to face us, but it's like I can feel his gaze on me.

"Keep shit-talking, Linc. When Lexington beats you up and down this field, you can give me your humble apology."

When we get to the mound, the guys have their bromance slap on the back before Anders leans in, pressing a kiss to my cheek. "Hey, Lexington." He lingers just a fraction longer than he should and much shorter than I'd like.

"Hi. Congrats on the win. I know I've said it on the phone but in person is different. You were amazing. You *are* amazing." I'm beginning to waffle. "I'll shut up now."

"Thanks. You ready? I need you to win tonight, or this guy's going to be insufferable. He can't have a World Series win *and* this."

"I'll do my best."

"I'm pretty sure you've studied my pitching more than my coach, so you'll be fine. Linc, here, never pays attention to any other player except himself." These two have such an easygoing rapport.

"And yet I still spank everyone else on the team during practice. I've got this in the bag."

"We'll see about that. You ready, Lexington? Ladies first."

"Actually, I'm going to let the lovely Linc go first. I just want a few minutes to drink this place in."

"It looks pretty great at night." Anders looks around with the same wonder in his eyes that I feel as I take it all in.

"Fine with me." Linc swings his bat, doing all those flashy tricks that I'm sure the ladies just lap up. I can do all that showboating, so it doesn't pack the same punch.

"Bring it on, bro." As Anders grabs a ball from the basket at his feet, I feel a little starstruck. He's just pitched in the World Series, and here I am, on a random Wednesday night, waiting to bat. It's surreal.

The sound of that first ball connecting with Linc's bat is like a crack of lightning echoing through the empty stadium. It's the most satisfying sound in the world.

"*Yes!* Did you see that, Brooke? Probably not because it was going so damn fast." Linc is feeling pretty good about his chances right now, and I don't blame him. That shot was the textbook definition of perfect. "Keep them coming, Beck, and try to pitch me something better. My grandma could do better."

"That's not what she said last night, Linc. She said I've got magic hands."

"Low blow, Beck. Low blow! I'm going to have to dial up my game now for the honor of Meemaw. I was going easy on you, but now, it's on like Donkey-Kong."

"Dream on, Linc. I can wipe the floor with you any day of the week. Tonight's going to be twice as sweet when Lexington makes you look like a minor league bench warmer."

His vote of confidence is fueled by ridicule of his best friend, but any compliment from Anders is high praise. It takes me a few minutes to relax and start throwing out the witty banter I'm known for on the team.

Just when I think I've got a shot at winning this bet, Linc hits a curveball so hard, his bat splinters. For someone who isn't a connoisseur of baseball bats, it might not hit home how much weight needs to go behind a strike like that to cause the bat to splinter. Suddenly, I realize it could've been foolish on my part to think I could out bat someone of Linc's stature.

My nerves return with a vengeance.

"Holy shit! Did you see that?" Linc is swinging what's left of his bat, laughing so hard his voice goes hoarse. "That ball is about to kiss the fucking moon! Get your dancing shoes dusted off, Brooke because we're going to be dancing on that date."

Anders turns and locks eyes with me. "You need to beat his ass. I can't deal with the gloating."

"He just obliterated his bat. There's no way I can top that."

"Fuck me. Trust Linc to bring out his A-game for the sake of a date."

"You guys just won the World Series. I hardly doubt that his batting prowess has anything to do with winning the bet."

"Shows how little you know about him."

Linc strolls over to meet us on the mound. "Can I borrow your bat?"

"Hell no! You just shredded your own. There's no way I'm letting you near my lucky bat."

"Then I guess you're up, pretty lady. Do you need a minute to recover from the majesty of me literally knocking it out of the park?"

I steel myself before meeting his gaze. "Bring it, pretty boy. Do you want to start writing that public statement now, or will you do it on the fly tomorrow?"

"I like your confidence, no matter how misplaced it may be." He slings his arm over my shoulder, and I can see a spark of something in Anders' eyes, but it's fleeting at best.

"Your ass is grass, Nash." Even if I don't feel it, I'm faking confidence as I slip from his side and make my way toward home base.

"If you bat with the same level of swagger that you walk, I'm definitely going to lose." Linc's voice is all gravel and sex appeal, but when I hear Anders, his deep baritone washes over me in a wave of desire.

"Can you stop hitting on her for three seconds?"

"I warned you, bro. If you don't ask her out, I will. Look at her, she's hotter than Hades." I pretend not to hear them and attempt to focus on the task at hand. Linc may have broken a bat, but he hit seven out of ten pitches. If I can hit eight, I win.

I wait until the very last second to turn and stare down the barrel of Anders Verbeck's pitching arm. Linc is riling him up, trying to put him off his game, but from the glint in Anders' eye, he wants me to win.

"Don't go easy on me, Anders. I want your best." I can see his wry smile from over here before he shouts back at me.

"I only have one setting, Lexington, and it's hell for leather." A jolt of electricity runs through me and straight to my core. "You ready?"

I shake it off, forcing myself to step up to the plate. "As I'll ever be."

Swinging the bat a couple of times, I adjust my stance, relying on muscle memory to overcome my nerves. I keep my eyes on Anders, my stomach doing somersaults and my hands bracing for impact as they flex on the bat. This is going to be faster and harder than any ball ever pitched to me.

My muscles are twitching as I anxiously wait, adrenaline coursing through my veins, amping me up. The second he lets the ball fly, my focus is on him for a fraction longer than necessary, making it impossible for me to hit such a fast-paced ball. It goes rushing past me as I swing too late, hitting nothing but air.

The noise as the ball slams into the wall behind me reeks of defeat. One down, and I am not convinced I'm going to be able to hit any of the upcoming balls.

"Strike one, Brooke!" Linc is enjoying this.

"You got this, Lexington. Tune everything else out. It's just you and the ball." I need Anders to stop talking because his gravelly voice is distracting as hell.

"Just pitch. I've got this." I take a deep breath and do as he says. Forcing my eye to the ball rather than the face of the man pitching it, I stand ready with my bat gripped firmly in my hands.

As it leaves his hand, I can read the pitch, remembering every video clip I've watched over the past few weeks. I know exactly when I need to swing, down to a fraction of a second, and when I do, the glorious sound of hard leather connecting with my slugger. It's not the best hit in the world, and if it were during a game, I doubt I'd make it to first base, but I don't care.

"I hit it!" If I had it in me to play it cool right now, I'd stop myself from jumping up and down like a maniac.

"One down, eight to go." Anders is all smiles and encouragement while Linc continues to psyche me out.

"No way you're hitting eight in a row. You're good, but not that good. Even I couldn't hit that."

"Watch me." I exaggerate my stance, wiggling my ass as I get into position. I'm not the only one who can be put off their game. Both of them look a little dazed. "Are you going to pitch or not?"

"You said to watch you. I'm just obeying orders." Anders runs his hand over the scruff on his jaw, and even from this distance, it does something to my insides. Why the hell did I have to vomit all over him the first time we met? This night would be going very differently if I hadn't.

"Go for it. And tell your buddy there to stop trying to mess with my game."

"You're making it too easy for me, Brooke!" I'm sure women fall over themselves for Linc's sexy, smart mouth.

"Just shut up and let me concentrate."

I send the next four pitches with a short but effective hit. The rules don't say anything about me having to hit it farther than Linc. I just need to hit the same or more. Sitting at five out of six right now, my confidence is soaring, even if the ball isn't. I'm two hits away from equalizing and three from winning.

Anders isn't going easy on me. The power behind his throwing arm is insane. As a curveball comes hurtling toward me, I feel it in the split second before it happens—I send it sky-high with one almighty swing of my bat. *Holy shit!*

As I stare to the heavens in disbelief, I don't even see him coming. Anders literally sweeps me off my feet and spins me around like I weigh nothing more than a feather.

"That was amazing. I could kiss you right now. Seriously, that was poetry in motion right there." My brain stutters over the mention of a kiss. My brain is screaming at me to grab his face and press my lips to his. When he sets me down, there's a fraction of a second when our eyes meet, and I think he feels the same sparks that are going off like fireworks in the pit of my stomach. God, he smells good.

"Hey, guys, can you save the high school sexual tension for after Brooke loses?" And just like that, Linc pours the proverbial water on the fire, extinguishing the moment.

"She's going to beat your ass, Linc. Didn't you just witness that hit? Holy fuck. Most of the guys on our team couldn't have knocked that out of the park."

"She's still got to hit another one for a draw. Two for a win."

"You sound a little concerned there, Linc. Worried you're going to be beaten by a girl?"

"Not at all. I love being beaten... off... by a girl."

I can't help but comment. "You have a disturbing way of turning any word or sentence into something sexual. You're aware of that, right?"

"Save the compliments for our first date. You're about to seal the deal on this next hit or lack thereof."

Anders takes a step back. "Let's just finish this already and go eat. I'm starving."

It didn't cross my mind that they would want me to tag along after this little session. I watch as he strides toward the pitcher's mound.

"Why haven't you two bumped uglies yet?" Linc is at my side.

"Stop trying to put me off my game."

"I'm not." He puts his hand over his heart. "It's a genuine question. You're smokin' hot, and you know everything about baseball. You're basically the perfect woman."

"Aside from all the introductory vomit."

"We've all blown chunks after a few too many drinks. It's not a big deal. I assume you've showered since then, and I see the way you're looking at Anders. Doesn't matter if you win or lose, I'm not the guy you want to go on a date with. Am I wrong?"

"Anders has already made it clear that he has no interest in dating me. We're friends. That's all. I just plan to bleed you both dry of your baseball knowledge. Anything to up my game in the women's league. Now step off so I can concentrate."

A baseball comes flying toward Linc, not particularly fast, but with expert precision. He reaches out and grabs it before it hits him in the nuts.

"I think he's ready to pitch."

"Great powers of deduction there, Watson."

"Why the hell am I Watson? I'm totally Sherlock." He feigns offense as he heads for the dugout.

"You ready to show his ass some grass?" Anders shouts across the field.

"Sure am. Let me have it!"

His stance is familiar from hours and hours of studying every pitch in his arsenal. A wicked curveball comes my way, and I already know my bat is never going to connect with it. I can only watch as it passes me by. I knew it was a long shot, but I was starting to believe my own hype. I can't even turn to witness what I'm sure is a shit-eating grin from Linc.

"Last chance, Brooke. You can't beat me, but you still have a chance to tie."

"Try to contain your jubilation, please."

I swing my bat a few times, trying to keep it together for this final pitch, and I can see in the way Anders is moving right now, he's annoyed that I didn't hit the last ball.

"You've got to hit this one, Lexington. Otherwise, Linc is going to be an insufferable asshole for the rest of time."

"Telling me that isn't helpful. Just throw the damn ball." My voice is hoarse from shouting back and forth tonight. As I wait with my bat at the ready, I try to anticipate what Anders will pitch, but I'm completely wrong. Why the hell would he pitch a screwball?

"Looks like you owe me a date, Brooke." Linc is smug as fuck right now. I drop on my haunches, running my fingertips over the plate beneath my feet. *Dammit!*

Anders strides toward me, messing with his ball cap. When he's standing in front of me, I chance an upward glance. He's impossibly handsome, but he doesn't look happy right now.

"I guess you really want me to go on a date with your best buddy. A screwball? Really?"

"I fucked up."

"So you don't want me to date Linc?"

"I don't meddle in his love life, or anyone's for that matter. You agreed to the bet."

"And your last pitch ensured I'd lose."

Linc looks like the cat that got the cream right now. "Feels good to be a winner. It's my default setting, after all. Now, can we blow this popsicle stand and go grab some drinks?"

"I think I'll pass. I've got an early practice in the morning." I push myself up onto my feet and hold out my hand to shake his. "Well played. You won fair and square."

"What's this shit?" He gestures to my outstretched hand before pulling me in for a hug. "When you hit like that against Beck and give me a run for my money at the plate, you get a hug."

"Wasn't enough." He gives me a tender squeeze before grabbing me by the shoulders.

"Don't act like you're that girl who needs to win all the time to know you're amazing. Seriously, there isn't a guy on our team who can hit that many balls when Beck is pitching. Obviously, I'm the exception because I'm Lincoln Nash, but mere mortals can't be held to my standards," he says with a chuckle.

The second he relinquishes his grasp on me, Anders pulls me into his arms. "That was pretty fucking awesome. I'm impressed. You've got skills, Lexington."

"And yet you still got me."

"Well, I don't know if you heard, but I'm kind of a big deal. World Series. Winning pitch. Best curveball in major league baseball right now."

I let myself linger a moment longer than I should before pushing out of his arms. "We're going to have to get drinks at an outside bar. I don't think your ego will fit inside the door. Even those double-wide ones."

"Don't be a hater."

I don't think I could hate Anders Verbeck even if I wanted to.

Chapter Six

ANDERS

I CAN'T BELIEVE how well Brooke hits. I keep tabs on all the great hitters and pitchers in the men's and women's leagues. It's one thing to watch her on a television screen, but I know how fast and hard I pitch. Linc and I weren't blowing smoke up her ass when we said most of our team couldn't hit the way she did—she's legit.

We decided on a bar that serves food, but as I slide into one of the booths in the back corner, Brooke slides in beside Linc, who's quick to spread his arm over her shoulder. I really want to punch him in the face, but I'm the maker of my fucking demise. If I hadn't thrown an impossible-to-hit screwball, he wouldn't be such a smug prick right about now.

Why the hell do I have zero game with this woman?

"So, where do you want to go on our date?"

"You're not really going to hold me to that, are you?"

Linc starts laughing. "Riddle me this, Batman, would you have held me to your end of the deal? Tell me you wouldn't be sitting feeding me lines for my public declaration of the awe and wonder that's Brooke Lexington."

"That's different!"

"Bullshit."

"As much as I hate to say it, he's right. A bet's a bet. You agreed. And I really hate saying that."

"Then I want to go to McDonald's on our date, and I'm going to have a chaperone." I can't help the wry grin that creeps at the corner of my lip. There's the feisty girl I'm quickly—I'm not even going to finish that thought.

"And who are you planning to bring as a third wheel?" Linc sounds a little irate, and it brings a huge fucking grin to my face.

"Anders." My eyes go wide as she kicks me under the table, staring me down like I'm a life raft, and she's onboard the Titanic.

"Ouch. I need my shins." Now, her eyes are bugging out of her head, and it's freaking me out a little.

"You're going to be my chaperone, right?" I rub my hand over the scruff on my jaw while Linc gives me an altogether different stare—the death stare.

"Why do you need someone to go with you? Are you afraid you won't be able to withstand the Nash charm? Or are you thinking you can get lucky with both of us?"

"Now, there's an interesting thought. I hadn't even considered that option." She has a devious grin on her face as she looks between us.

"Not going to happen. I don't share my women, Lexington."

"I'm not your woman, though. I'm your friend." She's playing with me now.

"Friends don't have threesomes." When I take her into my bed —and I know in this moment that it's *when* and not *if*—I won't be fucking sharing with anyone, male or female.

"Speak for yourself, Beck. I'd happily have a threesome with my new friend. My only stipulation is that the third participant is a chick. No guy-on-guy stuff for me."

"Nice to know you have boundaries, Linc," I jibe.

"You trying to impress her with your virtue? I think that ship sailed long ago, my friend. I know you've chowed down on double tacos. Don't try to be all innocent now." I'm going to hit him with a curveball to his testicles tomorrow. He can't be this dimwitted.

"And now I need to change my order. Thanks, Linc, you just put me off tacos for life." Any hope I had of getting myself out of the friendzone with Brooke may have just gone up in a puff of smoke.

"Way to paint a picture, brother." I grab my beer and drain the bottle before signaling the waitress for another.

"And here I thought you were a veritable saint. So, are you telling me you're not a virgin? That was the entire premise of our friendship. I'm cut to the bone." I'm glad she can see the funny side because I'm not feeling it right now.

"Anders Verbeck? I think he lost his virginity back in junior high. Sound about right, Beck?" Linc is enjoying this.

"Yeah, and your sister said it was the best she'd ever had."

Brooke laughs so hard beer shoots out of her nose and peppers my side of the table. "Oh my God." She looks horrified. "I'm so sorry." She starts scrambling for napkins.

"Not the worst bodily fluids you've covered me in. Don't sweat it."

"Don't remind me. I'm still mortified by that entire night."

"Why? If it were that terrible, I'd have left and never spoken to you again."

"True." She gives me a sly smile. "It probably says more about your low bar for friendship, which makes perfect sense when I see you hang with this guy all the time." She nods in Linc's direction.

"When did you puking on him all Exorcist style become about my worthiness as friend material? I think you guys are ganging up on me now."

"I'm one hundred percent certain that your ego will be just fine." She doesn't miss a beat—she's quick-witted.

"She's got you pegged already, bro."

"Well, if you're done ragging on me, there's a blonde at the bar giving me the bedroom eyes."

"I'm going to have to insist that you forfeit your winnings. If you think I'm going on a date with you when you're planning to leave the table to go have sex with some random woman, you're out of your mind."

"We all know I'm not the one you want to get jiggy with, so I relinquish my winnings, but only if you go on that date with my boy here." He gives me a conspiratorial wink, and it makes me cringe.

"Just go already. I don't need you brokering deals on my behalf."

"Your loss, bro. I always seal the deal." I'm relieved when he heads off to chat up the blonde.

"Is he always like that?"

"Like what?"

"A manwhore."

"Yep. You could be riding that train right now. Why did you think you'd need me to chaperone you?"

"I didn't, but you're fun to hang out with, and there's no way in hell I'd let myself become a notch on his bedpost. Clearly, you already know that I make questionable decisions when I'm under the influence of alcohol."

"We all do. You've got to let loose once in a while."

"True." She holds my gaze, biting down on her lip, making my cock twitch in my pants.

"So, tell me, Lexington, what do you like besides baseball, cocktails, Mario Kart, and the occasional bad choices?"

"What else is there? I've been obsessed with baseball since I made the boys' little league team let me play when I was five." I can just imagine her all tiny and full of fire. "Why are you smiling?"

"I'm not surprised that you were a ballbuster even when you were a kid."

"Is that a compliment?"

"Hell, yeah. It paid off in spades. You're an amazing hitter. I don't think I can adequately convey how impressed I was tonight. I pitch against the best there is, and you would give any one of them a run for their money."

"Thanks. It's daunting being on the receiving end of your curveball, and shit, when you threw that screwball, I was convinced you *wanted* me to go on a date with Linc."

"You said you hit a mean screwball. Trust me, I wasn't trying to aid and abet him."

"So, does that mean we can do this again sometime?" Her shy smile is super cute and betrays the air of confidence she exudes at all times. Somehow, she had me on the backfoot from the beginning, even in a vomitous haze.

"I'm down for that."

"Great. I know this is supposed to be your downtime after winning the World Series, so just whenever you feel like hanging out, text me."

"Sounds like a plan. I'm going to grab another drink at the bar. Can I get you anything?"

"I could be persuaded. Margarita, please."

"Coming up."

As I head to the bar, I grab my phone and type out a quick text. Before I hit send, thinking I'm a smooth operator, I turn to see Brooke already staring at her phone with a furrowed brow. There's a distinct possibility that she just let out a string of expletives—I'm no lip reader, but it doesn't take a genius to make out the word *fuck* over and over again. Shoving my phone back in my pocket, I order the drinks and head back to the table.

"Everything okay? You look pissed off."

"Nothing worth talking about." I know enough about women that when one says the word *nothing*, I know she's blazing mad. At least I know it wasn't anything I did.

"Spill before your head explodes. I don't need you blowing chunks of brain matter on me. A line needs to be drawn." She cracks a smile.

"Mom problems."

"You're a mom?" What the fuck? How did I not know this?

"No, dumbass. *My* mom."

"Oh. Okay. I have experience with mothers. Not to brag, but they love me."

"I bet they do. In fact, I'm certain my mom would trade me in for you." The waitress brings our drinks over, but I don't take my eyes off Brooke.

"So, what's she done to piss you off?"

"They are coming up on their thirty-fifth wedding anniversary, and my mom decided they were going to renew their vows and basically have a full-scale wedding."

"That's awesome. Your parents are still in love with each other after decades. Isn't that a good thing?"

"Yeah, except when my mom decided I can't go stag to her re-wedding. I have two weeks to find a date, and she has messaged me every fucking day for a month asking if I've magically pulled a boyfriend out of my ass. If I have to endure another lecture about the importance of personalized place settings, I'm going to pierce my eardrums for some fucking peace and quiet."

And so, a plan is born.

"I'll be your boyfriend." Her eyebrows shoot up so high, they almost leave her forehead.

"Come again?"

"I'll be your fake boyfriend for the wedding. Tell me it's not a great idea? Parents love me..." She cuts me off mid-sentence.

"My dad might call off the wedding and attempt to woo you. He's your biggest fan." She rolls her eyes at the prospect, but I know she's going to say yes.

"Perfect. I can swoop in with my fake boyfriend cape, wow your parents with your epic girlfriend potential, and then mosey on out when the weekend is over."

"You're going to regret this offer. You'll have to stay at my parents' house, my mom won't settle for anything less. You'll have to eat, sleep, and breathe a wedding... for two people you don't know and a woman you barely know, if we're being honest. Why would you even offer? You're... you." Her tone makes me laugh.

"I'm aware that I am, in fact, me. And I'm offering because I think it could be fun seeing you in your natural habitat."

"Being at my parents' house is in no way my natural anything these days. You're either going to love me or hate me by the time they say *I do*."

"I'll take my chances." I offer my hand across the table. "Shake on it. If I can win the World Series, I can win over your mom." She throws her head back and laughs.

"We'll see, I guess."

Linc reappears long enough to grab his jacket while the blonde he was talking to stands by the door. "I'm heading out. You two can handle being left alone, right?"

"I'll call you tomorrow, jackass."

"Not before noon. I'm planning to be up all night." He gives Brooke a sly wink. "You could've been the one swinging from my chandelier tonight."

"How will I ever forgive myself for passing up the chance to bang the great Lincoln Nash?" She can't even say it with a straight face.

"I guess you'll have to settle for this joker." He nods in my direction.

"Fuck off already. Your bimbo is getting impatient."

"And that's my cue." He gives me a mock, elaborate salute before heading in the direction of his conquest for the night.

When he disappears out the door, Brooke looks me up and down. "Do you want a napkin for that drool on your chin?" I love that she runs her hand over her lips as if she believes me.

"You're hot. It's not a crime to look. Besides, if you're going to be my fake boyfriend, we need to seem naturally affectionate, don't you think?"

"Why don't we go the whole hog and create a little buzz?"

"What do you mean?" She eyes me up and down like prime rib.

"If we let ourselves be seen hanging out like we are right now, we're bound to draw a little attention. Make it seem authentic. There's no reason we can't have some fun. What do you say?"

"You're crazy, but you also might be a devious genius."

"Scoot over here beside me. We'll start with a little selfie action." She does as I ask, sidling up good and close. I drape my arm over her shoulder and pull up the camera on my phone. "Ready?"

"Yep." She turns and grabs my face, pulling me in for a kiss. I drop my phone, the thud of it hitting off the table, startling Brooke. "You were supposed to take a picture."

"Stop talking." I slide my hands into her long chestnut brown hair, my eyes locked on her just long enough to ask permission without words before my lips crash down on hers. *Fuck!* She tastes so damn good. I lick the seam of her lips, and as she darts her tongue out to meet mine in a gentle caress, my cock strains against my pants. I'm desperate to deepen our kiss, but the moment I take a breath, she pulls back, putting some distance between us.

"Wow!" Her breath is labored, and her lips are kiss-swollen, but she quickly recovers herself. "Shrewd move, Verbeck. You almost had me believing you're into me. Holy shit, you're a good kisser."

My breath is ragged, each labored rise and fall of my chest giving me away. "Lexington, I'm a baseball player, not an actor."

"You have a new career path when you retire." She grabs my phone and thrusts it into my hand. "Will you actually take the picture this time?" Her eyes refuse to meet my gaze, and I know she enjoyed that kiss just as much as I did. This fake boyfriend thing is going to be fun.

"Sure. Maybe just plant one somewhere less boner-inducing this time." As she presses her breasts against my shoulder, she places a featherlight kiss on the rough stubble of my cheek while bracing herself with a hand on my leg. She inadvertently turns a semi into a full-on boner, and when the slightest tip of her finger brushes against it, I'm rewarded with her sharp intake of breath.

It takes all my self-control not to throw her over my shoulder like a caveman and head for my place. My mind is flooded with flashes of what I'd like to do to her—how glorious she would look naked with her legs parted, waiting for me to feast on her for hours.

I snap a quick picture and upload it to my Instagram account, tagging Brooke in it before I change my mind about this idiotic plan.

"I guess we should head out. It's getting late." When I chance a glance in her direction, she's biting down on her bottom lip, and it's sexy as hell.

"Anders."

"Yeah."

"Do you want to have dinner with me next weekend? A fake date."

"It's a date." I leave it hanging out there, letting her interpret my answer any way she chooses. For me, there's nothing fake about what I just felt when her lips were on mine. I want Brooke Lexington, and I'm going to be such a phenomenal fake boyfriend at this wedding. When it's over, I'm going to pull out all the stops to get her on a real date.

Fuck the friendzone. I'm going to hit a home run with this girl.

THE PICTURE I POSTED ON INSTAGRAM OF BROOKE AND ME LAST week has been reposted, tweeted, and plastered all over Facebook. I guess it did the trick. Brooke called me within twenty-four hours, waxing lyrical about the fact that her mom was going crazy over it, in a good way. I'm officially on the seating chart for this wedding, and our fake date tonight has turned into a dinner with her parents.

Nothing like a baptism of fire.

Her folks live in the Hamptons, so I offer to drive and have some fun in the Corvette. When she steps out of the front door of her apartment building, my jaw drops. She's not wearing anything fancy, but this woman makes jeans and a Yankees shirt look edible. Leaning against the hood of my car, I take a moment to drink her in before we hit the road.

"Hey, slugger. What's with the grin?"

"I've never seen a Yankees shirt look so good."

"I better not show you this then." She does a twirl, and I see my name on the back of her jersey. *Holy fuck!* "Thought it would be a nice touch."

"Damn." I bite down on my knuckles, my cock straining against my jeans.

"You like?" she asks with a knowing grin.

"I'd have to be dead or gay not to be completely turned on by you right now."

"You don't look too shabby yourself, Anders."

I open the passenger side door for her. "If I'm going to win over your mom, I thought I better be clean-shaven and wear a shirt."

"She's going to love you. I swear to God, she hasn't stopped messaging me all week. You probably need to worry more about my dad. He's your biggest fan when you are on the pitcher's mound, but he thinks you're sticking it to his daughter. You've probably gone from MLB rock star to top of his hit list."

"Well, shit. I didn't think of it like that." As I slide into the driver's seat, Brooke attempts to reverse the frown she just put on my face.

"Don't worry. It's all fake. A few weeks from now, you'll never need to see them again." She smiles brightly as I rev up the engine and pull into traffic.

"Yeah. Fake. Awesome. I hope the fake beating he gives me tonight will only fake hurt." At least I made her laugh. Not only do I need to be convincing with Brooke's parents, I need to be convincing to her so she doesn't suspect I'm not faking it at all.

Chapter Seven

BROOKE

THIS WAS A TERRIBLE IDEA. My mom is going to see right through me. She'll know I'm lying. As Anders pulls into my parents' driveway, I realize I should've just stood my ground on the vow renewal front. It's unreasonable for my mom to insist I bring a date.

I feel like I'm going to be sick.

He looks impossibly gorgeous tonight, and my mom will eat him alive, chew him up, and spit him out. Then, he's going to drop me home and will likely try to ghost me, and I couldn't even blame him. *Ugh.* Why did I have to meet him on a bad drunken night?

Before I can even get my seat belt off, my mom and dad are on the front porch. Mom is waving like a lunatic, and my dad has his arms crossed over his chest, the furrow of his brow evident from fifty feet away. He can be quite menacing-looking when he wants to.

Anders kills the engine. "I'll come around and open your door. I don't need strike one before we even get to the front door. Your dad looks pissed off. Does he always look that way? Whatever the male equivalent of resting bitch face is."

"Resting dick face?" He starts laughing.

"I'm trying to picture what that would be. Resting dick. Semi-hard and hung to the left?" He makes some goofball face at me before getting out and jogging around to my side of the car to open the door for me. He offers his hand to steady me as I try to extricate myself from the Corvette's low seat. As I slide my hand into his, a jolt of electricity rips through me.

I lift my gaze to his, and I'm met with the same heat I feel in every fiber of my being. "Game on." I take a deep breath to calm my nerves. Anders is so natural, his hand moving to the small of my back, guiding me over to the door where my mom is waiting impatiently. I don't remember the last time a man touched me in a chivalrous, protective way—fake or genuine.

"I've got your back, Lexington. Relax," he whispers. "All you have to do is pretend to be into me for a couple of hours." His lips brush over my ear in a delicate caress. "It's not that difficult, is it?"

I want to tell him there's no faking necessary. The way my body is sparking to life right now at just the faintest of touches, I want to get back in the car and speed to my apartment with him. Who wouldn't be into Anders? He's funny, smart, at the top of his game with the body of a god, and he's cool to hang out with.

My mom is too impatient to wait for us to reach the door, instead almost tackling Anders to the ground. "Anders Verbeck. Welcome to our humble abode."

I hate it when my mom says that. There's nothing humble about a mansion in the Hamptons.

"Thanks for inviting me, Mrs. Lexington." His voice oozes confidence and sex. The latter might be my libido interpreting everything he says with a sultry overtone.

"Please, call me Martha. Mrs. Lexington makes me feel old."

"You look young enough to be Brooke's sister. I don't think you have anything to worry about, Martha." I'm simultaneously impressed by Anders' game and annoyed that my mom is blushing and touching his arm like a shameless flirt.

"Oh, this one's a keeper, Brooke. If you don't marry him, I might have to ditch your father and snap young Anders up for myself."

"Mom! That's officially the grossest thing you've ever said to one of my boyfriends. Please, for the love of everything holy, stop."

She rests her hand on Anders' arm, ushering him toward the front steps, and my dad is staring at her with consternation in every line of his face. "She talks like we've met other boyfriends. I think the only boy Brooky brought home to meet us was her prom date and that's only because my husband insisted on it."

"Great. Thanks for painting such a rosy picture of me, Mom. I'm sure Anders is desperate to hear about my dating life."

"I'm only telling the truth, sweetheart." She turns her attention back to Anders. "Oh, I'm sure she's dated, or at least had some one-night stands under her belt, but she always gets mad when I ask her if she's making time for a healthy sex life."

"Dad! Will you please wrangle your wife? What the hell, Mom?"

My dad cracks a sliver of a smile as he walks toward me, enveloping me in his arms. "If I could wrangle your mother, none of this hoopla would be happening in the first place. There's no point in fighting it, baby, it's like swimming against the tides. She's a force of nature, and the only way to survive is to give in and go with the flow."

"Can you at least ask her to stop discussing my sex life in front of Anders? Or at all for that matter." He squeezes me tight, pressing a kiss to my forehead.

"That I can do. Trust me, I want to hear about that stuff about as much as I want to go and get my yearly prostate exam."

"You've got wine, right?"

"Of course. Unfortunately, I can't give you a glass without giving one to your mom, and she's going to be even more inappropriate after a few glasses of chardonnay."

As we head inside, I chance a glance behind me at my mom and Anders. When he meets my gaze, a beautiful, panty-dropping smile spreads across his gorgeous face, and my stomach begins to somersault. I guess he's laid back about this whole dinner thing. The pressure isn't there when it's not a real relationship to start with. Anyone can survive any situation for a few hours. Anders is obviously about to do it in style.

My mom is laughing and fawning all over him as they trail behind us. He's charming, that's for sure. As soon as the door closes, my mom goes into full-on hostess mode. "Can I get you a drink, Anders? You seem like a scotch kind of man. Classy with a devious streak."

"You've got me pegged already, Martha. Maybe another night. I'm driving, and I won't want to be impaired when I drive your lovely daughter home later. Water will do me just fine."

"Such a gentleman. Did you hear that, Richard?" She practically shouts at my dad.

"I'm standing two feet away, darling. Of course, I heard."

Anders immediately turns his attention to my dad, offering a handshake. "Thank you for the invite tonight, Mr. Lexington. It's a pleasure to meet you."

My dad gives him what I assume is more than a firm shake. "As long as you treat my daughter right, you're welcome in our home. Do her wrong, and I'll hunt you down."

Anders blanches at his words but quickly gives him the right answer. "I'd expect nothing less, Mr. Lexington. Your daughter is one of a kind." He looks to me, faking adoration, and for a moment, I bask in the glow. "I have no intention of getting on her bad side or yours."

My dad slaps him on the back, and just like that, we're over the first hump.

"You've pitched a hell of a season, son. Yankees haven't looked this good in years. How does it feel to be a World Series champion?" My dad leads us into the dining room.

"Pretty damn good, sir. I hit my stride with the team this year."

"That's an understatement. I just about hit the ceiling when you threw that last pitch that took us to the World Series."

"You're a Yankees fan?" Anders knows my dad's a huge baseball fan. He plays the unassuming boyfriend very well.

"Yep. Who do you think Brooke got her love of baseball from? I had her in a Yankees onesie the day she was born."

"I'd love to see a picture sometime." He gives me a genuine smile and a sly wink of his eye. "I bet you were a cute baby, Brooke."

My name seems foreign on his lips. I'm already used to him

calling me by my last name. "We don't need to break out the photo albums, thank you very much."

"On the contrary. I want to see if you're as cute in a onesie as you are in my jersey." He leans over, running a hand across his name emblazoned on my back. It's such a tender gesture.

Nothing gets past my dad, and he's quick to pick up on it. "Never thought I'd see the day when you had someone else's name on your back, kiddo. I hope you've given him your team's jersey. It's only fair, after all."

Anders drapes his arm lazily over my shoulder, pulling me into his side. "Yeah, where's my shirt? I want a jersey with Lexington scrawled on the back."

Before I can say anything else, my mom appears with a tray of drinks. "Dinner is almost ready. Here are your drinks."

"Can I help with anything, Martha?"

"Such a nice young man. Don't you lift a finger, dear." She disappears back toward the kitchen. "Richard! Come and help me, please."

My dad just rolls his eyes before following her foghorn request. "Apparently, you're the new favorite, Anders. Enjoy it while it lasts." He chuckles to himself as he leaves.

"He's right, you know. I don't think my mom has ever been so happy about one of my dinner guests."

"I'll take it as high praise." He doesn't retract his arm from the back of my chair. If anything, he leans in closer as he speaks. "Exactly how many boyfriends have made it to the dinner table?"

Heat rises in my cheeks, making me blush. "My mom wasn't exaggerating. My prom date is the only guy I ever introduced them to."

"Wow. Then I really am honored. Fake or not, I'm competitive as fuck. How lucky did the prom date get?"

"Why? Are you going to fake taking my virginity?" My attempt to be funny backfires as he tilts his head, pinning me with his ice-blue gaze.

"Only if you promise not to fake an orgasm like I'm sure you did with your prom date."

My breath catches. His voice so sexy—just hearing him say the word *orgasm* has me ready to cream my pants. "Something tells me I wouldn't need to fake anything with you."

He runs his thumb over my bottom lip, his eyes flitting to my tongue as I dart it out to lick the tip. The rapid rise and fall of his chest tell me I affect him. "I'd make sure of it, over and over again." His words are slow and measured.

I can't take my eyes off his lips, desperately wanting a taste of him, but before I get a chance, my mom comes bursting in with plates of food, yapping about something at my dad. The second she sees us mere inches away from what I know would be an explosive kiss, she can't help but comment.

"You two are so cute together. You'd have such gorgeous babies." She barely takes a breath as she sets down our plates of food. "Wouldn't they have beautiful babies, Richard?"

My dad grumbles something under his breath as he takes his seat across from me. "Yes, yes, Martha. Why don't we let them get through dinner before starting a family?"

The moment is squashed like a bug beneath my mother's over-bearing foot. I love her to death, but I'm beginning to think faking a boyfriend for their vow renewal is going to be harder than going stag.

"So, Anders, when did you start playing baseball?" My dad comes to my rescue, as usual.

"Please, call me Beck. And to answer your question, I think I was three when I started playing. Batting was never my strength, but lucky for me, I have a good arm."

"I can attest to that," I interject.

"I doubt your father wants to hear about your boyfriend's sexual prowess, but I'm all ears. Foreplay is so very important."

"What the hell are you talking about, Mom? How do you get from a pitcher's arm to foreplay? That's just weird."

She throws her head back and laughs. "I thought you meant he's good with his hands." When she wiggles her eyebrows at me, I want to crawl under the table and wait for death to take me.

"Let's just assume that whenever I'm talking, it's not about sex or anything remotely close to that topic of conversation."

"Don't be such a prude, darling. Anyway, if you're not talking about this gorgeous boy's skilled hands, what did you mean?"

"He took me to Yankee Stadium and pitched for me. It was amazing. *He's* amazing." I know I'm blushing again like a high school cheerleader. As much as I disgust myself at this moment, Anders has a beaming smile on his face that makes it all seem okay.

"Don't clam up now, Brooke. What was it like batting against this guy?" My dad can't hide his obvious excitement.

"Imagine how hard a baseball going at 105 mph would feel, and then triple it. That's what it actually feels like."

"And I bet you knocked at least one out of the park." My dad is grinning from ear to ear.

Anders answers for me, giddy to share how well I did. "She hit seven out of ten. It was incredible, and I assure you, I wasn't going easy on her."

"Holy crap!" My dad looks stunned.

"Still wasn't good enough to beat Linc."

"You were batting against Lincoln Nash? Why is this the first I'm hearing about this?"

"Daddy, this is the first you've seen me since it happened. Linc is Anders' best friend. You should've seen it. Anders pitched a top-speed curveball, and Linc hit it so hard, his bat splintered into a million pieces. It was insane."

"I'd love to have seen that. I always knew you could hit with the big dawgs."

"You should come sometime and watch Brooke giving me a run for my money. I can give you the unofficial tour of the stadium. Plus, now we've got the World Series trophy sitting pride of place."

My dad looks to me with a sly grin. "Your mom might be right, sweetheart. This one's a keeper." My parents are hopeless. A flashy smile and the promise of every New Yorker's Mecca, and they're ready to sell me off like cattle.

"You really don't have to do that, Anders. It's a kind offer, but

I'm sure you're way too busy to pander to these two crazies. Let's just eat before they call the minister and pay you a dowry for me."

"Sounds like a win-win situation, Lexington." He's enjoying my eternal discomfort.

"Oh, how adorable." I grab a bread roll and stuff it in my face. My mom isn't making it easy to tell a little white lie. I've never been much good at it, even when it would've saved me some heartache. "Brooky, that's so unattractive. You weren't raised by wolves. There's plenty of food, you don't have to shoehorn it into your mouth."

"It's so I don't say something I'll reg..." My inaudible protest makes me choke on the bread. Anders immediately goes into rescue mode as I struggle to cough up the inordinate amount of bread lodged in my throat. I reach for my glass, but I'm starting to panic, and my mom is freaking out.

Anders stands up, positioning himself behind me, lifting me into a standing position before pressing his chest to mine and wrapping his arms around my torso. With a short, sharp squeeze, he dislodges the bread, and I watch in horror as a globby mess tumbles into the center of the dining table. I don't think anyone will be eating the bowl of green beans that are now swimming in my saliva and bread chunks.

"Take a deep breath." Anders rubs my back as he sits me down and hands me a glass of water. "You can't stop spitting stuff on me, can you? You're lucky I like you." I really wish he hadn't just said that.

"If you came to give me a heart attack tonight, you succeeded." My mom is white as a sheet right now. "Thankfully, Anders was here to save your life."

Oh, my God! Really? "I think you're being a little dramatic, Mom." I turn to look at Anders, and I'm met with worry etched in his brow. "Thank you. I was starting to panic a little there. I promise I'll try to stop spitting on you."

"What's he talking about? Why would you spit on your boyfriend?"

My dad drops his head in his hands, his mind going to worse

things than a little vomit. "Martha, some things are better off unanswered."

"Dad. Don't you start as well. He only meant that I puked on him a few weeks ago." I immediately wish I'd kept my mouth shut.

"That's disgusting. Just because you're an athlete doesn't mean you need to forfeit being a lady, Brooky."

"I didn't do it on purpose." Anders steps in once again to save my ass. It seems to be a theme of our friendship thus far.

"The night I met your daughter, she was feeling a little under the weather. If she hadn't been, I wouldn't have insisted on escorting her home safely. When I was sure she felt better, we got to talking, and I knew I wanted to get to know her better. It all worked out for the best, or we wouldn't be sitting here together right now."

He tucks a loose curl behind my ear and presses a chaste kiss to my cheek.

"Well, aren't you just a unicorn of a gentleman. I thought that sort of chivalry ended with my generation." I think my mom is falling for Anders hook, line, and sinker.

"I do my best. Your daughter brings out the best in me. She's a credit to you both." He looks lovingly into my eyes, and I'm starting to worry that I'm buying into this charade. Anders is a great liar. This could backfire on me, big time.

The rest of the evening goes by without incident, and by the time we're ready to leave, my dad is making plans to visit Yankee Stadium, and my mom has my wedding china picked out. When we finally get into the car and close the doors, my entire body sags under the weight of an evening of deception. I love my mom and dad, and I've never been one for secrets and lies when it comes to them. We're close, and I like it that way. This just feels wrong.

As Anders pulls out the driveway and heads back in the direction we came, he's grinning from ear to ear. "Admit it, I'm the model boyfriend."

"Hands down. All of the benefits and none of the commitment. I'm pretty sure my mom is in love with you. If you're into it, I bet she'd swap my dad out for you at the ceremony next weekend." He throws his head back and laughs.

"Cougars don't do it for me."

"You realize I won't hold you to schmoozing my dad, right?"

"I wouldn't have offered if I didn't want to. He's a Yankees fan. What better time to take a tour than right after a World Series win?"

"You only signed up for a wedding date. Not a dinner where you had to give me the fricking Heimlich maneuver and a job as a tour guide for my old man." Being in the confined space of the car makes me edgy.

"A job? You're starting to make me feel like a gigolo."

"A gigolo gets copious quantities of sex. Totally not the same thing."

"Damn. Why didn't I sign up for the gigolo gig? Can I change my status from helpful friend to super serious, overachieving gigolo? No payment required. Just an enthusiastic orgasm when I'm writhing between your thighs."

Every fiber of my being comes alive at the mention of it. Could I really enjoy the intimacies that a boyfriend affords without getting attached? Not likely, given that I already want to hang out with him after this arrangement is over.

"Don't temp me, Anders."

"You don't know me well enough yet, but let me assure you, Lexington, when someone tells me not to do something, it makes me want to do it all the more." My stomach does somersaults as he gives me a quick glance full of sex, desire, and the most delicious, wicked intent.

"Are you going to try to seduce me at the wedding?"

"Who says I haven't already started?"

God help me!

Chapter Eight

ANDERS

I GOT a call this morning from my agent. We've been fielding new offers from all the big brands since the World Series win. I already had great endorsement deals, but the silver tuna of baseball has come knocking on my door again. This time they don't just want me, they also want my 'girlfriend.'

Brooke and I leave today for our four-day wedding extravaganza of fake relationship bliss. I figured it would be better to discuss this with her face to face. She's been busy this week, or at least that's what she's telling me. Ever since I declared that I might be tempted to seduce her, Brooke has kept me at arm's length. We've spoken and texted back and forth, but even at that, her responses are short, clipped, and less than enthusiastic.

I fire off a quick message to let her know I'm on my way.

Me: *Be there in 15 to pick you up. Remember to pack your dancing shoes.*

Brooke: *OK.*

Me: *Do you want to just go to this thing yourself? If you've changed your mind, it's fine. You seem... off.*

Brooke: *Sorry. Sorry I'm crabby. Sorry I dragged you into all this.*

Me: *I'll be there shortly. We can talk.*

I drop my phone onto the passenger seat and step on the gas.

Whatever is going on with Brooke, I want to figure it out sooner rather than later.

When I pull up outside her building, she's ready and waiting with a small suitcase at her side. I kill the engine and get out to help with her bag.

"Hey, beautiful." I lean in, giving her a small kiss on the cheek to say hello. The smell of her perfume is intoxicating. "Let me get that for you." I manage to squeeze her suitcase into the tiny trunk on this thing. It might have been a better idea to bring my Expedition.

She stands at the passenger door, staring off in the distance, lost in her thoughts. "Why did you agree to this? What are we doing?"

"We're going to a wedding, and we're going to have fun. It's an excuse to get dressed up, get drunk, dance, and make some poor choices."

"My whole family is going to be there. How are we going to convince everyone that we're a real couple? We know nothing about each other. Not really."

"For a start, that's not true. We know plenty about each other's careers. I know you can't hold your liquor. You chew on your bottom lip when you get nervous, and you can't hold my gaze for more than three seconds. You've got a great sense of humor, but you're fierce and the highest-paid female baseball player of all time. I know you, Lexington, better than you care to admit."

"I… we…" I close the trunk and walk over to her. With her lips only inches from mine, I answer for her.

"I think you know me better than you think. What's real?" I hold her gaze. "Are you afraid that it won't feel authentic when we touch each other? The devil is in the details, after all."

"People notice that stuff. We're not used to holding hands, kissing, or showing affection the way boyfriend and girlfriend do so effortlessly."

My eyes flit to her lips. Her breath is erratic. "Does this feel forced or fake to you?" I slide my hands up into her hair, my eyes searching hers for permission. Then, I slowly press my lips to hers in a soft caress. Every nerve ending in my body goes off like fireworks. An ache I didn't know was there, blossoms in my chest, constricting as I deepen the kiss, licking the seam of her lips before darting my tongue in to meet hers.

My pulse is racing as she rakes her hands down my back, pulling me closer with an urgency that makes me hard as a fucking rock. "Tell me this doesn't feel real to you." My words are lost on her lips as she moans, sending me into a tailspin. There's nothing fake about this moment—about this woman.

I back her up against the car, my hands fisting in her hair, my body begging for more. Cars are honking their horns for one of two reasons—either the show we're putting on right now on a busy street or, more likely, they want me to move my double-parked car. She tastes so damn good it takes everything inside me to stop—to push myself back and take a breath. I wipe my thumb over my bottom lip, sticky with Brooke's cherry lip gloss.

"We better get going if we're going to make it to dinner at your folks' house." Her breath is labored, her chest heaving in the most enticing of ways as she reaches for the door handle. "I think maybe you should drive."

"What?" Her eyes snap to mine, a grin spreading on her kiss-smudged lips.

"My dick is in the driver's seat right now. I don't think I'm in any shape to concentrate on the road. Not when you're sitting next to me looking so fucking sexy, I want to rip your clothes off."

"Anders."

I don't want her to say anything because one of two things will happen. Either I'll take her right here on the bonnet of my car without a care for who watches, or she's going to send me away. "Can you just drive?"

"Okay." She rests her hand on my chest, my heart beating wildly against her palm. "Your heart's racing." Looking up at me through hooded lashes, I'm the one who has to avert my gaze. I think we just crossed over the barrier and out of the friendzone, and my timing couldn't be worse.

The ride to the Hamptons is shorter than it should be, but only because Brooke was breaking every speed limit between Manhattan and her parents' house. This time, the driveway is full of cars, and the second she cuts the engine, we can hear a party going on in the backyard.

"About earlier." She can't even look at me.

"We don't need to talk about it right now. I know what this is, Lexington. You don't have to spell it out. I'll grab the bags from the trunk and meet you inside. Go and say hi to your family, I'll be right behind you."

She gives me a tight smile and heads inside. I take a minute to center myself. We took advantage of the radio on the drive up here, letting music fill the silence between us. I pull my phone out and text Linc.

Me: *What the fuck was I thinking? Why didn't you stop me?*

Linc: *I told you so, bro. Don't do fake shit with a real woman, and don't do real shit with a fake woman. It's the only piece of wisdom I've ever bestowed on you. It ain't my fault you're dumber than a bag of rocks.*

Me: *Thanks. I feel so much better.*

Linc: *You've got four days to turn it around. I guarantee if you come back to Manhattan without sealing the deal, the deal is dead in the water.*

Me: *I fucking know that.*

Linc: *Then stop pissing around talking to me and go use your charm and good looks. Do I have to spell it out for you? G-O. A-N-D. F-U-C-K. H-E-R. B-R-A-I-N-S. O-U-T.*

Me: *You're a dick.*

Linc: *At least my dick is getting some action this weekend. It's more than yours will be getting if you don't get your head out of your ass and stop being this chick's friend.*

Me: *When everyone in the locker room starts calling you Limp Dick Linc, just know that I started the rumor. Today. After your shit advice.*

Linc: *Do that, and I'll make you the Yankees' new eunuch. You're my wingman. You have more game than anyone other than me. Stop overthinking with your dimwitted brain, and let your dick steer the ship. Later, eunuch.*

Me: *Later, limp dick.*

As much as I hate to admit it, Linc might have a point. I've gotten way too in my head about this woman. If I had any sense and self-respect right now, I'd get back in the car and leave. This is a job for a guy who has zero interest in sleeping with Brooke, and *if* that guy exists, he's asexual.

I grab the bags and head for the door, but before I get a chance to knock, a woman opens the door, eyeing me warily. I recognize her.

"Lacey. The best friend, right?" She narrows her gaze as if she's trying to see down to the depths of my soul.

"Yep. Remember when I told you not to hurt her?"

"I sure do."

"Then, what the hell are you doing here leading her on with some fake-ass-pretend-boyfriend shit?"

"She told you?"

"No, but you just did." Shit.

"What do you want, Lacey?"

"I want to know why a World Series champion, who can bag any woman he wants, is playing the role of dutiful fake boyfriend to my best friend? What's your angle?"

"Do I have to have one? Did you ever contemplate that I like spending time with her? We're friends." I need to work on my lying before I meet everyone else.

"Bullshit. I'll be watching you this weekend. If you put a toe out of line or try to take advantage of Brooke, I'll rip your balls off."

"What is it with everyone wanting to rip my balls off today?"

Brooke appears in the doorway before I dig myself a deeper hole. "Can you let him in the door, Lace? I sort of need him in here. He's not a vampire, it's okay to invite him in."

"He may not have fangs, but he's just as deadly, I'm sure." She gives me a sickly-sweet smile as Brooke pulls her out of the way. "I'll be watching you, Verbeck."

"Awesome." What the fuck am I doing?

Brooke grabs my arm and hauls me through the living room and upstairs.

"Welcome to *our* room." I look around. It's nice.

"Great. Why do you look pissed?"

"I thought we'd be in separate rooms. But, my mom, being the wildly inappropriate woman she is, wanted us to have time together to, and I quote, 'explore our physical connection' while we're here. Geez, why can't she be like every other mother in America and frown on unmarried daughters having a lover under her roof." Brooke starts pacing the floor like a caged animal.

"We're grown adults. I was expecting to share a room with you. Apparently, the only person bothered by it is you."

"For once, I just wish my mom wouldn't be so fucking cool about everything. I want lectures about *why buy the cow when you can get the milk for free*. Is it too much to ask?"

I drop our bags and stop Brooke in her tracks, pulling her into my arms. "Take a breath. It's fine. Your parents are good people. You're not a 'cow' giving away your milk or whatever. We're here. It's going to be a great weekend. We'll have some laughs, your parents will get married a second time, and I can sleep on the floor. It's not a big deal."

Before she can answer, there's a knock on the door. "Brooky, are you going to bring Anders downstairs. The sex can wait until later. Everyone's dying to meet him. Your dad's been bragging that the star pitcher for the Yankees is here."

"Mom, we're not having sex. What's wrong with you?" Brooke storms over to the door, practically swinging it off the hinges.

"If I were thirty years younger, I'd be jumping this handsome man's bones in a hot minute."

"It's official. I'm never having sex again because you just scarred me beyond measure."

Brooke's mom pulls her into her arms, hugging her tight, and whispers in her ear. I don't think I'm supposed to hear what she's saying, but Martha doesn't have the quietest of voices, even when she's trying to whisper. "Stop getting in your own way, sweetheart."

"I'm not," Brook replies.

When she lets her daughter go, her gaze flits from Brooke to me. "I beg to differ. Now, I expect both of you in the backyard in five minutes, or I'm coming back up here to drag you downstairs. Understood?"

"Yes, ma'am. We'll be right there," I answer for us both.

Satisfied, her mom leaves us, tapping her watch to remind

Brooke that we're on a five-minute countdown. As soon as we're alone, she covers her face with her hands. "God, I'm so mortified."

I close the distance between us, gently tugging her hands down, forcing her to look at me. "So, it's not a big deal your mom's a bit of a cougar with a very healthy libido. She has eyes. I'm hot. You can't hold it against her that she appreciates all of this."

I'd be offended that she bursts out laughing if it weren't for the fact that it was my intention. "She's probably attracted to how humble you are." A little snort escapes her, and it's so stinking cute, it's ridiculous.

"You like that I'm cocky. I've got the goods to back it up." If I were to brush up against her right now, she'd feel my goods straining against my pants. She takes a step back, extricating herself from my grasp, but she can't hide the way her breath quickens when her eyes meet mine.

"We better get downstairs before she comes back up here with a packet of condoms." Now I'm the one laughing.

"She wouldn't."

"She did… my senior year of high school. The prom date guy. The only reason I can look back and laugh about it was because she bought the XXX Trojans. I guess she was giving him the benefit of the doubt, but he may as well have tried to roll a trash bag onto his cock." She starts swinging her hips from side to side, mimicking what I can only assume is a make-believe cock. "It took me like a week to find his teeny tiny erection in amongst all that latex."

I laugh so hard I can barely breathe. This girl is so funny, and I'm not sure she knows how endearing it is. With every gasp for air, she repeats her little cock shake, making me laugh harder and harder until tears form in my eyes. I don't remember the last time I laughed this much.

"You're killing me, Lexington." She's about to launch into another shake, but I reach out and pull her into my arms. "You've got to stop before I pee myself."

"Go for it. Then I'd feel like we're even on the bodily fluid projectiles."

"Get over it, already. It wasn't that big a deal."

She sobers as she pulls back just far enough to look me in the eye. "It's a big deal to me that you looked out for me. That you made sure I was safe."

"Most guys would do that. I'm nothing special."

"I think the opposite is true." I want to ravish her, but just as I lean in for a kiss, her mom yells up the stairs, and I feel like a teenager again.

"We better get down there." She doesn't move, her hands sliding around my waist. "Are you ready to be my girlfriend for the next four days?"

"Yes." One word that could change everything. There's nothing playful in her tone, but that one word is laced with desire, and dare I hope, affection.

"Brooke Olivia Lexington!" Brooke's best friend, Lacey, appears in the doorway, killing the moment. "Your mom is going to blow a gasket if you don't get down there, now." Lacey literally rips her out of my arms, and I have to take a deep breath before I say something I'll regret. I came here to help Brooke. I can schmooze these people.

I follow behind, steeling myself for an onslaught of hellos, Yankee fan handshakes, and the Spanish Inquisition from at least one protective family member. Then it dawns on me—we didn't come up with a backstory or a timeline for how long we've been 'dating.'

I guess we're winging it.

The moment we step out through the French doors and into the backyard, all eyes are on us. Before I can take Brooke's hand in mine, her father strides over to me and pulls me off in the direction of a big-screen television and the outdoor grill. I'm met with applause and raised bottles of beer.

"I don't think this guy needs an introduction, but fellas, this is Anders Verbeck." A collective rabble of welcoming words ring out. They each shake my hand with congratulations on winning the World Series. I forget most of their names before I get a beer in hand.

"Nice to meet you all." I can talk about baseball for hours, so small talk isn't hard with Richard's friends. Everyone is in the party mood, and drinks are flowing freely and in abundance. Whenever there's a gap in conversation, I search the yard for Brooke, smiling whenever I catch her eye. As she laughs and jokes with her mom and sister, I enjoy seeing how close they all are.

Every now and again, I find Lacey staring at me. It's as if she's waiting for me to slip up. I make a mental note to get on her good side this weekend. If the best friend hates you, you have no chance with a woman.

After what feels like hours, Brooke weaves her way through the crowd to stand at my side. "Daddy, can I steal Anders for a little while? Mom wants to show him off." She rolls her eyes.

"Sure thing, sweetheart. Sorry we've been hogging him. We're enjoying all his baseball stories."

I drape my arm over her shoulder the way a boyfriend would. She looks up at me, and I seize the opportunity of her closeness, planting a soft kiss on her lips. "I'm all yours."

As we head over to where her mom and sister are chatting with Lacey, she whispers under her breath. "You don't have to do the PDA stuff. It's okay. Some couples aren't into public displays of affection."

I stop her for a second, just long enough to hand her my beer. "Can you hold this for a second?"

"Sure."

I clasp her face with my hands and press my lips to hers, not so gently this time. When she's good and breathless, I move to her ear so only she can hear. "We do the PDA stuff, Lexington. Public, private, anywhere, anytime, and whatever you want. At least for the next few days. Are you good with that?"

"Mmm... yeah." She's flustered, and it only serves to turn me on.

"I'm your boyfriend for the next four days. Anything, and I mean *anything* you want from me, is yours."

Chapter Nine

BROOKE

EVERY NERVE ENDING in my body goes into overdrive at the sound of Anders' deep rasping voice in my ear.

"Anything?"

He brushes his lips against my neck, just below my ear. "Any… thing." A thrill runs through me, and I can feel my nipples pebble at the thought of what a night with Anders could be like. I want to play it cool, but the rapid rise and fall of my chest betray me.

"You're bluffing." The smell of his cologne invades my senses, and all I can think of is watching him writhe between my thighs. He doesn't move, his lips still ghosting a kiss on my neck.

"Try me. I never bluff, Lexington." Everything and everyone fades into the background as Anders darts his tongue out to taste me.

I'm about to pull him into the house and up to the guest room—anywhere with a door that locks will do—but Lacey grabs my hand and drags me over to my mom. "You don't need to go overboard with the PDA. Besides, that's a kiss or a handhold. You two looked about ready to fuck right here on the lawn."

Anders follows, the firm set of his brow telling me he's as frustrated as I feel at this moment. Maybe he was being serious.

"Brooky! Time to introduce your lovely boyfriend to my bridge club ladies." My mom breezes right past me, taking Anders by the hand. "Ladies, this is Brooky's boyfriend, Anders Verbeck."

I'm surprised when one of them congratulates him on the World Series. I didn't think any of my mom's bridge cronies would be into baseball. She practically shoves me out the way to shake his hand and stroke his arm. *Cougar.* "You're even more handsome in person if that's possible. Is this why you got into baseball, Brooke? I see the appeal."

"We don't play in the same league, so no, I didn't get into base-ball as a toddler with the view of finding a boyfriend." My voice is more clipped than it should be, but none of these women have ever shown interest in my baseball career, and the way she's pawing Anders just makes me mad. Jealous.

My mom is quick to chastise me for my tone. "Brooky, there's no need to be snippy. We're all very proud of you and how successful you are. Cheryl is just overexcited to have such a handsome young celebrity in our midst." I'm pleased when my mom gives her friend a death stare until she backs off and stops touching my fake boyfriend.

Anders is every inch the gentleman, and his stunning smile has every woman within a hundred-foot radius going weak at the knees. "It's a pleasure to meet you, ladies. I hope you'll be keeping a spot open for me on your dance card this weekend."

They all swoon like idiots, and I hate that my stomach is in knots at the thought of it. I don't consider myself a jealous person, and I have no right to feel possessive over Anders, but I do. "We're so thrilled to have you here. If you and Brooky need anything at all, you come to me."

"This weekend is all about you and your husband. Don't give us a second thought. I'm sure Brooke and I can muddle through on our own." He slings his arm over my shoulder and pulls me close. "Right?"

I'm dazed. He plays this role so well, and with his earlier revela-tion, all I want to do is get him alone.

"Brooke, can I talk to you for a minute?" Lacey appears at my side.

"Sure." I look to Anders. "I'll be right back. Don't go anywhere."

Lacey drags me into the house under the guise of grabbing a few more bottles of champagne. Not a bad idea. I make a mental note to take one upstairs later.

"How are things with Verbeck? Are your parents buying the whole boyfriend scenario?"

"Of course. Have you seen him out there? They love him. Everyone loves him. And God, did you see how fucking edible he looks? Men shouldn't be made that hot *and* talented."

"Yeah. I see him. He's hot, but he is also as fake as a boyfriend comes. Tell me you'll remember that. I don't want you getting all the feels for this guy."

"Would that be so terrible?"

"Yes! You've worked your ass off to make a name for yourself in baseball. If you become Anders Verbeck's arm candy, that's all you'll be known for. Don't be that stupid, Brooke."

"We're just having fun. He's helping me out, and I can flirt without falling for a guy and becoming a 1950s housewife."

"As long as that's all you're doing." She seems on edge tonight.

"Where's your date?"

"I dumped him last night. I'll suffer your mom's wrath for flying solo. He was just so damn dull. I couldn't stand him another minute. Besides, there's got to be a few single guys coming to the wedding. I'm sure I can snag a hot guy to warm my bed for a night." I'm surprised she dumped whatever his name is. Lacey is always on the lookout for her next bedfellow, but she would normally make the transition seamless.

"So, was there something else you wanted to talk to me about or just the lecture?" My tone reflects my mood—I'm ticked off that she feels the need to chastise me. I'm well aware of what I'm doing right now, and if I choose to take Anders into my bed this weekend, I'm a grown woman, and my choices are my own. Not even Lacey gets a say when it comes to my love life, genuine or fake.

"You need to be careful with guys like him, Brooke. He has an angle. They always do. Ask yourself why a multi-millionaire baseball god is voluntarily at your parents' vow renewal playing the part of the devoted boyfriend?"

"That's not your concern, Lacey. Nothing about Anders is your concern. Got it?" I swipe a bottle of champagne from the ice bucket and leave her standing in the kitchen.

"Loud and clear." I don't look back. She's been a little off since the night she met Anders. When he turned up on my doorstep to take me to the charity ball, she has had nothing good to say about him.

I make my way back outside and find Anders smooth-talking all of my mom and dad's country club friends. He has his phone out, letting them see a few pictures of behind-the-scenes at the last World Series game. Everyone is enthralled by him. His confidence is evident in every word and the way he carries himself. He knows he's hot stuff, and I find it sexy as hell.

The moment his eyes find mine, he makes his excuses and strides over to where I stand, watching him.

"Enjoying the view, Lexington?"

"I'd enjoy it more if all these people were gone, and you were naked." He rubs his thumb over his bottom lip, a wry smile spreading across his flawless mouth.

"You're considering my offer?"

"Maybe. If I say yes, does it make me slutty?"

He takes the bottle of champagne from my hand, leaning in to whisper in my ear. "God, I hope so."

I try to duck out on the party a thousand times, desperate to get Anders alone, but every time I do, someone else wants to talk to him. It's as if he is the sun, and the rest of the partygoers are caught in his orbit.

It's ten o'clock by the time everyone is either too drunk to notice us leave or they've headed to their hotels. I help clean up the kitchen before saying goodnight to my folks and leading Anders back to our room.

The second I close and lock the door behind us, I launch myself at him, taking his lips in a fierce kiss. I've been waiting all night to touch and taste him, and he doesn't disappoint. He's quick to take over, pinning me against the door, his lips crashing down on mine, our tongues twisting and tangling with overwhelming desire.

"Fuck." I adore the sensation of Anders' muscular physique covering every inch of my body. His erection strains against my thigh, and it makes me groan, which only serves to make him grind harder.

Desire explodes deep in my core, and I begin to moan his name, my hands sliding between us, feeling the length of his cock. "Anders... fuck... me."

My words have the opposite effect. He pushes himself away, putting some distance between us. "My cock is going to hate me, but we can't do this here."

"What? But you said..."

He steps forward, and my words are lost on his lips. "I said I'm yours to do with as you please. But if you want to do this, then it can't be here." He continues to kiss me, trailing up and down my neck, driving me wild.

"The door is locked."

"It's locked, but it isn't soundproof. I want to hear you scream my name, Lexington. I plan to take you over and over again, and when that happens, you're definitely going to be screaming."

"I can't wait... I need..."

He runs his hand down my body and between my legs. "I promise it will be worth the wait. Tomorrow night, we're staying at a hotel."

A thrill runs through me, but I'm not sure I can stand to wait another twenty-four hours to feel Anders driving into me.

"I don't want to waste a night. I only have you for four days."

He blazes a trail up my neck before capturing my lips in a kiss. "I guess we're going to have to extend our timeline a little. If you haven't had your fill by the time we leave the Hamptons, I'll let you have your wicked way with me back in Manhattan."

Fuck.

"Are you always this much of a tease?"

"A tease has no intention of following through. Trust me, I will one hundred percent be fucking you tomorrow night, in a hotel suite, where you can scream my name until you're hoarse and saddle sore."

"Okay." I'm speechless.

"Now, I'm going to need you to go to bed before I throw any shred of decency out the window and fuck you right here, right now, for everyone in this house to hear."

"Would that be so bad?"

"As much as I want to, I'm partial to my cock, and I don't need your daddy trying to shoot it off with a shotgun."

"Good point." My pulse is racing, so I close my eyes and focus on my breathing in a vain attempt to calm the storm of desire waging war inside me.

It takes me a minute to force myself out of his arms and into the bathroom. Staring at my reflection in the mirror, I see my cheeks are flushed, and my hair has the beginnings of that sex-mussed look I'm eager to have at the hands of Anders.

Hiding out for a few minutes is all I can do at this point. If I had my way, we'd already be in a cab heading for a hotel. I wash off my makeup and throw my hair in a messy bun before putting on my favorite, oversized raglan shirt. When I've composed myself, I open the door to see Anders with his crisp white shirt unbuttoned and his belt unbuckled. *Fuck me.*

His eyes rake me from top to toe as he lets out a deep groan. "You don't want to make it easy on me, do you, Lexington?"

"What?" I bite down on my bottom lip, loving the way he eyes me greedily.

"You know exactly what. You were a knockout in that dress at the charity event, but this… you right now… hottest woman I've ever laid eyes on. No contest."

"Pretty hot yourself, slugger. Just unzip that fly and give me a look at the good stuff." He runs his hands through his hair, accentuating that delicious 'V' that disappears beneath his waistband.

"Get into bed, Brooke." A thrill runs through me.

"When did you become so demanding?"

"This is the tip of the iceberg. Wait until you're writhing beneath me, then you'll see just how demanding I can be." I'm physically squirming with anticipation.

"We can be quiet. This is torture. I'll never get any sleep."

"You will because you'll need your strength for tomorrow night." His stare is dark and intense and full of promise.

I slide under the covers, my eyes fixed on him as he lets his shirt drop off his broad shoulders. Every toned, corded muscle is bathed in moonlight, and he's mouthwatering to behold. The way he moves —so comfortable and graceful in his own skin—has me pressing my thighs together. I should probably avert my gaze as he unzips his fly and pushes his pants to the floor.

"Holy sweet mother of all that's good and pure. Come to mama."

"What?"

"What? Did I say that out loud?"

He gives me a mischievous grin and a deep, hearty chuckle. "I'm beginning to realize that the only predictable thing about you is that you're unpredictable, Lexington."

"Is that good or bad?"

"Definitely a good thing." He grabs a blanket off the sofa in the corner and sets up a makeshift bed for the night. He's way too tall and broad to enjoy any kind of real sleep over there.

I lean over and switch off the bedside lamp, plunging us into darkness. My heart is galloping in my chest.

"Lexington."

"Yeah."

"You don't snore like a mother-trucker, do you? Tell me you're not one of those cute women who defy the laws of physics with a noise so big coming out of someone so itty-bitty." A snort escapes me. "Jesus, you're a snorter."

I grab a pillow and throw it in his direction, completely missing the mark. "Now I'm horny *and* self-conscious. I'm never going to sleep. Thanks."

"I can see why you're not a pitcher. That throw was pitiful. You missed me by a good six feet."

"It's pitch black!"

"Exactly. It's in the title. *PITCH-er.* I could get within six inches of you with my eyes closed and one hand tied behind my back."

"You know what they say, you only need a good six inches."

"Who the fuck says that? A six-inch boner is only half a cock. That's no good to anyone."

"Bullshit. Are you telling me you've got a twelve-inch cock? It's not like Pinocchio, it won't grow if you lie about it." I make myself laugh with that one, and I'm rewarded with the sound of Anders chuckling in the dark.

"You'll find out tomorrow. Solid wood, Lexington." There he goes again, making me squirm.

"You don't have to sleep over there, you know. You could share the bed with me."

"Are you trying to get into my pants?"

"Why would I try? I have a guarantee that I'm getting lucky tomorrow. I just…" Before I finish my sentence, he slides beneath the covers next to me and pulls me into his arms.

"Go to sleep before I ravish you."

"Ravish? Oh, Mr. Darcy!"

"What?"

"Jane Austen, *Pride and Prejudice.* Come on, everyone knows who Mr. Darcy is."

"I'm going to erase that sentence from my brain, and yes, I said ravish. Deal with it. Goodnight, Lexington."

"Night." Lying here, wrapped in his arms, a sense of content-ment washes over me, but my stomach doesn't get the memo, somersaulting as I drink him in. "Thank you for coming here with me."

"You're pretty good company."

"You're not so bad yourself, slugger." He silences me with a kiss. Soft and slow, sensual and wickedly seductive. I don't remember the last time I just laid in bed making out with a guy. In my experience, the second you put out, guys have zero interest in the finer points of seduction. Anders is a breath of fresh air, and yet his very presence knocks the wind right out of me.

———————

"What do you mean you're not staying here tonight? I asked for four days, and you're jumping ship after one night."

"It's just a lot. Everyone wants to bombard Anders with questions, and I just think it might be good to give him some peace and quiet after the rehearsal dinner. It's a lot of pressure, Mom. We haven't been seeing each other for that long, and I love our family, but they all have wedding fever. Aunt Rose grilled him for a solid hour about how he's planning to propose. Seriously? It's stressing me out."

A sly grin tugs at the corner of her mouth. "If you want a night to make some noise, you should've just said. Honestly, you're a little prude sometimes, Brooky."

"I'm going to go and see if Daddy needs any help setting up the bar."

"Have fun tonight!"

"*God.* Can you just be normal?"

"Where's the fun in that?" As I listen to her giggle, I follow her gaze to where my dad is unloading crates of champagne. I'm sort of in awe of her. Sure, I'd rather my mom didn't overshare, but what she has with my dad—it's what everyone aspires to.

My dad has a goofy grin on his face when he finds her staring. I can't imagine how that must feel to have a man look at you like that after decades together. The new and exciting buds of a new relationship long since bloomed.

I set about helping my dad with more champagne bottles than I've ever seen, and that's saying something. When I made the USA baseball team, my parents threw a massive party with everyone I've ever met in attendance. It was sweet and so over the top—not my style—but I loved it because they were so damn proud of me. For me, it wasn't a celebration of my talent but about all of the blood, sweat, and tears my mom and dad put into nurturing my dreams. They never once complained about all the weekends, evenings, or expensive equipment. They gave their all to help me succeed, and I couldn't even bring a real date to their vow renewal.

I stamp out the gnawing feeling in the pit of my stomach and focus on what I have to get done today. My dad doesn't need small talk. He and I can just co-exist in the same space and be quite content, so he catches me off guard when he speaks.

"That boy has got it bad." He nods toward the back door, and I follow his line of sight. Anders is leaning against the doorjamb with his arms crossed, and he looks effortlessly gorgeous. Fresh out of the shower, his hair is still damp. Everything about him draws me in. His eyes are fixed on me, and he has a wry smile tugging at the corner of his lips. It does something to me, especially after falling asleep in his arms last night.

When I awoke this morning, he was sound asleep but still held me tight against his chest. In truth, I didn't want to move a muscle. I didn't want the moment to end, but my mom was blowing up my phone to come down and help, so I left him sleeping with the sheets pooled around his waist. It's probably a creepy stalker warning sign, but I could've watched him deep in slumber for hours. He's breathtaking, and he isn't mine. I need to get my fill in the next three days before my carriage turns into a pumpkin.

Chapter Ten

ANDERS

GOD, she's beautiful. It doesn't matter if she's in an oversized t-shirt or a ballgown, Brooke is stunning.

Last night was torture, self-imposed, but torture all the same. I called the top hotel in the Hamptons the moment she fell asleep last night. I lay awake for hours, unwilling to miss out on the feel of having her wrapped in my arms. I grabbed my phone off the nightstand and booked out the entire hotel with one hand typing away. It's amazing what you can do when you're motivated by sex! I had them offer every guest a long weekend, all expenses paid, at any other time, if they just cleared out at a moment's notice.

I'm counting down the hours until the rehearsal dinner is over, and I can whisk Brooke away for a romantic evening. If I don't seal the deal tonight, I'm going to be relegated to the friendzone for the rest of my natural life. I should've ignored my good-guy instinct last night. We could still have had hot sex and kept the noise level down. Except, I don't want her to be a quick, silent fuck. I want to fuck her so hard and so loud that she'll be begging for more.

I've been standing at the back door, just enjoying seeing her interact with her dad. He seems like a good guy, and considering my dad is non-existent, it's nice to see what that relationship can be. She looks happy and content with no need to force a conversation for the sake of it. When she finally turns to see me, her smile is so beautiful it makes me weak at the knees.

As I stride down the grand steps of this Hamptons' mansion, I'm so focused on Brooke that I don't notice a power cord running from the house to the marquee. The tip of my shoe catches under the cord, throwing me off balance. I manage not to fall on my ass, but my smooth, alpha male swagger is gone.

When I reach Brooke, she's trying not to laugh, but I can see it's a losing battle. "Just go for it. Let it out. My bravado has all but vanished. Just do it before you pop that vein in your forehead."

I knew she was going to laugh, but the guffaw that bursts from her lips would make a lesser man retreat with his cock between his legs. Not me.

"Well, that was quite the entrance, slugger." She's adorable when she's taunting me, so I do what any boyfriend would do. I pull her into my arms and kiss her as if my life depends on it.

"Morning, Brooke." I press my lips to hers once more, and her goofy grin is a bonus.

"Your recovery was stellar."

"I thought it might be." I cup her face with my hands. "I'm not perfect, but when I stumble, I always come back stronger."

Her eyes search mine for any hint that I'm playing around right now, and I know the moment she realizes I'm deadly serious. She shies away from me. "You could give Faith Vaughn a run for her money."

"Do you know her?"

"Everyone knows who Lady Fumble is. She's the most accident-prone person on the planet."

"I can't argue. Hunter's totally smitten with her. Sometimes attraction just hits you out of nowhere, and no matter how hard you try to shake it off, you can't."

"Do you know him?"

"Yeah. We used to go out drinking together. His teammate, Coop, is a good friend of mine."

"Cooper Danford?"

"Why do you seem so surprised? We're in sports. I went to college with Coop."

"I can't even picture what a night out for the three of you looks like. That much hotness shouldn't be able to co-exist in the same space."

"You think they're hot?" It irks me.

"There isn't a woman in America who doesn't think they're hot. Add you and your ridiculously handsome face and rock-hard body, and I'd be playing slip and slide having creamed my pants."

"That's both arousing and completely disturbing."

"I tell it like it is. It might not be sexy or elegant, but it's true." She scrunches her nose, and all I want to do is kiss her again.

"Elegant… no. Sexy… yes. Anything that involves you and me, and you creaming in my vicinity is hot as fuck."

"You have a devious mind, Anders."

"Something tells me you're a little sexual deviant yourself," he leans in, whispering in my ear. "I guess I'll find out tonight."

"Where are we going?"

"It's a surprise. Just make sure you have your bags packed."

"For one night? Don't I just need some clean underwear?"

"One night? You really think I'll be done wringing every ounce of pleasure from your body after one night?"

"I…"

"You're mine until Monday, Lexington. Remember that when you're sitting at dinner tonight. I want you wet with anticipation. And when I get you alone, I'm going to indulge in the taste of your arousal on my tongue."

She doesn't speak, but the way her breath catches at my words lets me know she's turned on. If this event were anything other than a family occasion, I'd have convinced Brooke to ditch it and spend the weekend naked in my bed.

"This is just a wedding reboot. We don't really need to be here for the rehearsal of the reboot. It's like *Star Wars*—the original trilogy was amazing, and then episodes one to three were decent, but then they couldn't just leave it alone, and it ruined the whole thing."

"Harsh. You're basically calling your parents' rehearsal dinner episode eight, or as the rest of us call it, the *Star Wars* that shall not be named." She's trying to keep a straight face, but her mouth twitches when she's trying not to laugh, and I can't help but chuckle, which sets her off.

"I'm the worst daughter in the world, aren't I? *I'm* episode eight." She screws up her face, completely exaggerating her dismay. It's hilarious.

"Never say those words again. I can't, in all good conscious, seduce *The Last Jedi.*"

"But I need your mighty light saber to thrust inside me." She descends into a fit of giggles.

"It's unsettling that your disturbing analogy has me hard right now."

She presses her body to mine, sliding her hand between us so no one will see as she caresses her hand over my cock. Fuck, that feels good. "I just wanted to see if you were telling the truth."

"And?"

"And you weren't lying. Although, if this is you at half-mast, I'm a tad concerned that you're going to break me."

I thrust my hips forward, harder against her palm. "Don't worry, Lexington, I know what I'm doing. Now, you need to take your hand off my cock, so I don't get a beating from your best friend who's giving me the evil eye right now."

She turns to see Lacey standing over by her mom. "She's protective. Don't worry about it. If anything, you should be worried about my sister, Diana. When we were teenagers, she'd beat any guy who came near me."

"I'm pretty sure I can handle your sister. In twenty-eight years, I've never been beaten up by a girl."

"Have you ever gone toe-to-toe with an MMA fighter?"

"Shut the front door." I look in the direction of where her sister is helping set up tables in the marquee. "I thought she was familiar. Your sister is Dee Lex?"

"Yes, Sherlock."

"Holy fuck. Your mom and dad deserve this party if only to

celebrate some insanely awesome genetic mingling. Wow. Two athletes at the top of their game. That's amazing."

"Yeah, my dad always says *who needs sons when you have Lexington women.*"

"He's not wrong. You realize you can never introduce your sister to Linc. He's a huge MMA fan. He'd be trying to get her naked within minutes."

"Thanks for the mental scarring that you just conjured in my mind."

"I'll make it up to you later." I love to see the spark in her eyes every time I mention us getting physical, but I'm at my limit when it comes to anticipation. Tonight will be an exercise in self-control. At this moment, one more stroke of my cock, and she'll send me into an early grave—an early, jizz-filled grave.

"Promises, promises. You've yet to make good on one."

"I beg to differ. I promised you a night of dancing at the charity ball. *Check.* I took you to Yankee Stadium and pitched for you. *Check.*"

"True."

"And, am I or am I not the best fake boyfriend you've ever had?"

"Well, yes. You're the only one."

We're interrupted by Brooke's mom yanking on her arm. "Kiss your boyfriend goodbye. I need to steal you until dinner."

"Duty calls." She starts to walk off, but her mom is not having it.

"Give the poor man a kiss. Were you raised by wolves? It's common courtesy to share a little PDA with your man. Look at him, he's already forlorn at the thought of being away from you." Her mom doesn't hold back. Now I know where Brooke gets her frank, no-nonsense attitude.

"Don't worry, Martha. I've got it covered." I give her a sly wink and pull Brooke into my arms, dipping her down like they do in the movies, and plant a heartfelt, hot-as-hell kiss on her lips. When we come up for air, she's speechless and boneless in my arms. It takes her a moment to find her feet. "I'll see you later, baby. Have fun."

"Mmm." It's all she can muster, and it gives me deep satisfaction to know I've sent her off horny and thinking of me. My heart is pounding as her mom and Lacey drag her off toward the house.

I help Richard and the rest of the guys get set up for the evening, and as soon as I'm able, I sneak out to the hotel to set up one or two personal touches that I think Brooke will enjoy. Thankfully, time flies. I got showered and dressed at the hotel, so when I step inside the marquee and see Brooke standing laughing with her sister, I'm completely floored at the sight of her.

She's wearing a figure-hugging burgundy dress that accentuates her athletic body. Her hair cascades down her back in soft waves, and her eyes have that smokey look that all guys find really fucking sexy. The term jaw-dropping was invented for moments like this.

"You're drooling, big boy." Lacey appears behind me, whispering in my ear like a creeper. I immediately step out of her way.

"I'm allowed to appreciate my girlfriend looking beautiful." She eyes me with a cunning glare.

"Except she's not your girlfriend, is she? This is all fake."

"The way I feel about her isn't fake."

She throws her head back and laughs like some maniacal villain who thinks I'm the village idiot. "If she were into you, she wouldn't have asked you here."

"She didn't. I offered, and I don't see why it's any of your business."

"I told you the first time that we met, if you hurt her, I'll hurt you."

"I have no intention of hurting her. She wanted a date for her parents' vow renewal, and I'm the date."

"So you're not together?"

"Again, why is this any of your concern?"

"Are you sleeping with her? It's a simple yes or no answer." She has a smug grin on her face.

"Relationships are complicated. But, no, we haven't slept together yet."

"Good." She slides her hand into mine, giving me a hard-plastic keycard. "I've got a room at the Maidstone. If you get tired of playing Brooke's fake boyfriend, come by after the rehearsal dinner.

I don't fake… anything. You're hot. I'm hot. And Brooke would've jumped your bones long ago if she really wanted to. I suspect you already know that, but you have a sappy look in your eyes, so I'll spell it out." She trails her finger over my shoulder.

"And what's that?"

"You've never had a woman say no to you before, especially after you hit the major league. There hasn't been a woman in your life who dropped you in the friendzone… ever. You're horny as fuck with no release but your own hand. I can take care of that for you. I'm a Yankees fan, big time, and you're sexy as hell." She pushes herself up onto her tiptoes to whisper in my ear. "You won't regret using that keycard."

Her hand moves lower, but I grab it before she does something to really fuck me off. I shove the keycard back into her hand. "There are a few things I need to set you straight on. One, my relationship or lack thereof with Brooke is none of your fucking business. Second, I'm not an animal, I don't need a woman to put out for me every two seconds. I do possess a modicum of self-control. Thirdly, and this is the most important one, you're a sorry excuse for a friend. Brooke deserves better. She might never see me as anything more than a friend, but I'll take that any day over a lazy, mediocre night between the sheets with you. So, I suggest you keep your fucking hands to yourself from this point on, and I won't tell her what a colossal bitch you are."

I don't wait for her to respond because nothing good can come from further conversation with this woman. I'm pissed as I make my way over to Brooke. I want to tell her what just transpired with her so-called best friend, but when her eyes find mine and a stunning smile spreads across her pretty, pouty lips, everything else melts away.

"Wow. I thought you looked hot in the penguin suit, but the no-tie, open-collar thing is seriously hot. You should always wear this outfit. Twenty-four-seven. While you're pitching. Just all the damn time." It's been a hell of a long time since I've blushed—maybe not ever as an adult man—but I can feel my cheeks heat from her appreciation of my wardrobe choice this evening.

"Trust me, it's going to look much better on the hotel floor, alongside this figure-hugging dress of yours."

"Let's get this dinner over and done with. I'm ravenous." From the look in her eyes, I know what she's hungry for, and it isn't food." I hold my arm out to escort her to our table, which she gladly takes, giving me a little squeeze as we wind our way through the marquee to our much-discussed place cards. I can't help but laugh when I see mine.

"Remember when we hatched this plan, and it was all about your mom's deep desire for the perfect place cards with a date for you?"

"Ah, yes, the great *plus one* debate. I hope she's happy."

"As long as you don't tell her that my name is misspelled, I think we're golden."

She throws her head back and laughs, so hard she does that little snort thing she does when she's truly amused. "Fuck me! Seriously?"

"Yes, to both statements."

"Let me see it." She grabs the entire reason for the situation we now find ourselves in and almost starts crying and laughing at the same time. "Verbeek! I love it. You realize this will spawn a nickname that you'll forever be known by." She takes the card and taps my shoulders. "I now dub thee, Dawson!"

"What?"

"Come on. You don't know who Dawson Leery is?"

"Of course, I do. I fail to see how you get from the misspelling of Verbeck to a lame nineties' teen drama."

"Ugh. I thought you and I were on the same wavelength, but clearly, I was wrong."

"Enlighten me, oh wise one."

"Verbeck became Ver*BEEK*. The guy who played Dawson is called James Van Der *Beek*. It's the logical go-to."

"Your mind is a strange place, Lexington."

"You're not the first guy to tell me that."

"I'll be the last." Her eyes snap to mine, but before she can say anything, her dad taps the microphone.

"Good evening, everyone. Martha and I would like to thank you all for coming to share this weekend with us. I'm looking forward to seeing the woman of my dreams walking down the aisle to me for a second time tomorrow. Apparently, when she asked me if I'd do it all over again, she took me at my word and planned this shindig. If you could all take your seats, dinner is about to be served."

I pull the chair out for Brooke to sit down just as Lacey appears at her side. "Well, isn't that fake chivalry something special?" She gives me a sickly-sweet smile as she takes her seat next to Brooke.

"Can you keep the volume down, Lace? The ruse doesn't work when you announce it to everyone."

"Sorry, bestie." She grabs a champagne flute from a passing tray, but she's clearly had a few already. "My lips are sealed." I have an intense dislike for this woman. She's two-faced and fawning over her 'bestie' as if she didn't just proposition me.

"You okay?" Brooke rests her hand on my knee under the table —a small gesture, but it feels so intimate.

"I'm good."

Dinner seems to drag on as we eat our way through a three-course meal. The drinks are flowing, and when it comes time to take to the dance floor, Brooke is quick to grab my hand and pull me out of my chair.

"Dance with me, Dawson." I love how carefree she seems tonight. Her smile is bright and beautiful, and when a slow song comes on, she throws her hands around my neck, pinning me with her gaze.

"Are you having fun?"

"Yes. I have the perfect date, and dinner is over."

"You didn't like the food?"

"It didn't satisfy my appetite." With her body pressed tight to mine, I can't stand it any longer. I'm done playing around and pretending that what we're feeling isn't real.

"Say the word, Brooke. Tell me what you want, and I'll make it happen."

"Fuck. Me." Before she can say anything else, I scoop her up into my arms and stride off the dance floor.

"What the lady wants, the lady gets."

She chuckles. "That's a first. I don't think I've ever been called a lady before."

"Maybe you just needed the right guy to see it."

"Anders…"

"Yes."

"Remember that you think I'm a lady right now because the second we reach our hotel room, I'm going to be anything but."

"I'm counting on it."

Chapter Eleven

BROOKE

THE SECOND ANDERS puts the car in park outside Topping Rose House, I practically launch myself out the door. He's quick to throw the keys at the valet. "A hundred bucks if you take good care of my girl." The guy's eyes go wide as saucers. "Not my woman. Touch her and you'll be getting a different number... six feet under. I'm talking about my car. The other woman in my life."

The feminist in me—that I thought made up a good ninety-five percent of my being—is disgusted with the butterflies running rampant in the pit of my stomach. Hearing him so possessive of me does strange and exciting things to my insides.

I can't move quick enough in these damn heels, so I stop for a second to take them off, but as soon as I do, Anders picks me up in a fireman's lift.

"Put me down! I can walk."

He slaps my ass, his hand lingering as he strides through the lobby. Thankfully, there's no one to see me thrown over his shoulder like a ragdoll. "You're too slow in this dress. I can't wait another second. I need to get you beneath me and sink inside you more than I need my next breath." A thrill courses through me as we head into the elevator.

When the doors close behind us, Anders sets me down before pinning me against the wall. "Tell me you want this, Brooke. I won't do anything until you spell it out." His lips are almost touching mine, the scent of his cologne invading my senses. My heart is hammering in my chest as my breath quickens.

"I. Want. You."

His lips crash down on mine before I can say anything else, his body pressed tight against me as his hands begin to roam, hitching my dress up to my waist. "Fuck, Brooke, I want to rip this dress off you."

"I want that too, but not in the elevator. What if someone sees us?"

He smiles as he continues to run his hand up to cup my ass. "Why do you think I bought out the entire hotel for the next few nights? And I may have told them to make sure the staff sticks to the ground floor unless we want room service."

"You're a genius. An evil, sexual genius."

"If you think this is genius, just wait until you see what I can do with my head between your thighs."

"Do it. Do it now."

"I thought you said not in the elevator?"

"No one will see us. You've made sure of that. So, drop to your knees and show me what you've got, slugger." I don't need to tell him twice.

"Yes, ma'am." He pulls the emergency stop button on the elevator before sliding down my body, hitching my leg over his shoulder, and pressing a kiss between my thighs and over my black lace panties. He snakes his arms around my waist, holding me steady. "Like this?"

He tilts his head to meet my gaze, and I'm entranced as he continues to kiss me. "Not quite."

"Maybe this?" He moves from where I want him most, nibbling and kissing my thigh.

I can't stand it another minute, so I reach down and pull my black lace panties to the side, letting him see just how wet I am for him. He can't take his eyes off me, and it's so empowering. I grab a fistful of his hair, guiding his head to where I desperately crave him at this moment.

Without another word, he devours me, his mouth hot against my skin as his tongue flicks over my clit, sending a jolt of desire straight to my core. I ride his face with wild abandon, his deep groans of pleasure vibrating through me, amping me up even further.

"Brooke, you taste so fucking good." Seeing him on his knees for me is so erotic. I've never been an exhibitionist, but I want to be naked, letting him see every inch of me as I fall apart on his tongue. The entire staff could get on this elevator right now, and I wouldn't be able to stop myself from continuing to ride his face until I come.

I grab the hem of my dress and pull it up over my head before dropping it on the floor. Reaching around, I unclasp my bra and let it fall. Left in nothing but a pair of heels and my panties pulled to the side, I feel freer than I've ever felt before. Naked and unabashed.

"*Fuck.*" Anders' hands begin to roam up and down over my naked flesh, his tongue driving me to the brink of orgasm. I've never wanted a man more than I want him at this moment.

"Oh God, Anders. I… oh God, yes… right there. Don't stop."

He doubles down, and grasping my panties, he rips them from my body, removing the only barrier between us. With that last scrap of material gone, Anders doesn't hold back, kissing my pussy with the same reverence and urgency he kisses my lips—hard, sensual, and devastatingly sublime. When I can't hold back any longer, I brace my hands against the elevator wall, seeing myself naked in the mirrors, watching Anders push me over the edge, headlong into an intense orgasm, wave after wave pulling me under.

I barely recognize my voice as I scream his name over and over again. He sends me spiraling out of control until I want to feel him inside me so badly, I'd sell my soul to the devil himself.

"Fuck me, Anders. I need you." He restarts the elevator, and seconds later, the doors open, and he hoists me into his arms. "Wait. My clothes."

"Trust me, Lexington, you're not going to need them." He doesn't miss a step. With me cradled, naked in his arms, he reaches into his pocket and pulls out a keycard, holding it over the door handle.

His lips don't leave mine, the air between us thick with anticipation. I've been ready for this moment since I woke up in my apartment with a dreadful hangover and saw him asleep on my couch.

The second we're through the door, Anders kicks it shut and heads straight for the bed. My pulse is racing as my heart pounds in my chest. I never got the phrase you see in romance novels when they say *her breasts were heaving*. What even is that? And do I want it? I like my breasts the way they are, and yet at this moment, as Anders lowers me onto the bed, my brain is filled with desire and imagining my heaving breasts.

I can't help but let out a giggle as he starts unzipping his fly. "Is there a reason you're laughing right now? Not exactly the reaction I'm going for. I've got to tell you, Lexington, a lesser man would shrivel up when a woman starts laughing at the unzip."

"I'm not laughing at you. I'm nervous. And I don't know why, but I can't help thinking my breasts are heaving right now." He cracks a smile as he unbuttons his shirt, exposing some seriously hot abs.

"Heaving? Really?"

"That's what they say in romance novels. Are they heaving?" I grab my breasts and squeeze them. "Is that even a real thing?"

Shirtless and oh so mouthwatering, he shoves his pants and boxers to the floor, kicking them off along with his socks. I'm so glad he did that. I hate when a guy keeps his socks on. It's an instant libido killer.

"I'm so happy you're not a sock guy."

"Brooke." He takes himself in hand, drawing my attention.

"Yes." My stomach does somersaults at the sight of his cock. Big, thick, and beautiful.

"I'm going to need you to stop talking now. No socks or heaving anything. I'm going to grab a condom, and then I'm going to fuck you until you can't think of anything but me. Are you good with that?" Stroking himself, I'm suddenly lost for words or a coherent thought. He has the body of a god. Hercules would be jealous of his lean, muscular frame and his impressive cock.

"I…" Seriously, I can't form a sentence right now. My nerves dissipate, replaced by a deep desire that takes over my entire body. I want him more than my next breath.

"Is this what you want, Brooke?" He brushes his thumb over the crest of his cock, and I'm mesmerized. "Nod or say something."

"Yes." His eyes shift to the bedside table and a family-size box of XXX Trojan. When he moves his hand, I see him in all his glory. An erection that could split me in two, but I want it so bad I could beg. "Don't stop. I'll get the condom."

"You like watching me?" His gaze is dark and full of promise.

"It's hot. You're hot." I reach for the box, but overshoot, tumbling onto the floor with a thud.

"Jesus, are you okay?"

I hold the box of condoms up like a trophy. "I'm okay. I'm okay. You saw nothing. Reset. I gracefully grabbed the condoms, and I'm about to slide one on like a pro."

"Like a pro? You realize *pro* sexual partners are hookers, right?"

"Fuck. Can you just ignore anything I say, so I don't make even more of a fool of myself?"

"Brooke, give me the condom already. You aren't a fool, and if my rock-hard boner doesn't tell you that, I guess I'll have to prove it."

I rip the box open, sending little foil packets flying like confetti. Scrambling for one, my cheeks flush, and my entire body prickles with the sensation—embarrassment.

Grabbing a packet, I tear it open, ready to redeem myself. I try to slink over to him with some semblance of seduction, but the look on his face tells me I'm not pulling it off. "What's wrong? I can roll the condom on for you. I promise I won't break your cock. I'm usually pretty good at the whole sex-kitten vibe, but apparently, not today."

He reaches down and tugs at my hair. "You've got a condom packet in your hair." My shoulders sag. This wasn't what I had planned when I got naked in the elevator. I was going to be much sexier than I am right now. I thought I couldn't embarrass myself more than I did the first night we met, but apparently, I can.

"I'm sorry."

"Why are you apologizing?"

"Because you're naked and hot as hell, and I'm ruining it with my inability to be any kind of sensual."

He lifts me onto the edge of the bed. "You're sexy as hell, and there's nothing you could do tonight that will make me think otherwise. Open the condom, Brooke." I do as he asks, but my fingers are shaking. "Now, take a deep breath."

"I…"

"I'm in control now. No talking. Breathe." I close my eyes and take a breath and then blow out my nerves. "Good. Now, roll it on for me."

The second my hand touches his cock, his entire body reacts as he lets out a shuddering groan of pleasure. "*Fuck!*"

He can't take his eyes off where our skin meets. His cock is hard as steel, and as I roll the condom into place, my mind is flooded with desire and urgency I've never felt before.

"I want you, Anders. Now."

"Not before I get another taste of you." He drops to his knees before pushing my legs apart, opening me to his gaze. He doesn't take his eyes off me as he flicks his tongue over my clit.

My pulse is racing as I watch him, my whole body on fire for this man. We're crossing the line from friendship and a fake relationship to him feasting on my pussy. He's as skilled with his tongue as he is with a baseball.

"Oh God, Anders. Right there."

"That's it, baby, let me hear you. You taste so fucking good." I try to press my thighs together to alleviate the growing ache pooling where his lips meet my most intimate flesh, but he pushes back, forcing my legs as wide as they'll go.

His groans of pleasure reverberate through me, pushing me to the brink of orgasm before pulling back. "Don't stop. I'm so close. Please, Anders!" I've never been one to beg for release, but he knows exactly how far to push to leave me right on the edge.

"Not yet. I've not had my fill of you. Your arousal is sweeter than honey. I could lick you for days and never tire of your pussy on my lips."

"I can't. I need to come." He runs his tongue up the length of me, from my entrance to my clit in one long, languorous lick. I let myself drop to the mattress, arching my back as he continues his ministrations. It's torture, and yet I never want it to end.

"Come for me, Brooke." He sucks my clit into his mouth before pulling in a sharp, cold breath. He follows it with the warmth of his tongue, flicking over me, sending me crashing over the edge, again and again.

"Oh God, yes! Anders... yes... oh God!" I scream his name over and over. He doesn't relent, letting me ride his face into one orgasm after another until my legs are shaking so violently that he has to steady me, pressing my hips down. Wave after wave crashes over me, one orgasm after another. I grab the sheets, fisting them in my hands in an attempt to steady myself, but it's no use. Anders owns me, tearing pleasure from my body time and time again.

When he finally relents, I watch with delight as he wipes the evidence of my arousal from his lips before positioning himself at my entrance and slamming into me with one hard thrust.

"*Jesus Christ.* Brooke." He looms over me, lowering his lips to mine. "Taste yourself on my lips. Taste the effect I have on you."

Holy shit, he's hot as hell. I grab his face in my hands and pull him in for a kiss. Licking the seam of his lips, I taste myself, and it drives me wild. Our tongues twist and tangle, lost in the sensation of the way our bodies come together as one. I wrap my legs around his waist, urging him deeper. Harder. Faster.

"Anders..." I can't contain my desire.

"Do you like the way you taste, Brooke?"

"Yes." I slide my hand between us, pressing two fingers inside me, alongside his huge cock, stretching me to the edge of pain. Then, I keep my eyes on him as I pull back and take my slick fingers in my mouth.

"Fuck!" His lips crash down on mine, primal and unrepentant.

"Brooke… oh fuck… Brooke." My name falls from his lips in a litany of worship.

I scratch my nails down his back, pulling him closer, hungry for more. His long, measured thrusts become frenzied as he loses control, chasing his release.

"I want to hear you come, Anders." I can feel myself climbing again, his cock filling me, stroking me with expert precision. I didn't believe in the G-spot until now. The way his cock hits it with every thrust—delicious and mind-altering pleasure.

"Come with me. I want to feel you come around my cock." As if he flicked a switch, I let go, overwhelmed with sensation. Pleasure radiates from every nerve ending in my body, hurtling me over the edge, pulling Anders with me.

"Fuck, yes!"

"Brooke… fuck…" I detonate around him, my muscles contracting, milking his cock as he finds his release, thrusting so hard the headboard slams against the wall. A guttural roar escapes his chest, and I scream his name as I ride out the aftershocks of the most intense orgasm of my life.

When Anders' arms can no longer hold him over me, he pulls out and discards the used condom on the floor before slumping down on the bed beside me. I'm left bereft, already wanting to feel him filling me.

"I've never come so many times in one night. You deserve a World Series sex trophy."

His deep raspy chuckle makes me squirm. "I'll take it."

"Was it okay for you?" My questions shock him out of his blissed-out moment.

"Were you not just present for me coming so fucking hard I thought my cock might fall off?"

"That's not a good thing."

"If that's the price I pay for having mind-blowing sex with you, I'll gladly die a happy man. Fuck me, Lexington. When you did that thing with your fingers, I almost shot my load. Hottest. Thing. Ever."

"We'll see if you still think that after watching me give you a blow job."

"Holy shit. You're going to kill me, and I'm going to be okay with it. You might need to give me a few minutes to regain my strength."

"You're already rocking a semi."

"Exactly, give me a minute, and I'll be ready to go again."

I grab the sheet and pull it up over my naked body, but Anders is quick to tug it off and shove it over the side of the bed.

"Why'd you do that? I feel weird now."

"You just spent the better part of an hour riding my face. I think the time for shyness has been and gone, Lexington. Besides, I want to look at you."

I roll onto my front. If I'm going to be on display, it's a little more comfortable when only my ass is out catching a breeze. "You have some serious tongue skills, my friend. Like… wow."

"Tip of the iceberg."

"I don't believe you. I came about ten times. I didn't even know that was possible. I've bragged to Lacey about having three orgasms in one night, but you just blew that out of the water. Unfortunately, she'll never believe me. I doubt any woman who hasn't slept with you would believe double digits can happen in one night."

"The night isn't over yet. Keep that tally running. I'm a competitive man, and I like to break my own records. Plus, can we not talk about your friend?" There's a slight furrow to his brow—fleeting, but it's definitely there.

"Is something wrong?"

He lazily runs his fingers down my spine, sending a shiver through me. "No. I just want to forget everyone else in the world exists tonight. In this room, in this hotel, it's just you and me. There's no baseball, no expectations, no public appearances, or friends and family to deal with."

"I guess if we're having a fake relationship, we can suspend our disbelief that the rest of the world exists for a night or two."

He leans in, pressing his lips to mine. "As long as those ten orgasms weren't fake, I'm good."

"They were very real and quite possibly some of the best I've ever had."

"There's a question about it? I should be a clear winner." I love that he seems disgruntled by that.

"It's not all about quantity."

He grabs me around the waist and rolls me over before straddling me, his erection heavy against my thigh. "Is the quality not up to par?" He traces the line of my neck with his tongue.

"I… I think I need more data to make an informed decision." He bites down on my earlobe, sending a jolt of desire straight to my core.

"Your wish is my command. I'm an advocate of data. I'll give you all the data you need until you can't take any more. Now grab another condom and try not to fall off the bed this time."

I arch my back off the bed, my breasts pushed tight to his chest. "I can't when you're on top of me. Besides, why should I get it?"

"Because I want to watch you bend that fine ass of yours over to reach it." He gives me just enough space to wriggle out from under him. "Come to think of it, why don't you just grab a handful since we're going to need them." A thrill courses through me as I shimmy off the bed and bend down to get the condom confetti off the floor. Knowing he's watching my every move is a rush, and an air of confidence settles over me.

I toss five condom packets on the bed. "There's no way you can use all these tonight. It's a physical impossibility."

"Would making balloon animals out of three of them count?"

I slide my hand between my legs, holding his gaze as he rips open a packet with his teeth. "Nope. Five condoms, five fucks, at least five orgasms. You're a champion on the field, so show me how much stamina you have in the bedroom."

"Challenge accepted."

Chapter Twelve

ANDERS

I CAN'T TAKE my eyes off her. I've turned into a simpering idiot overnight. Everything has changed. Watching Brooke standing at the altar with her sister, waiting for her mom to walk down the aisle a second time, I'm speechless at the sight of how beautiful she looks.

I knew she was gorgeous yesterday, the day before that, and the week before that. There have been feelings on my side since the moment I laid eyes on her, and it's been a long time since I've felt the desire to care for another person. I'm not even sure how or why I got to a place in my life where I stopped looking for someone to share it with. My friends and my career took over, and it's been incredible, but it wasn't until I sat down next to Brooke that night in the bar, and I realized something was missing.

Maybe I needed a pukey hot mess of a woman to come crashing into my life and assert herself as a friend rather than a lover. In all likelihood, if we'd slept together that night, it would've been a one-night stand. Her emptying the contents of her stomach might be the best thing that ever happened to me.

As she scans the crowd, I love that I know the moment she spies me, her face lights up with a stunning smile. She shifts from side to side, the same way she does when she steps up to the plate. She's nervous, and I've come to realize this is one of her tells.

When the music starts to play, her mom appears, all eyes going to the bride. Not me. I'm more interested in Brooke's dad. He lit up the second he saw her, and thirty-five years after their first wedding, he suddenly looks like a young man, seeing his blushing bride for the first time. The years melt away, and he's a man in love. I envy him.

It's not until my eyes gravitate back to Brooke that I realize she's staring at me. Undressing me with her eyes, I want to steal her away and keep her all to myself for as long as possible—until my dick falls off from pleasuring her so much neither of us will have the energy to leave the bed. Last night is a testament to that. Every muscle in my body is feeling it today, but I was true to my word. Brooke now knows better than to question my stamina. We fucked until we were both so exhausted, we passed out, tangled in each other's arms. Just the thought of waking up next to her this morning brings a smile to my face.

I barely register the ceremony or the crowd around me, my gaze fixed on Brooke the entire time. My skin is burning, desperate to touch her, aching as the heat in her eyes pushes me to a fever pitch. It's not until there's a collective chuckle from the crowd that the spell is broken.

"Earth to Brooke. Can we have the rings, please? We can't get to the dinner and drinking part of the evening if you don't hand them over." Her dad follows the line of her sight, and he gives me a—I'm not certain if it's a good or bad stare.

"Sorry." Brooke's cheeks flush as she hands her dad a small jewelry box. "You know me, I have the attention span of a goldfish."

"You seem pretty focused… on your boyfriend." Her dad is being playful, but Brooke's body language changes on a dime. Her gaze plummets to the ground, and she shifts her whole body to avoid eye contact with me for the rest of the ceremony.

I'm used to being conspicuous. Being a major league baseball star doesn't exactly lend itself to the quiet life. This is different. It's as if everyone here is suddenly laser-focused on every move I make —the way I glance at Brooke or whether I'm smiling when I look at her. Now I see why she warned me about the scrutiny of her family and their friends.

When the ceremony is over, everyone stands to clap for the happy couple as they walk down the aisle together, still very much in love. I grab Brooke's hand as she walks behind them, coaxing her to follow me, and she doesn't hesitate. Just the small brush of her fingertips against my skin is different after last night. I worshiped every inch of her body into the early hours of this morning, and as I look at her now, I want her even more.

Her pleasure is addictive.

"Where are we going?"

"I don't know. Somewhere we can be alone, so I can ravish you." Sparks of desire flicker in her eyes.

"I know just the place. Follow me." She leans on me for a second. Just long enough to take off her heels and hitch up the hem of her dress so she doesn't fall over it.

"Oh, you mean business, Lexington."

"Hey, don't complain. You started it. The moment you used the word *ravish*, I had a sense of urgency. Why is it that even though I'm saddle sore from last night, all I can think about is feeling your cock inside me?"

"Because I'm a lucky motherfucker."

Her laughter rings out as she yanks on my hand, quickening her pace, pulling me down onto the beach.

"Hurry up."

"Do I need to throw over my shoulder again? You don't seriously want to have sex on the beach, do you? I'll be picking sand out my ass for days."

"Well, that visual just dampened my urge to mount you. Besides, I'd make it worth your while."

"I don't doubt it. And scratch that visual."

"Scratch the thought of you scratching your ass? Will do."

"You're the only woman I've ever slept with who can make fun of me and turn me on in a five-second window."

"It's a talent. Get used to it." Her stride falters, just for a moment. "Or not. I forgot you don't have to get used to it at all."

"Brooke. Can we do that thing where we don't talk while we're turned on? We both seem to have a knack for saying the least sexy things in the world to each other."

"Don't worry, slugger, I find your asshole sexy."

"Case in point."

Her laughter is carried on the breeze, out into the ocean like a siren song. "True. I'm shutting up now. The next time I bump my gums, it'll be for a mouthful of your cock."

"Second half of that sentence was so hot, I'm hard as a rock, but gums shouldn't be used in the same breath. Just for future reference."

"For the next guy or future reference for me offering to suck your cock?" A swell of jealousy takes over like a rush of adrenaline. It's a primal, possessive, and completely overwhelming feeling. I'm not a jealous guy by nature. I'm used to seeing what I want and figuring out the best way to get it. That has been true for every aspect of my life until I sat down next to Brooke that first night.

It wasn't a conscious decision to become the antithesis of everything I believed myself to be in a relationship. She brings out a side of me that has been dormant until now. When I'd see previous girlfriends flirting with another guy or vice versa, it didn't bother me. I'm not sure if it was misplaced confidence that made me think it was harmless. Why would a woman want to hook up with someone else when she was dating me?

Brooke is a completely different story. I stop her in her tracks, my lips crashing down on hers. I want to claim her, which is so Dickensian. She's not a possession for me to own, and yet as her tongue darts out to meet mine in a sultry dance, my brain and my cock are screaming *mine*.

"If only for now, you're mine, Lexington. There's no next guy. I'm here, and fake or not, I want you. Your pleasure. Your laughter. Your climax." My words are like a red rag to a bull. She goes straight for my belt, trying to undress me in broad daylight.

"Fuck me, Anders. Now."

"Anyone could see us. I don't want someone else seeing you

naked." She continues to undress me, shoving my suit jacket off my shoulders.

"I don't care. I want you."

"Then tell me where we won't be seen. I'm serious, Brooke, I don't want anyone but me seeing you naked."

"There's a lighthouse two minutes from here." As soon as she points me in the right direction, I'm desperate to get her underneath me, and I'm practically running to get there. "You're going too fast. I can't keep up with your insanely long strides."

"Hop on my back. If I don't have you out of that dress in the next ninety seconds, I think my cock is going to explode."

"You want to give me a piggyback? We're not eight."

"Unless you want another fireman's lift, jump up on my back." She hitches her dress up to her thighs and does as I ask.

"This needs to be added to the weird chronicles of Brooke and Anders."

"We have chronicles?"

"Your cock skills deserve chronicles." She giggles as I lift her, cupping her ass in the name of a piggyback.

"Why, thank you. I do my best with the equipment I've got."

"Don't say it like this is news to you. Before we met, I knew just from watching you pitch, that you had been blessed in the trouser snake department. You're graceful like you are at ease in your own skin. Plus, I'm certain you know that your snake is an anaconda compared to most men's garden snake, if you know what I mean."

"Why don't you just say I'm rocking a huge cock?"

"Fine, you have a huge cock, and you're not afraid to use it. My vagina bows to the majesty of your girth! Good enough for you?"

"If only for the mention of your vagina."

"There it is." The lighthouse comes into view, and my cock twitches at the imminent prospect of sinking balls deep inside Brooke. She squeezes her thighs around my waist. "Giddy up."

"You want a ride? I'm your man." Brooke tightens her arms around my neck, and this small show of genuine affection is heart-warming to me.

"Hell, yes. A ride. A home run. A down and dirty fuck. I say yes to it all."

When I set her down, she reaches for a rock next to the doorway and lifts a key from underneath.

"Is this place your family's?"

"No, but my friends and I used to come here during senior year. Many a drunken night has been spent in this place."

"I should've snagged a bottle of champagne from the reception."

She grabs me by my tie, pulling me inside before letting the door slam behind us. "I don't need alcohol. I'm about to get drunk on your cock."

Dropping her heels on the floor, she pushes me against the wall before sinking to her knees. "Fuck, you're hot on her knees."

She makes short work of my zipper and pulls my boxers just low enough to let my erection spring free. I'm so hard it's almost painful. A rush of desire shoots straight to my core as she wraps her fist around the base of my cock before flicking her tongue over the tip.

Lifting her gaze to meet mine, she pulls back, leaving me bereft. "Is this what you want, Anders?"

"I'll take that pretty little mouth of yours any way I can." I have to look away when she slides her lips around my cock, the warm wet of her mouth so divine I could come in ten seconds flat. I let my head drop back against the cold, hard brick wall, giving myself over to the sensation of her lips on me. She swirls her tongue over the crest of my cock before taking me in as far as she can. When I feel the tip hitting the back of her throat, I let out a roar, unable to contain how amazing she is.

Her small, mewling moans of pleasure vibrate against my skin, pushing me closer, making me desperate for more.

"Jesus, Brooke, you have to slow down. It feels so fucking good." She ignores me, taking my admission as a greenlight to quicken her pace. Her eyes stay locked on me as she moves up and down the length of me, kissing my cock like she can't get enough. I never want this sensation to end—on the brink of ecstasy—lost to the pleasure she's commanding from my body.

"Shit. Brooke, you need to stop. I'm not going to come before you." The dark twinkle in her eye says everything. She knows how powerless I am at this moment. Here with her, she owns me, not the other way around.

"Then I guess I better stop." I ache for her as she moves to stand up, licking her lips as if she's just finished a delicious lollipop. "I'm going to want more of that later." My pulse is racing as she unzips her dress and lets it drop, pooling at her feet. She's not wearing a bra, and she hooks her fingers at the sides of the tiny scrap of lace she's calling underwear. Pushing them down, she stands before me, stunningly confident in her own skin.

"You're so beautiful, Brooke."

"I want to feel you fucking me so hard I can barely breathe." Without another word, my lips crash down on hers as I grab her ass and lift her to wrap her legs around my waist.

I'm ravenous for her pleasure, pressing her back against the wall as I kiss her with a passion so urgent, I lose all rational thought.

"Oh God, Anders. I... please."

"I've got you. I'm right here." Reaching her hand between us, she positions me at her entrance, and I can't contain the roar in my chest as she leverages her weight against the wall and pulls me in. She feels so fucking good, and the second she starts to move, I can't hold back. Taking over, I set a punishing rhythm, hammering into her, seated to the hilt. "Brooke..." She captures me in an urgent kiss, our tongues twisting and tangling in a frenzied fuck. "Shirt." It's all I can manage, but she understands.

She pushes my open shirt off my shoulders and scrambles to get it off me as I continue to thrust, unable to tear myself away long enough to get naked. All that matters is Brooke. Having unfettered access to her body, slick with a sheen of sweat as I continue my ministrations, is all I ever want. In this moment, I'd give anything to stay right here, nestled deep inside her. *Forever.*

I can already read Brooke's body. One explosive night was all I needed to commit every line and curve of her to memory. She's close.

"God, Anders, I'm close. I can't... I need... I..." She can't form a coherent thought, and it drives me wild, desperate to crash over the edge with her.

"Tell me you're mine."

Without hesitation, she speaks those two little words that are my undoing. "I'm yours."

"Come for me, Brooke." I thrust harder and faster, the beginnings of my release pulsing through me as she crashes over the edge, pulling me with her as she screams my name over and over again.

"Anders... yes... oh God... yes!"

My mind splinters with a thousand different sensations firing in my synapses as I come harder and longer than I ever have before. Brooke tightens around me, sending aftershocks coursing through every fiber of my being. I can barely stay standing, leaning my head against the wall, bracing myself as I struggle to catch my breath.

"Holy shit."

"Is that a good or a bad *holy shit?*" Brooke's voice is hoarse, sultry, and tantalizing.

"Best orgasm of my life. I fucking love you." Her whole body tightens and not in a good way.

"Don't get carried away there, slugger."

I know I should play it down and take it back, but I don't want to. This is a lightbulb moment for me—I meant it. I'm in love with Brooke.

It's not until I move to withdraw that I realize what just happened. How could I be so stupid? "*Fuck!*"

"We just did." I set her down and go in search of her dress.

"Yeah, and without protection. I'm so sorry, Brooke. I'm never this careless. I don't know what came over me."

"Technically, you came *in* me, not *over* yourself." How is she this calm, flippant even?

"I'm clean if that's any consolation."

"In all honesty, that didn't even cross my mind. I know it should, but it didn't. I trust you, and I'm also clean, just to put your mind at ease." I feel like such a dick that we even need to have this conversation after—no word of a lie—the best sex I've ever had.

"What about contraception?" I'm a fucking schmuck.

"Don't worry. There will be no bun in my oven. I've got you covered on that one."

"I swear, I'm not that guy. At least I wasn't until just now. I've never gone bareback before."

"I took your bareback virginity? I'm touched."

"How are you so chill about this?"

"Because I enjoyed it… more than enjoyed it. Did it feel okay for you?"

"Are you kidding? No barriers between us, skin to skin, you're without a doubt the hottest, sexiest woman alive. If I died from being balls deep inside you, I'd die a happy man. It would be totally worth it."

She scrunches up her nose as she slips back into her panties and dress. "God, that would be awful. Crossing over from hot, sweaty sex to necrophilia in a matter of seconds. I'd never have sex again, and I'd have to rename my pussy the black widow."

"Rename? Does it currently have a name? And if so, what is it?"

"Don't laugh. I've never told anyone this."

"Before you tell me, can I just point out that in this scenario, you don't give a rat's ass about me dying from the hot sex."

"You'd be dead, so you wouldn't care. I'd be the one left traumatized by the whole thing."

"Fine. You owe me the current name choice."

"Can I preface it by saying I was eleven when I came up with it?"

"Spit it out."

"Virginia."

I can't hold in my amusement. "Wow! I'm glad you didn't tell me that before we slept together. Not sure I could get down and dirty with *Virginia*."

"You said you wouldn't laugh." She feigns upset.

"Why Virginia of all names?"

"I was eleven! My mom had just given me *the talk* because we were going to watch the puberty video at school that week, and I didn't want to be surprised by what was in it. I cringed when my mom said vagina, and you've met my mom, you know she has zero filters when it comes to these things, so I told her I'd just use the word Virginia instead."

"I suppose that makes sense. I really wish I didn't know the name of your vagina, though. I feel a little violated."

"Then you really won't like the fact that I renamed every penis in the world."

"That's a lot of names." I jibe as I button my shirt.

"Ha-ha. One generic name."

"All penises are not created equal, Brooke. Dare I ask what you named them?"

"Pennsylvania."

"Jesus."

"So when my mom explained the mechanics of sex, we talked about how Pennsylvania entered Virginia, and that's how babies are made. It was all very disturbing at the time."

"It's disturbing now."

"I just let you put your huge Pennsylvania in my Virginia, so you're not allowed to judge me."

"And on that note, we better head back for the reception."

"Did I just kill your desire to sleep with me tonight? Was my confession a bucket of ice to your libido?"

"Brooke, I could be in an ice bath and still get a hard-on at the sight of you naked and wet for me."

"Good answer."

As we head out the door, I'm achingly aware that we're breezing right past my 'cum confession.' If I were truly honest with her right now, I'd tell her that she'll always turn me on because she has something no other woman on earth has—my love.

Chapter Thirteen

BROOKE

I CAN'T BELIEVE the weekend has gone by so fast. Anders and I have had so much fun in and out of the bedroom. My parents love him already, as did everyone else who came for the vow renewal. He charmed the pants off everyone, and there wasn't a hint of fakeness in the way he took an interest in what people had to say. Ironic when you consider the circumstances.

Lacey and my sister are the only people who seem overly interested in us, and I think half of that is because they want an introduction to Linc. Apparently, he's the hottest sex on a stick after my date. My sister, Diana, finds my story about the bet I had with Linc mildly amusing, but Lacey just seems pissed off, and I have no idea why.

"What do you have that makes the two rock stars of baseball want you?"

"Not going to lie, I feel a tad offended by that, Lace. Do I have the face of a troll, and no one thought to tell me? Or is it my personality that should be off-putting to them?"

"That's not what I said."

"Linc just wanted to beat me. Even when he won, he didn't

demand his date. And as for Anders, I'm not sure why he's here with me. I just know that I'm happy about it."

"Barf."

"Geez, who shoved a bug up your ass this weekend?" She seems a little off recently, but she gets angry at me whenever I ask her if she's okay. I don't want to ruin my last day with Anders, so I opt not to poke the bear.

"I just hate weddings when there aren't any single, hot guys to have questionable sex with. The average age at this shindig is at least fifty, and that's with us bringing it way down. I'm all for a sugar daddy, but their rickety old wives are all here."

"Well, it's over now. You can resume normal service back in Manhattan."

"True. Do you want to come out with me tonight? We can hit a few clubs and get slutty."

"I'm not sure what we're doing when we get back to the city. Let me talk to Anders, and I'll give you a call."

That was absolutely the wrong thing to say.

"So now you need permission from a guy to hang out with me? He must be hung like a donkey. Forget about it. I'll talk to you later if you can find the time and Anders lets you answer the phone."

"Come on, Lace, you know that's not who I am."

"I thought so, but right now, I don't recognize the simpering idiot you've become over a guy. I'll see you later." She grabs her bag and heads for the door.

Diana looks at me with the same confused expression I'm sure I have at this moment. "She's a bit of a nutcase, don't you think? There's something off about her."

"You cage fight for a living, I reckon most people would call you a nutcase. Who enjoys getting punched in the face?"

She shoves my shoulder, and I stumble a few steps. "You know what I mean. She's a little intense. So you want to spend the day banging your hot boyfriend, wouldn't we all. It's no big deal."

"Can you not shove me so hard?"

She throws her head back and laughs. "You're kidding, right?"

"No. That hurt, and I'm not exactly a snowflake. Professional baseball player here."

"You'll always be a snowflake to me, princess Brooke."

Anders walks in through the front door, looking disgruntled.

"I grabbed the bags from the hotel. Are you ready to hit the road?"

Before I get a chance to answer, Diana buts in. "Do you know what would turn that frown upside down, Beck?"

"Enlighten me."

"Giving me your buddy Linc's number." She winks at him and hands over her phone.

Anders looks to me as if I have any control over my sister. She's not exactly the shy and retiring type.

"You know he's a player, right?"

"So were you until you met my sister."

"Touché, but I value my life, and your sister wanting me in hers." He hands the phone back without giving her Linc's number.

"I'm good with a player. I need a plaything, no feelings required. Don't be a buzzkill."

"Then you're perfect for each other, but I'm still not going to be the one who facilitates Brooke's sister hooking up with Linc." Anders drapes his arm over my shoulder and gives me a relaxed kiss. "You ready?"

"Yeah."

Diana gives us a sappy wave as we head out the door. "Bye, love-birds. Anders, I'm going to weasel that number out of you at some point."

"My lips are sealed. I'm a vault. Besides, I'm sure you'll cross paths at some point."

Before she berates him any further, I turn and stare her down. "Goodbye, Dee."

"Yeah, yeah. Go have amazing sex with your baseball boy toy."

"Will do!"

The second the door closes behind us, Anders drops his arm, leaving me bereft. "I don't think it's the best idea in the world that your sister hooks up with Linc."

"I'm sure she'd say the same thing about us, and we're doing just fine with our arrangement." Why did I call it that? It sounds so cold as I hear it fall from my lips.

"Time to turn back into a pumpkin." He opens the passenger door for me. "Your carriage awaits." I slide in, and a swarm of butterflies takes flight in my stomach. I don't want this weekend to end. Sure, I've had enough of smiling and making small talk with my parents' country club friends, but I'm not ready to give up my fairy tale with Anders.

When he gets in, and the engine roars to life, he turns to me with a concerned look in his eye and a furrowed brow. "Did I do okay? You don't seem too happy that we pulled it off."

"You did great. You even had me believing we were boyfriend and girlfriend for a while there."

"Is that so bad?" Before pulling out the driveway, he leans in, pressing his lips to mine as he cups my face in his hands. I love the smell of his cologne—not too much and distinctly him—comforting and at the same time, seductive.

"I guess not."

"Don't sound too enthused."

"I'm just going to miss the hot hotel sex. You're almost as skilled between the sheets as you are on the pitcher's mound."

"Almost? Was I doing something wrong? I might have to beg you for one last inning."

"That could be arranged." My pulse quickens at the prospect.

"Come home with me tonight, Brooke. Let me satisfy you in any way you desire."

"Anything goes?"

"Any. Thing. One night, no holds barred."

"You don't know me well enough to make that kind of promise. What if I'm into some freaky shit?"

"Then let me sign on the dotted line, and my safe word is *mango*."

"You're a funny guy."

"True, but I was serious. You get a free pass tonight." I don't want a free pass for one night, it won't be enough to quench my thirst for him. "So, are you in? Am I driving you home, or are we going to my place?" His voice is dripping with sex, low and raspy. It's a no-brainer.

"Your place." My pulse quickens, my heart hammering in my chest. Everything about Anders excites me. His voice, his body, and the way the muscles in his forearms cord as he grips the steering wheel and puts his foot on the gas.

We reach Manhattan in record time, and with every minute that passes, anticipation builds, and the sexual tension between us is at fever pitch when he finally puts the car in park. He doesn't speak, leading me up to his penthouse apartment with his hand on the small of my back. I know he wants to ravish me in the elevator, but tonight he's drawing it out.

A pang of sadness tugs at my heartstrings when I realize he's letting the anticipation build because this could be the last night we spend together as lovers. The vow renewal is over, and he fulfilled his role as my boyfriend with expert ease. Now, we're just two friends who have amazing sex. I want more, but I'd rather have him in my life as a friend than not at all.

The moment the doors open, he grabs my hand and pulls me into his arms. "Remember what I told you, Brooke," he says, trailing kisses down my neck. "Tonight, you can have anything you want. I'm yours. One night, no judgment."

"Anders… stop talking and get naked." I can be as take charge as I want tonight. Why not ask for what I really want? I have nothing to lose at this point.

He slowly unbuttons his shirt as he walks through the living room before turning to face me with his glorious abs on display. I want to lick that sexy 'V' disappearing under his belt. "Are you coming?" He rubs his hand over the scruff on his jaw, looking at me with fire in his eyes.

"God, I hope so."

"See something you want, Lexington?"

"Understatement of the century."

"Come and get it." He unbuckles his belt and flicks open the fly of his pants. "Am I seriously going to have to undress myself?"

"Yes, and I'm going to watch. I want to see every glorious, hard inch of you and commit it to memory."

I follow him down the hallway, unable to focus on anything but him. His voice is like silk as he coaxes me into his bedroom. "I won't bite, Brooke. Not unless you want me to."

He reaches for the cufflinks on his shirt, and it's such a turn-on. I practically tackle him as he opens the door into what I assume is his bedroom.

"I want… something from you. Rather, I want to do something *with* you." I feel embarrassed that I'm even contemplating asking him for this. It's not something I've done with a fling. Long-term boyfriends, yes. He said no rules. "I want… I mean, I like… anal play." My voice is barely a whisper, but I know he hears me as he pushes his pants just low enough for his erection to spring free.

"You're going to have to say that a little louder. I'm not sure I heard you properly." He's loving this, and as calmness washes over me at the sight of his smile, so am I.

"You heard me right. I want you to fill me, Anders. Everywhere." I don't undress, loving how powerful and confident I feel having him strip for me right now. He's hard as a rock as I walk toward him.

"Lose the pants completely. I want to see every inch of your body."

"Fuck me, you're hot when you take charge. I could get used to you being a dominatrix in the bedroom."

"You say that, but you're way too alpha male to give up that kind of control. Why do you think I find it so hot that I'm in charge right now?"

A wry smile creeps at the corner of his mouth as he steps out of his pants, relishing my voyeurism for a minute. "Then you better take advantage before I take over, spread your legs, and watch you make yourself come at my command."

Holy shit. If he were anyone else, I'd laugh at the very thought of it, but I know what he can do to my body and the pleasure he rips from me with a single word or caress.

"There's plenty of time for that when I'm done with you. We have all night."

"One night? If this is genuinely the last night you want with me, then we need to stop talking and make the most of it."

"Agreed." I push aside the idea of tomorrow morning being the final curtain on the past few weeks with Anders. He's become so much more than a fake boyfriend, and what I feel for him goes far beyond friendship.

I stalk toward him, my heart galloping out of my chest. I've always enjoyed a naked sexy guy, but not like this. I want to lick him like a freaking lollipop. A huge, gorgeous, hard, cock pop. With a word, I drop to my knees in front of him, taking his impressive length into my mouth before reaching my hands around to cup his ass, steadying myself.

"Jesus Christ, Brooke. That feels so fucking good." I groan in delight, swirling my tongue over the crest of his cock. My desire for him is out of control, my core tightening as I enjoy this most intimate of acts.

I'm already wet for him.

His moans of pleasure spur me on, pulling me under in a haze of sexual ecstasy. It's never going to be enough when it comes to Anders. I want more. I want all of him, and I can't bear the thought that someone else will be warming his bed soon.

As I work him with my mouth, his hands fist in my hair, his head dropping back as he loses himself to the sensation. I can't take my eyes off him. He's the most stunning man I've ever been with, chiseled to perfection, as if the gods themselves had carved him from stone.

"Brooke... fuck... you need to stop. I'm not coming in your mouth." He pulls out, leaving me bereft but only for a second. He tears my clothes off with animalistic desire and an urgency that turns me on so much I feel like I'm on the verge of orgasm before he even touches me.

"Anders." His name is a plea for more, for everything. I've never wanted someone so much it's a physical ache burning through every fiber of my being. But here, tonight, I'm consumed by Anders. The way his hands caress the length of my legs before he snakes his fingertips under my panties and sliding them down my legs until I'm exposed to his gaze.

"You're already wet for me. Does it turn you on when I fuck your mouth?"

"Yes." My pulse is racing, my heart hammering in my chest.

He dips his head between my thighs, kissing me, savoring my arousal. "Do you want to know how good you taste, Brooke?" I nod, barely able to catch my breath. "I want to hear you say it."

"I want to taste myself on your lips."

He stalks up and over me, bracing his arms on either side of my body, teasing me. "You want it, you take it, Brooke."

I grab his face with my hands and pull him in, licking the evidence of my arousal from his lips. He groans as his tongue meets mine, deepening our kiss. I'm overwhelmed with desire, desperate to feel his hard length inside me, setting a punishing rhythm. I want it hard so that tomorrow when I leave, I'll still feel the effects on my body—of being owned by him for one last night.

"Anders, I can't wait any longer. Fuck me. I need your cock." Our kiss becomes frenzied as his hands roam my body, and I'm not prepared when he breaks away and flips me onto my front.

"All fours, Brooke. Tell me where you want me." He runs his finger down the length of me, circling my clit before moving back, pushing two fingers inside me. "Here?" He pulls out before tracing a line to my ass, pressing his slick fingers just enough to cause my stomach to somersault. "Or here?"

"Everywhere."

"You don't get to give up control now, Brooke. Tell me. Where. You. Want. Me." His cock rests heavily between my legs, and it's all I can do not to beg for more.

"I want your cock hammering deep inside me while your fingers claim my ass."

"Fingers, plural?"

"Yes."

He takes a long, shuddering breath before clutching my hips and thrusting into me with one hard stroke. "*Fuck.*"

"Fill me, Anders. I want all of you." Any embarrassment or shyness is long gone, lost in the midst of his primal roar.

He steadies himself, sinking to the hilt before trailing his fingers over my ass, driving me wild before slipping two fingers inside. All of my muscles contract around him, so full as he starts to move, slowly easing his cock in and out of me in measured, controlled thrusts. He works his fingers in the same lazy rhythm while his other arm holds me steady.

"Brooke..." He speaks my name with such reverence, making me feel conflicted in the best of ways. Having his fingers inside me is a dark, almost naughty high, and yet the way his voice caresses my name, I feel loved. Cherished.

"More. I want more." My words mean more than I care to admit, but he doesn't need to know that.

He slips a third finger inside me, quickening his pace, filling me so completely I can't contain the ecstasy building with every hard thrust—the familiar tightening deep in my core, hanging on the brink of orgasm.

"God, Brooke. You're so fucking tight."

"Yes! Oh God, yes! I don't know how much longer I can hold back. I'm so close." A slick sheen of sweat covers my body as my legs begin to shake, pleasure taking over all of my senses.

He fucks me harder, his pace becoming frenzied as he chases toward his release. "Let me hear you, Brooke. I want you to come with me. I'm so fucking ready." His hand tightens on my waist, his fingers digging into my hip as he thrusts so hard the headboard starts slamming against the wall. He doesn't let up, his fingers continuing to work my ass, filling me so much it's almost painful and yet pleasurable beyond measure.

"Oh God, Anders, yes! I'm coming. I... yes... *yes!*" Every nerve ending in my body splinters into a million pieces, pleasure ripping through me like a tornado, spinning me out of control, over and over again as Anders hammers into me, shouting my name until his voice is hoarse. The moment he finds release, he releases my hip, slipping his fingers round my waist and down to my clit.

I can't take it, my body detonating on overload. I collapse on the bed as he slows his pace, riding out the aftershocks of his orgasm as I ride mine.

"Best. Sex. Ever." Anders pulls out, leaving me empty as he collapses at my side. "You're even more of a minx than I gave you credit for, Lexington. Holy shit, that was hot." He's breathing hard, trying to catch his breath.

I swipe my hair off my face, it's so damp with sweat. My entire body is still tingling, involuntary shudders coursing through me from head to toe. "I… oh my God."

"Was that what you wanted?"

"So much better. You're a sex god. A boner-fide sex god."

"It must be good if you're breaking out the puns."

"Seriously. I've never felt so thoroughly, utterly, and completely fucked in my life. In the best possible sense of the word."

I turn to face him, his eyes fixed on my lips, a sated expression softening his features. "Glad I could be of service. I wanted you to have something to remember me by." He leans in, pressing a chaste kiss to my lips. "I'll settle for the best orgasm of your life."

"We really have amazing chemistry. It's not just me, right? Our sex is off the charts, brain-exploding, I-could-die-happy kind of orgasms."

"I'd say that's a mild assessment of how good we are together." I search his eyes for any hint that he might want what I'm about to ask.

I don't know why I can't just ask him if we're more than fake fuck buddies. Instead, I tiptoe around the subject. "It seems like a waste to stop."

"You mean tonight? I'm not even close to done with you."

"Yes." I take a deep breath and then blurt it out. "And maybe beyond tonight, if that's something you want too? I've enjoyed spending time with you since we met, and this weekend…" I stutter through it, "… it felt… *not* fake."

"You mean real?"

"It's the same thing, isn't it?"

"Just clarifying."

"I'm rambling. I'm not good at this stuff. I can talk a good game all day long with confidence for days, but I know we're friends, and you want it to stay that way. You've been clear from the start. But, the sex, I feel like maybe it changed things. Just tell me to shut up any moment now. I'm down the rabbit hole, digging it deeper, and if you don't say something soon, I may just lie down and call it my grave because I'm dying of embarrassment now. You speak. For the love of God."

"It didn't change things for me, Brooke."

"Oh." My heart sinks. He lifts my chin, forcing me to look at him.

"It didn't change because I already wanted more. I have from the beginning."

"Why didn't you say anything before now? You're not exactly the shy and retiring type."

"You kept talking about the *friendzone* and bringing up the vomit incident. I was hoping that my lame offer to be your fake date for your parents' vow renewal might give me the chance to show you we could be more than friends. The sex was unexpected. I don't think I could let you go now, even if you wanted me to."

I launch myself at him, straddling his thighs. "So, we're dating, for real?"

"I'm all in. Are you?"

"Of course, I am."

We stay up long into the night talking and making love, stopping now and again for some snacks to replenish our energy for the next round. As I fall asleep tangled in the sheets beside him, I think for a moment—what would I have done if he'd said no? If I had to walk away? I'm so glad I won't need to find that out.

Chapter Fourteen

ANDERS WON'T TELL me where we're going today. I suspect he knows it's my birthday. I didn't mention it because we've not been dating long, and I didn't want him feeling pressured to make a big deal about it.

He looks breathtakingly handsome as he pulls up in the Corvette. As always, he won't let me just jump in the car, instead getting out to open the door for me. In a pair of low-slung jeans and a white t-shirt, he's every bit the sexy baseball star.

"Hey, gorgeous." He pulls me in for a kiss before holding the passenger door for me.

"Hey, yourself." Even the smallest of touches quickens my pulse, my breathing shallow and full of desire. As he slides in beside me, I bite down on my bottom lip, pressing my thighs together in an attempt to quash the need burning inside me.

"If you keep looking at me like that, we won't be going anywhere. I'll take you back up to your apartment and fuck you senseless."

"I'm good with that. Kill the engine."

"Damn." He adjusts himself, the outline of his cock thickening, straining against his jeans. "I just shot myself in the foot there."

"Where are we going? It can't be better than a naked Saturday afternoon."

"True. Now, it'll be lame by comparison."

"Then, it's settled. Turn the car around, and let's get freaky."

His knuckles turn white as he grips the steering wheel. "We can't. Places to go."

I slide my hand over his thigh, tracing the line of his growing erection. "Are you sure?"

"Fuck. Babe Ruth's stats. Wins above replacement 182.50. At bat 8,399. Runs 2,174. Hits 2,873. Runs batted in 2,214. Walks 2,062. Strikeouts 488. Home runs 714. Stolen bases 123. Batting average 0.342."

"Fun trivia, but what the hell?"

"I run baseball stats in my head when I need to get rid of a chubby. Or if I need to make it last longer. No one likes a guy who's done in sixty seconds."

"So, you're reciting stats when we're in the throes of passion? That's not very romantic. I'm all focused on you and how hot you are."

"You can come over and over again. Once I shoot my load, I need at least a few minutes to regain my strength. So, you can have ninety seconds of romance or an hour of screaming orgasms and a long, hard ride. Which is it going to be?"

"Women like a quickie every now and then. It's hot when a guy just can't hold back. I feel really sexy when I know I can make a guy lose control."

"Nice way to avoid the question. You want romance or longevity. For me, they go hand in hand. I want you. I have feelings for you. I have to recite stats so I don't become a jizz fountain the second I'm inside you. It's a testament to how much I love being with you. It's easy to make it last when someone doesn't get your blood pumping, other than it being a snooze fest and wanting to get it over with."

"Here's a crazy idea. What if you just don't sleep with women that you don't have feelings for?"

"Are you telling me you've never had a one-night stand?

Someone you had heat and chemistry with but who you knew wasn't boyfriend material?"

"That's not what you're talking about. You said the words, *snooze fest*. Where's the chemistry there?"

"People can be deceiving. You could be really attracted to someone, and then when you get down to business, you just aren't compatible. I'm right, and you know it."

"Why is your jaw so tight?"

"Because even talking about your sexual partners makes me feel sort of murderous."

"Sort of? I'm not sure there's a *maybe* version of murderous." I can't help but laugh. He's the one who started talking sex.

"Fine. Completely, over the top, seeing red, murderous rage. I'm not this guy. I don't get jealous of ex-boyfriends or one-time Charlies. The past is the past, and I get to warm your bed now, and I don't plan on letting some other schmuck come along and snake you out from under me."

"Wow, that was an extremely possessive sentence in a 1950s kind of way. There's no one waiting to 'snake me.' The only serpent I'm interested in is the one in your pants. So, take a deep breath and chill out."

"Sorry. I don't know where that came from."

I'm about to tell him I have the same sinking feeling at the thought of the women who've seen him when he comes, but my phone rings, and it's my manager.

"Hey, can whatever it is wait until tomorrow?"

"It's good news and happy birthday." I'm glad he's not on speaker.

"Thanks. No big deal. What's the good news?"

"You've just been offered a huge endorsement by the biggest brand in baseball."

"What?" I didn't know he was looking for any new deals, so this is truly a surprise.

"Did they come to you?"

"Yes, which means they are willing to pay the big bucks."

"Wow."

"They want you and Verbeck to do a joint campaign."

"Oh." It suddenly makes sense. They want Anders. "I'm not sure that's such a great idea."

"Don't turn it down just because it might not last with boy wonder. This will skyrocket your profile. It might not make a big difference while you're still playing, but when you retire and want to branch out into other aspects of the game, it'll be a huge sway in your favor."

"I don't know if he'll be interested in that. Can you leave it with me for a few days?"

"Sure, but the second you convince him, call me. It's free money for him. Checks with seven figures. It's a no-brainer."

"I'll call you tomorrow. Thanks for letting me know."

"I'm not going to lie, I thought you'd be screaming with joy. Millions of dollars are literally falling into your lap right now."

"I get it. We'll talk later. Bye." I shut off my phone, knowing he'll send me emails and texts, trying to get me signing on the dotted line.

"Sorry about that. I'm putting it on silent for the rest of the day."

"Everything okay?"

"Yeah."

"I don't mean to pry, but I couldn't exactly block out your voice. You said, *I don't know if he'll be interested in that.* If it's me you're referring to, I'm up for anything if it involves you."

"That's sweet, but it's not a dinner with friends or a small favor."

Concern is etched in his brow. "Spill. Whatever it is, I don't want it on your mind today. I have plans for us, and I want you relaxed."

Ugh. I really don't want to do this right now, but he's not the kind of guy who'd be happy to let me stew and stress. "That was my manager. He said he got an offer for a new endorsement campaign."

"That's awesome. Congratulations."

"I'm not done." I wring my hands, nervous to tell him. Everything with us is so new, and we've already had a less-than-normal introduction to dating. "Their offer is for both of us. They want some baseball power couple thing, I guess. Not that we're a power couple. It's stupid."

"It's smart. These companies want maximum bang for their buck and the widest audience they can get. What better way to marry men's and women's baseball?"

"Sure, but then we're out there. If things go south, we can't erase it."

"And you think we can do that now? I don't know if you missed the memo, we're sort of a big deal." He gives me the warmest smile, reaching his hand over to squeeze my thigh.

"If you want to do it, I'm fine with it. I don't plan on being *erased* from your life anytime soon."

"I appreciate you saying that, but can we not talk about it right now? I just want to enjoy whatever you have planned today. They don't need an answer straightaway. We can talk about it another day."

"Don't overthink it, Brooke."

"Have you met me?"

He chuckles as he puts his hand back on the wheel. "You're too hard on yourself. Things like this are supposed to be enjoyable. You're right, though, it can wait. Today I want you to chill and have fun."

"I'm with you, so it's already fun."

"Shucks."

"Are we almost there?"

"Yep."

"Is it somewhere busy or quiet?"

"You'll find out in five minutes."

"I'm not great with surprises."

"I promise you'll like it." I don't recognize our surroundings, but I'm pleasantly surprised when we pull in next to a beautiful little restaurant. It's out of the way and set back from the road. You wouldn't know it was here unless you know that it's here. I realize how dumb that sounds, and I'm happy I didn't say it out loud.

"It's so pretty." There are twinkling lights everywhere, and I can imagine how stunning it must look after dark.

"I'm glad you like it. I own it."

"Seriously?"

"Yep. A buddy of mine is a Michelin star chef, and when I hit my first big contract, I bought this place. I don't have anything to do with it other than on paper, but I come out whenever I get the chance. His food is insane."

"How have I never heard of this place?"

"It thrives on word of mouth with the Manhattan millionaires. I don't publicize that I'm the owner. You're the only person other than Linc who knows." My heart skips a beat, knowing that he's trusting me with this little secret.

"Thanks for bringing me. I can't wait to taste the food. I'm starving."

"He can make you whatever you want. Literally anything. He'll ruin you for any other restaurant." When we get out of the car, Anders wraps his arm around my shoulder, tucking me in close at his side.

"I'm so happy it's just us today. Life has been so hectic lately."

"Huh. I should probably tell you something."

I reach for the door, much to Anders' dismay. He really takes the chivalry thing to a new level. I pull it open as I speak. "Honestly, sometimes I just want to tell everyone to piss off. People just randomly get on my nerves, and I really didn't want to fake giving a shit about anyone but us today. Just you and me."

"But you're so good at faking things." A cold chill runs through me at the sound of her voice, along with a ripple of nervous laughter.

"Happy Birthday!" A crowd of my nearest and dearest friends shout in unison.

Fuck.

Lacey rushes over, pulling me into her arms. "You sure know how to make an entrance."

I turn to look at Anders, who's suitably horrified, mouthing the words *I'm sorry* as he greets everyone. I am such a colossal idiot.

"How did Anders know it's my birthday?" I know the answer before she speaks.

"I told him, of course. You didn't think I'd forgotten, did you?"

"No. I didn't really think about it."

"Wow. Way to make your bestie feel special. You get a fake boyfriend and just ditch me?"

"That came out all wrong. I didn't mean to sound like a bitch. After my ungracious entrance, I'm sure no one is in the mood to celebrate me."

Anders arrives at my side with a glass of champagne. "Can I steal the guest of honor for a minute?"

He and Lacey stare each other down. "Sure."

"I'm so sorry, I thought you'd enjoy an afternoon with your friends. I've been hogging your time lately."

"Don't apologize. I can't believe I said that in front of everyone."

"Is it too soon to laugh about it? It was pretty funny." I can't keep a straight face when he gives me that winning smile. The one that makes his eyes sparkle.

"Not funny. I think I just lost half of my Christmas card list."

"Don't sweat it, everyone loves you." He pulls me into his arms, pressing a kiss to the top of my head as he towers over me.

"Thank you for doing this."

"It'd be better if I'd done something you actually wanted. Why didn't you tell me your birthday was coming up?"

"I didn't want you to feel like you had to make a big deal of it."

"Of course, I want to celebrate you."

"Thanks."

"Anytime."

"What's the deal with you and Lacey? You both looked like you were chewing wasps when you came over."

"Nothing. Maybe she's not too enamored that we're dating. She's used to spending a lot of time with you."

"There's an easy way to fix that. Let's hang out tomorrow. Maybe you can invite Linc?"

"I'd say he already knows her just fine." He nods to the hallway that leads to the restrooms. Linc and Lacey seem to be getting acquainted all on their own.

"Still, I want you to get to know her."

He gives me a tight smile. "Sure. Anything for you."

I reach up onto my tiptoes and kiss him—heartfelt and full of promise. "Thank you. You're too sweet to me. I really do appreciate you going to all this trouble. Sorry I messed it up by putting my big fat foot in my big fat mouth."

"Let's just try to have fun, and the minute I can chuck everyone out, I will. Then I spread you out on one of the tables and eat dessert."

A thrill courses through me. "Can we throw them out now?"

"Not if you want to recover your very important Christmas card list."

"Damn. I guess dessert will have to wait a few hours. Right now, I'm going to go and rescue Lacey from your lush of a best friend."

"He can take care of himself, and the way it looks to me, he might be the one in need of rescue. Besides, you need to make the rounds and say hi to everyone who just heard you say you want them to piss off."

"Fuck me." I feel so awkward as I look around the room, and all eyes are on me.

"I plan to. Repeatedly. Later."

"Don't make promises you can't keep, Verbeck." He runs his hand down my spine, caressing my neck with his lips.

"I always keep my promises. I'll be feasting on you for hours."

"Happy birthday to me."

"Now go and be your endearing self. My attempt at your birthday surprise can't end in dead friendships."

"Yes, sir."

"Say it again. That's sexy as hell."

"Yes, sir." He slaps my ass as I turn on my Chucks and start the task of being a hundred and fifty percent sociable.

I may not have been stoked on the idea of having all my friends in one room and all the attention on me, but I've really enjoyed myself. Thankfully, everyone knows I have a tendency to be abrasive at times, and they see the funny side of my outburst.

Anders wasn't kidding when he said the chef is outstanding. I don't think I've ever tasted such amazing dishes before. The drinks are flowing freely, and I've laughed so hard, champagne came shooting out of my nose. The silver lining is that Anders didn't see my disgusting party trick.

As friends say their goodbyes, I'm suddenly aware that Anders is nowhere to be found. Linc is flirting with one of my teammates, so I head over to see if he knows where his friend disappeared off to.

"Hey, birthday girl. Your entrance tonight bumped you several spots up my friend list. You seriously had no idea he put this together for you?" He throws his arm over my shoulder, giving me a little squeeze. Linc likes to come across as all bravado, but he has a sweet side that's very charming. I can see why he's so popular with the ladies.

"No clue. I'm mortified."

"You're too cute to be embarrassed about shit that doesn't matter. Isn't that right… Penny?"

"Judy. We've been talking for forty minutes, and you don't know my name. I think that's my cue to leave." She rolls her eyes and grabs her purse off the bar. "I'll see you at practice, Brooke. Happy birthday."

"Thanks for coming." She's about to leave when she gives Linc another glance, reaches into her bag, and pulls out a pen. Grabbing his hand, she writes her number in chicken scratch."

"If you call me and say anything other than, 'Hey, Judy,' I'll block your ass."

He smiles with a sly wink as she turns to leave, but the second she's out of earshot, he signals the bartender for more drinks. "I need something to wake me up. She might be the most boring person I've ever met."

"Then why did you talk to her all that time?"

"I was trying to be nice. Plus, she's hot. Unfortunately, not hot enough to warrant an evening spent being regaled with her stories of baseball camp as a teenager. If anyone can ruin stories about girls bunking up together at summer camp, it's her."

"You mean you don't want to hear about how my best friend taught me to French kiss at one of those camps? We played baseball all day long, could recite World Series winners by year, and then late at night, we'd sneak into each other's beds and…"

"And…"

"Nothing. Don't be a perv."

"Not fair! I'll tell you my stories if you tell me yours." He has that wry grin that I'm sure gets him into all kinds of trouble, spreading wide across his face.

"Like I want to hear about you as a pimply teenager, sticking your teeny weeny somewhere it shouldn't have been. To think some poor girl out there has the accolade of losing her virginity to the great Lincoln Nash, but the disappointment of it being before you could grow facial hair and had zero idea what you were doing."

"Margot Ellis left the back of my dad's beat-up old Camaro with a smile on her face."

"You were old enough to drive? I had you pegged as losing your V-Card earlier than that."

"Of course, I was younger. Look at this face. I snuck out with the keys to the Camaro and drove Margot around town at midnight until we pulled into the school parking lot and hopped into the backseat. I knew exactly what I was doing. None of that amateur bullshit."

"Swear on your life?"

He tries to keep a straight face but descends into a fit of laughter. "Hell, no. I didn't know my ass from my elbow. It was awful. I had a false start, rutting between her legs, thinking I was in. When she had to ask the dreaded question, I realized my error. So, I went rooting around down there to make sure I got it in there. The condom was the wrong size. Thankfully, it was too small for my giant cock. If I'd been wearing a baggy condom, I don't think I'd ever have recovered."

I can't stop laughing. "Oh my God. She asked you if you were in yet? That's priceless."

"Don't worry, I've had plenty of practice since then. Now cough up your story."

"I never agreed to swap virginity stories with you. I haven't told Anders that one, so you're definitely not getting it."

"Low, Lexington, low."

"Maybe I'll spill over drinks another night."

He hands me another glass of champagne. "Drink up. I want to hear this tonight."

"Hear what?" Anders strides out of the kitchen, his brow furrowed.

"What's wrong?"

"Nothing. Everything's fine. Are you ready to get out of here?"

"I thought we were staying after everyone else leaves." I search his gaze for a hint of what's got him visibly ticked off.

"I'll take that as a 'fuck off, Linc' we want to have dirty restaurant sex." Linc lightens the mood. "Just please, for the love of God, thrash whatever tables you do the nasty on. I like the food here, and it'll completely ruin it for me if I have to be left wondering if I'm eating off a table that's had Beck's naked ass on it."

Lacey comes barreling out of—I'm not sure where—and practically barks in Linc's direction. "You want to get out of here? We can go back to your place and continue the party."

"Sure. We'll leave you guys to get freaky. Apparently, I have naked plans of my own."

Anders looks annoyed, shaking his head at Linc. "Not a good idea, bro. You know the rules." Something unspoken passes between them before Linc gives him a nod and follows Lacey out the door.

"She didn't even say goodbye. I think I pissed her off earlier. You were right." Lacey avoided me for most of the party other than her first dig about me ditching her for Anders.

"About what?"

"She thinks I'm not spending time with her because you and I started dating. I think her words were, 'you get a fake boyfriend and ditch me.' She's annoyed."

"Forget about her. Let's just go back to my place or your place, and I'll make good on my dessert promise."

"Are you sure? You seem upset about something. If you want to just drop me at my place and go home, it's fine."

"Sorry." He wraps his arms around me, holding me tight to his chest. "I just wish I'd done things differently today."

"I had fun, and it really is the thought that counts. I love that you were so thoughtful. Please, don't let my initial reaction ruin our night."

"It's not you."

"Then what's wrong?"

"Nothing for you to worry about, and I don't want to go home alone. Let me lose myself in you and give you a night to remember. I have a gift for you too."

"A night in your bed is gift enough for me."

"Are you getting all sappy on me, Lexington? It's so unlike you."

"Maybe you just bring it out in me." As we head for the door, I know it's him who makes me feel like a silly, sappy schoolgirl. I've never wanted to be super feminine or swept off my feet, but Anders has turned everything I thought I wanted on its head. With him, I have so many new and exciting hopes for my future—for *our* future.

Chapter Fifteen

ANDERS

TODAY IS the day we sign the contract on the joint endorsement—Brooke and I, together, in a huge campaign. I told my agent I could take it or leave it, basically leaving it up to Brooke to decide if she wanted to do it or not. I made him sit on it until the brand went to Brooke with an offer, which took more convincing than I thought. He was eager to get his fifteen percent of the deal, which shouldn't surprise me, but I've already made him millions.

There was no pressure from me where this is concerned. I know it'll help her career branding, and for me, being heralded as the new power couple of baseball is the part that's of value to me. She's the only part of this deal that matters.

Brooke and I connect on so many levels, and it's been a long time since I felt an emotional connection with a woman. She just came vomiting into my life and burrowed her way under my skin. I hoped the fake boyfriend routine would result in me getting the chance to woo her, and I'm so glad I did. What I feel now is so far beyond that.

The night Brooke and I finally slept together, there was such a long buildup, I didn't think it could possibly live up to my expectations. In reality, it was so much better. *She* is so much more than I bargained for. But it wasn't until she fell asleep, naked in my arms that night, that it hit me like a tidal wave—I'm in love with her. For me, the chicken came before the egg. I was in love with her before we actually started dating. Since we decided to get real, it's been amazing. We rarely spend a night apart, which I found stifling with previous girlfriends, but with her, the nights we're not together, I miss her. I've gotten used to the way she curls in at my side and falls asleep with her head on my chest and one leg slung over my body.

Last night, I missed her. She stayed at her place to get ready for today. I'm not sure what that means. We're signing a contract. I'm just putting my pants on one leg at a time like every other day.

My phone starts to ring, and as I stand in my closet sporting nothing but a pair of boxer shorts, I realize it's Brooke trying to FaceTime me. I'm quick to answer.

"Hey, Lexington. Your timing is impeccable."

"Looks like I'm a few minutes late. That pesky underwear is covering the goodies."

"Did you just call my cock 'the goodies?' I can honestly say that's a first for me." She laughs. "I'm glad you're enjoying my emasculation. You couldn't come up with another nickname for my manhood?"

"What do you want me to call it? The destroyer? Your yardstick? The Louisville sex slugger?"

"Your mind is a strange place, Lexington. None of those sound particularly inviting. I mean… *the destroyer*… really?"

"My personal favorite is the Louisville sex slugger. Come on, I'm passionate about batting, it's endearing to me. I spend a lot of time and effort taking care of my slugger, and it turns out I enjoy taking care of yours."

"Well, now you've got me standing at attention."

"Tilt the phone, I want to see."

"It's a phone, not a cinema screen. There's no way it'll fit. You'll only see a fraction."

"Sometimes all you need is the tip, big boy. Now let me get a peek."

"If you peek at mine, do I get to see yours?"

"Play your cards right, and you'll be seeing a whole lot more of me, up close and personal after the meeting today."

"Now we're talking!"

"I'll see you there."

"Wait, why aren't we riding together? I can swing by and pick you up on my way." She scrunches her face up at the suggestion.

"I'm capable of getting myself there."

"I know that. I just want to see you, and I actually hate driving alone. It's boring. You'd be doing me a favor, not the other way around."

"Sorry, but I want to be professional. This is business."

"Yes, it is, but the whole reason they want to work with us is because we're a couple. Therefore, it's not unprofessional to arrive together. If anything, it would make them more secure in the knowledge that we're the real deal."

"Nice try. Show me the sex slugger, and I'll consider it."

"Extorting a dick pic? I'm impressed." I tease her a little, tugging on the waistband, letting her follow the happy trail for just a second before angling my phone back up to my face. "That's all you're getting."

"No. You were just at the best part. Go back."

"Are you saying my face isn't the best part? I'm a handsome devil."

"You are, but I really want to look at your big beautiful cock right now."

"I'm hanging up now."

"Will I at least get the full show later?"

"I'm sure I can manage that. Now, go and get ready, and I'll see you at the meeting."

"See you soon, sex slugger."

"Please don't let that be my new nickname."

"Okay, destroyer. I'll see you later." She chuckles as she ends the call, amusing herself at my expense. Life with Brooke is definitely not boring.

Excitement blooms in my chest, not for the contract or for myself, but for Brooke. It took me a few days to convince her that this was a good idea. I get why she was hesitant—she's not in the same place as me right now. Her clock on our relationship started when we decided to date. For me, it's been since day one. I know I need to give her some time to catch up. This contract isn't a risk. She and I are going to work out, and years from now, she'll look back and see how important this moment was for her.

As I finish getting ready, I'm eager to get this done and celebrate with her. Unfortunately, our day doesn't quite turn out that way. Brooke invited Lacey to come and have a few drinks with us after dinner, so I mitigate the discomfort by asking Linc to take her off my hands. He's already made that mistake once, and I know he won't mind a repeat performance.

I consider it a win that we get through one night without Lacey offering to warm my bed, but she's clearly moving on from having the hots for me to setting her sights on tying Linc down in some way. I'm going to need to fill him in on what's been going on, but not tonight. Tonight, I just want to take my girl home and get lost in the sheets with her.

"Hey, slugger. Is it okay if I bring Lacey tonight?" I'm always thrilled to see Brooke's name come up on my phone, but her opening line dashed my hopes of an easy day.

"Why would she want to hang with us? Three's a crowd."

"I thought you could invite Linc to come hit a few balls with us." Fucking Lacey.

"I think he's busy tonight. Maybe we could do it another night."

"She's just feeling a bit down, and I don't want to leave her."

"Then stay with her, and you and I can rearrange our date for another night. I'll still get to see you today at the photo shoot, and then you can go be a good friend. It's not a problem." It's taking all my self-control not to let loose on what I really think of her best friend, but I rein it in. Now isn't the time to talk about all this.

"What's going on? You don't like her?"

"She's fine. You're reading too much into this. My idea of a good night isn't being a third wheel. If she needs you, then hang with her. I'm sure she'd rather have you to herself anyway if she's feeling like crap."

Our first shoot is in Central Park, then I was going to surprise her with a picnic in the Stadium, wining and dining her on the pitcher's mound. It's become one of our favorite places to hang out together, lying back on the grass and staring up into the night sky. Plus, it never gets old that my girl enjoys baseball as much as I do. We strategize, talk through different players' style, and I pitch for her. She's literally the perfect woman for me.

When I arrive at the park, photographers and their crew are scurrying around like ants, getting everything set up to put Brooke and me under the microscope. I thought I'd get here before her, but as I take in the set they're creating for us, I spy Brooke being primped and preened by a stylist, and she doesn't look happy. As I stride toward her, ready to calm her down when she turns to face me, getting a smear of lipstick up her cheek. She looks like the Joker.

"Hey, baby. You've got a little something on your face," I say with a chuckle.

"What?" Her eyes are frantic.

The stylist grabs her face and pulls her back around. "I'm going to need to start over now. Can you please try to stay still?"

I walk over so Brooke can see me without craning her neck. "Are you okay? You seem a little on edge."

"I'm nervous. I know I've done photo shoots before, but this is us, and I don't want to make you look bad, and what if people hate that I'm your girlfriend?"

"Okay, take a deep breath, Lexington. For starters, I don't give a flying fuck what anyone thinks of us. They can like it, dislike it, but the only people who matter are you and me. Secondly, how could you make me look bad? Have you seen me today?" I adjust my ball cap, giving her my best panty-melting grin. "I'm hot. You're hot. It'll be great. Just relax and try not to overthink it. It's just you and me, and the rest of these people are window dressing to our day."

"You do look hot today, but you look hot every day. I look like Coco the Clown."

"If you'd stay still, I can do your makeup properly and then no clown face." The stylist is clearly frustrated but trying to remain professional. "I'll have you looking just as hot as your boyfriend."

Brooke gives me a sly smile before she stops moving or talking, letting the makeup artist do her thing. She looks stunning when she's done, and we're ready to shoot. It's more fun than I thought it would be, but it's a little weird having to kiss her on cue and pose on the edge of a kiss so many times. I've done many photo shoots in my career, but they were just me and a baseball. I love the game, but I don't have to make out with the ball. This feels like some sort of acting, and I wasn't exactly the drama student at school. I was every bit the stereotypical jock.

It's clear Brooke is a natural, giving off the siren vibes as she drapes herself over my body on command. I'm used to her with her Chucks on and a backward ball cap. Sure, I've seen her dressed up, but this isn't just her clothes. The camera loves her, and she's definitely feeding off the photographer's direction.

When we're done, I'm desperate to get her alone and strip her out of these clothes. "Are those heels yours?"

"Yes, why?"

"Because they're sexy as hell. I might need you to keep them on while I have my wicked way with you later."

She bites down on her bottom lip, her breath quickening at the thought of it. "That can be arranged. I just need to go and check on Lacey first."

"Look, we'll just do what I had planned for tonight, tomorrow."

"No. I don't want to ruin whatever you were planning. I'll be an hour, tops."

"Are you sure?" I have a bad feeling about this.

"Yes. Just tell me where and when to meet you."

"The stadium. Meet me on the pitcher's mound. I'll be there, so just come when you're ready. No rush."

"See you soon, slugger."

She strides off in those heels, and there's nothing I can do but watch. It's official, I'm the luckiest son of a bitch in the world. The way she looks right now, the saying definitely applies—I hate to see her go, but I love to watch her leave. Damn, you could bounce a quarter off her ass in those jeans.

I think we can safely say our first foray into working together was a huge success. I stick around for a while to see some of the rough shots the photographer is pulling up on his laptop. They look incredible. *She* looks incredible.

I've been waiting on Brooke for well over an hour, and I'm pretty sure the chilled champagne is no longer chilled. Room temperature Cristal isn't what I had planned. Thankfully, the rest of our picnic isn't heat-sensitive, so I stretch out on the blanket with my arms under my head and stare up into the night sky. I guess I must nod off at some point because I'm coaxed awake by Brooke's lips on mine.

"Hey, sorry I'm late. I tried calling you, but it went straight to voicemail." I pull her down on top of me, my lips crashing down on hers in a proper hello.

"Room for one more on that blanket? I didn't realize this was a ménage à trois scenario. I could be convinced with a glass or two of that fancy-looking wine."

My stomach lurches up into my throat. Lacey. Brooke feels my body sag underneath her. "Sorry, I tried calling you, and I sent you messages."

"It's fine." I roll her off me and busy myself pouring two glasses of champagne. I guess I'm drinking straight from the bottle. I only brought two glasses and two of everything else.

When I hand them each a drink, Lacey purposely runs her fingers over my hand, and it just sickens me. "Thank you, Anders. Sorry for gatecrashing your date."

"Not a problem."

"I don't suppose it's really a date, anyway, is it with you two 'dating' for the cameras?"

Brooke steps in before I blow my top. "I've told you, Lace, we're together now, for real."

"Yeah, but I know that's just the story. Don't worry, I won't tell the tabloids or anything."

"It's not just a story, Lacey, Brooke and I are together. We're dating."

"For the money. That's not really a proper relationship. Sex and money. You guys are basically millionaire hookers for each other." She takes a seat like it's nothing and starts pulling stuff out of the picnic basket.

"It's actually nothing like that at all." Now, I'm really pissed.

"If you were dating for real, you wouldn't have tried to bed me."

"What the fuck is wrong with you?" I look to Brooke and watch in abject horror as the color drains from her face. "It's bullshit, Brooke. I haven't done anything."

"Yeah, only because I turned you down. Even if you're only fake dating, I'd never do that to my best friend. You know that, right, Brooke?" Lacey is cool as a cucumber, and it all falls into place. This is why she stopped with the inappropriate advances and decided on lying through her teeth to make me look bad. I should've told Brooke about this long ago, and now I don't have a leg to stand on.

"I…"

"We've been friends since we were eighteen, and you know me better than anyone."

"You're a sandwich short of a packed lunch, Lacey. You need help. Why would you want to hurt Brooke like this? Lying about me."

"I'm not the one who's hurting her right now. I was willing to forget your drunken advances, but when Linc told me that you kept this whole fake thing going on for the endorsement money, well, I couldn't ignore it anymore. Brooke is my friend, and I can see that she's starting to believe the shit you're spinning about your fuck buddy situation becoming something more. You don't get to treat women that way just because you're famous."

"Anders, what's she talking about? Why would Linc say something like that?"

"She's lying."

"Call him. The last time I took him home, he said you got the offer for the endorsement way before Brooke and that it was worth faking it a bit longer."

"Is that true? You knew about the offer and made out like it was brand-new-fucking-information when I told you about it."

"Yes, I knew, but I wasn't faking anything. I didn't want to pressure you, and I was more concerned about getting a chance to date you properly. I told my agent I didn't care and that *if* you got an offer and wanted to consider it, then I'd be fine with whatever you wanted to do."

"So, you did lie?"

"Not the way she's making out."

"Why should I believe you? Lacey has no reason to lie."

"Because you know me. I'm in love with you, and I'd never jeopardize that with so much as a look in another woman's direction."

"I've seen you at events. I kept wondering why you looked pissed and Lacey looked upset. I brushed it off because I didn't want to see what was right in front of me."

"Exactly. I tried to shield you from it, Brooke, but he was so persistent. I didn't know how to tell you, and I didn't think he'd take it this far, duping you to make a quick buck." She pulls a stunned Brooke into her arms. "I'm so sorry. I should've told you everything sooner."

Tears well in Brooke's eyes as she clings to her best friend, the traitorous, conniving bitch. I'm losing her. I don't even know what the fuck is happening.

"Don't listen to her, Brooke. I didn't try to sleep with her. She was the one trying to get in my pants. I told her no. I figured she got the message, and I wouldn't need to upset you."

"He's a player, Brooke, just like the rest of them. They think they can treat us like crap and just discard us when they're done."

I pace a ten-foot square, running my hands through my hair, frantically trying to figure out how to reassure Brooke that I'm telling the truth. If I'd just told her about the contract offer, she'd have zero reasons to doubt me.

"I can't believe this."

"Good, you shouldn't. It's a load of bullshit. I have zero interest in her. I never have, and I never will. It's always been you, Brooke. Only you."

"Lacey doesn't lie, Anders."

"She's a fucking fruit loop."

"Don't start talking shit about her to cover your tracks." The second those words leave her lips, and she steps in front of Lacey in a defensive stance, I know I'm fighting a losing battle, and I'm kicking myself for trying to leave their friendship intact after all of Lacey's bullshit.

"I have no tracks to cover, Brooke. I can't believe you're listing to this. Two hours ago, you knew beyond a shadow of a doubt how I feel about you. A few words from her, and you disregard everything between us?" I know the answer before she opens her mouth. Everything is crumbling before my eyes, and I'm unable to hold all the pieces together.

Chapter Sixteen

ANDERS

"NONE OF IT WAS REAL. You fucked me for an endorsement. You lied about it."

"Good to know you hold me in such high esteem. I've done nothing but bend over backward to help you, and this is the thanks I get?"

"You already got your thanks. Consider the enthusiastic blow job and the way I was riding your cock as payment."

"Good to know you've got your price. Do you spread your legs for every guy you want something from?" Her hand connects with my face in an almighty slap.

"Fuck you, Anders. I should've known. Guys like you aren't nice for the sake of it. Your life is so fucking easy, so you take what you want and discard the rest." I know I should walk away and take some time to cool down, but I'm so fucking angry.

"Are you listening to yourself right now? I'm the one who had an easy life… are you shitting me? You're a fucking trust fund baby with the summer mansion in the Hamptons who doesn't know the meaning of the word struggle. I earned every damn dime and accolade. I was raised by an incredible single mother who worked three jobs to pay for my little league. I worked my ass off for everything I have. I don't have a daddy with stacks of hundred-dollar bills to wipe my fucking tears."

"You don't know the first thing about me."

"Obviously not. And apparently, you know sweet-fuck-all about me. You think I slept with you for a measly endorsement? I don't need shit from you, Lexington. I'm the fucking golden child of baseball right now. I was doing that campaign for you because I know it's harder to be in baseball and get paid what you're worth as a woman. And let's just chalk the rest of the fake crap up to momentary insanity on my part."

"Lacey's right about you. I thought we were friends, but you just wanted to get laid." Lacey is standing back, crossing her arms in satisfaction. She's achieving exactly what she wants—my relationship with Brooke to implode.

I throw my head back and laugh at how ridiculous this is. "Are you fucking kidding me? Little Miss Two-Faced? She knows even less about me than you, if that's possible. There are easier ways for me to get laid. If all I wanted were to get my rocks off, I'd have left you in a pool of your own vomit the night I met you. I could've had any pussy in that bar. When it comes to sex, don't fucking flatter yourself that I'd go through all of this for a few nights with your magical cunt."

The second the words leave my mouth in an angry torrent of hurt and sheer disbelief, I regret them. I'm reacting to the smug grin on Lacey's face. How did I let myself get put in this position? Brooke doesn't play around, and this time she's not content with a slap. Her right hook catches me off guard, and I instantly taste blood.

"I hate you, Anders."

"That's what your little best friend here said when I declined her advances over and over again. Don't you see what she's doing? Open your fucking eyes, Brooke." She throws another punch, but this time I see it coming and duck.

"Lacey would never do that to me. You're lying." If I were a lesser man, I'd slap that self-satisfied, fake-ass grin off Lacey's face.

"From the mouth of a liar. All you've done since we met is lie to everyone around you. You needed me so that you could lie to your entire family. That was all you. Lie to yourself all you want, but I'm telling the truth. She came onto me at your parents' house and your fucking birthday party. Who does that to their best friend? I told her no, and she's been gunning for me ever since. You're playing right into her hands. Don't be that stupid, Brooke."

"I don't believe you."

I throw my hands in the air, dumbfounded that she can't see what's right in front of her. I only have myself to blame. I waited too long, and now there's no going back.

"I'm done. I should never have entertained this bullshit chemistry between us. Whatever this is, it's over. I'm out."

I don't wait around for more verbal or physical abuse. I've had enough. If Brooke can turn on me so quickly, she's not the woman I thought she was. My jaw aches as I head for the tunnel, leaving her on the pitcher's mound. I'm not going to keep loving a woman who doesn't want to be loved by me. I've been busting my ass to turn something fake into something real with Brooke, but Linc was right —*don't do real shit with a fake woman.*

I can still feel the sting of her right hook when I reach my car, so I don't bother looking at what I know will be a black eye in my rearview mirror. The roar of the engine coming to life is a balm to my rage, and I peel out of the parking lot at break-neck speed. It seems dumb now that I was complaining earlier that she wanted just to meet me here. If I'd picked her up, I wouldn't have been able to leave her here. I know she'd just call an Uber, but I still believe in chivalry—whatever that looks like these days.

I make a call to the one person I know will be happy to drown my sorrows with me.

"What up, shit face?"

"Apt nickname. I'm about to get shitfaced. You in?"

"That doesn't sound good. I thought you had a date with your one true love tonight."

"There are two rules tonight. Don't talk about Brooke, and don't even think about curbing my alcohol intake. I'm going to drop my car at the house, and then I'm heading for Viper."

"I'll meet you there in an hour. But can I say one thing before the rules of the evening are enforced? Maybe you should talk to Brooke about whatever has got you so bent out of shape."

"No, you can't say one thing. You warned me not to do real shit with fake women. Lesson learned." His silence tells me he understands what his friend duties are tonight—drinking and avoiding any kind of discussion about my love life.

"Fuck. Okay, I'll be there."

I hang up the call and speed toward home. My pulse is racing, fueled by the need to put as much distance as possible between myself and Brooke. If I don't, I'll go crawling back with no dignity and apologize for nothing, just so she'll give me the time of day. She stood there and looked me dead in the eye and then sided with Lacey. I asked her to believe in me, and she couldn't. I love her, but I'm not going to grovel and beg her to love me in return.

I don't waste time at the house, unable to sit with my own thoughts. The silence would be too loud. After a quick change, I order an Uber and head off to meet Linc. Usually, I drink in moderation. I'm not a guy who needs Dutch courage to get lucky in a bar. I can have a good time without drinking to excess. Confidence has never been an issue for me—until I met Brooke. She makes me question myself, and tonight, I'm not up for self-reflection.

I'm going to drink. In excess until she's a fuzzy thought at the back of my mind.

When I pull up outside Viper, the bouncer ushers me inside.

"Good evening, Mr. Verbeck. Mr. Nash is waiting for you up in the VIP lounge."

"Thanks."

Under normal circumstances, I love this club. The owner knows how to operate with discretion, and as I open the door to the VIP lounge, I can see him talking to Linc. Time to put on my game face. I have zero intentions of pouring my heart out. The only thing I'll be pouring tonight is a bottle of tequila.

"Hello, gentlemen. Are we a merry trio tonight?"

The owner, Carter de Rossi, turns to greet me. "I'm sure I can swing a few drinks with friends. How the hell are you, Anders?

Sorry I missed you the last time you were here. Fucking World Series champions!" He shakes my hand and pulls me in for a slap on the back. "You made this Yankees fan really fucking happy. Sit down, take a load off. What's your poison?"

"Bottle of tequila."

He doesn't question me and simply signals the bartender. "Can you bring a bottle of top-shelf tequila for my friend here? And three shot glasses."

"Make that two bottles," I interject.

Linc chimes in, "I'm sure we can split a bottle three ways. How fucked up are you planning on getting tonight?"

"Can't-remember-my-own-name drunk." They both look at me with pity in their eyes. "Don't lecture me. I can get drunk by myself or with one of the fine-looking women in here tonight."

Carter gives a simple nod to the bartender. "Two bottles of tequila coming up."

I pull my phone out of my back pocket and hate that I'm disappointed when I see Brooke hasn't tried to contact me.

"A watched pot never rings." Trust Linc to get it wrong.

"Never boils. Fucktit."

"Fucktit? That's a new one. I'm down for fucking some tits. Are you seriously not going to tell me why you're out here ready to drink until you puke and talking about the fact that you could just drink with the VIP groupies? You have a girlfriend. Lacey was stirring the pot, so what untruths has she been spouting?"

The bartender arrives with two bottles of tequila and shot glasses. I bypass the glass and grab a bottle. I take a long swig and fuck me, this stuff would put hairs on your chest. "I told you, no talking about Brooke Lexington and her magical pussy."

"You had a fight. No big deal. Couples fight all the time."

I take another gulp of tequila. "Shut the fuck up, Linc. When was the last time you were part of a couple? You fuck and chuck."

"So did you until the puke princess came along. Why are you letting this chick get you so bent out of shape?"

"Because he's in love with her." Carter's voice is calm, collected, and clearly speaking from experience. "No man comes in here to down a bottle of liquor unless his heart is all in with a woman. I've been there, done that, lost the girl, and spent a good bit of time getting fucked up and fucking everything that moved. It doesn't work."

"How'd that turn out for you?"

"A very long road, but I married her. She's the love of my life."

"Then, I guess that's where the similarities end. She obviously loved you back."

"And are you sure enough that she doesn't feel the same? If you're not sure, then whatever you do, with whoever, could be your downfall. Trust me."

"I don't need advice. I just want to drink. That's not so hard, is it?"

Linc is quiet on the sidelines—it's so unlike him. I know I'm pathetic when Lincoln Nash doesn't make fun of the predicament I find myself in.

"I have all the tequila you can handle, man. Just don't go off half-cocked and stick your cock where it doesn't belong. That's the last piece of advice you'll get from me tonight." Carter's a cool guy, and from what I know, he was the biggest manwhore in Manhattan before he met his wife. He's the guy who gives you hope that there's life after the sowing-of-wild-oats years.

They try to keep pace with me for an hour or two, but they're wasting time pouring tiny little shot glasses. "We need salt, lime, and a willing female to lick them off. It's the only way to really do shots."

As much as Linc doesn't want to indulge my bad decisions tonight, he perks up at the mention of licking salt off a hot chick and biting into a lime wedge from her lips. He heads for the bar and quickly returns with the ingredients and a hot blonde.

"This is Brandy. Brandy, these are my friends, Anders Verbeck, Yankees star pitcher, and Carter de Rossi, the distinguished owner of this place."

"Nice to meet you." She's wearing a dress that leaves nothing to the imagination and heels that could technically be classed as stilts.

"Brandy here loves a good tequila shot."

"I bet she does." Sure enough, she grabs the salt and shakes it

onto her wrist before holding it out like some bad vampire movie—
the stupid woman who inevitably offers herself up as a meal.

"I'm good, thanks." Carter is quick to decline. "I have a wife to
go home to. I suggest you do the same, Anders."

"I don't have a wife."

He pins me with an unsympathetic stare. "Whose fault is that?
You want her for the long haul, don't do whatever your very
drunken brain is telling you to right now. You'll regret it in the
morning."

"She told me she hates me."

"So? Stop playing around like a boy and start acting like a man.
I don't even know her, but I guarantee she's not out trolling for some
random guy to fuck. No one said relationships are easy, but if you
cheat, she won't forgive you."

"It's not cheating if you're not together."

"True, but this happened tonight, yes?"

"Yes."

"Then I don't care what she said to you, if you sleep with
someone else tonight and then get back with your girlfriend
tomorrow when she's had some time to cool off, you can't use the
we- were-on-a-break defense."

"Duly noted. Enjoy your wife, Carter. You're living the fucking
dream."

"Yep, and it took walking across a desert of broken glass to
reach the happily ever after part. So, yes, I'm going to go home and
crawl into bed with her and enjoy listening to her scream my name
as I lose myself in her."

"I envy you. But I also hate that you're rubbing your happy in
my face."

"Consider it a friendly reminder not to be *that* guy." He nudges
Linc. "Don't let him do anything he'll regret."

"I'm not his keeper. If it's over, it's over."

"Just because you miss your wingman doesn't mean it's okay to
stand idly by while he sabotages himself."

"When did you become the fucking Dalia Lama of
relationships?"

"I have a best friend who was willing to kick my ass and make me see what was right in front of me. He needs that right now. Don't let him down."

"Fine."

They talk as if I'm not even here, and it pisses me off. "You're breaking the rules of fight club. No fucking talking about it." I clutch my half-empty bottle of tequila and leave them to their conversation. There's an empty seat at the bar where I plan on taking up residence until I see the bottom of the bottle.

I tell myself a thousand times to switch off my phone—don't look—then I can convince myself it's Schrodinger's missed call. I set it face down on the bar and take another long swig of tequila.

"Is this seat taken?" A familiar voice comes from my right.

"What the fuck are you doing here?"

"Linc told me you were here drowning your sorrows. Can I sit?"

"No. With all due respect, fuck off. I have nothing to say to you." They let any old riff-raff up here. I make a mental note to tell Carter his VIP room policy is douchey.

"We don't need to talk, Anders. We could just go back to your place and fuck. You know what they say, angry sex is the best. I like it hard. The harder, the better."

My head is spinning, and I don't know if it's the alcohol or this moment. I stare at the liquor bottle in my hand and wonder if I'm so drunk that I'm hallucinating.

"You're shitting me, right? What the fuck makes you think that I want to take you back to my place and fuck you?"

"Because my sweet best friend won't give you the time of day. She's tucked up in bed with her bottle of wine, celebrating the fact that she knows the truth about you now."

"You're sick, You know that, right? I turned you down every time you tried to seduce me, Lacey. When are you going to realize that I don't want you? I want nothing to do with you."

She runs her hand down my chest. "As I said, angry sex is the best. I don't need you to like me, Anders. But I want you to fuck me."

"Jesus Christ. For a smart woman, I have no earthly idea why Brooke doesn't see right through you."

"Because she trusts me. I'm her best friend, and when her boyfriends inevitably fail her, I'm always there to console her. She's my family. I won't let you take her away from me."

"You're a fucking psycho." A chill runs through me at the realization. This is about more than Lacey disliking me or wanting to prove that she can bed me. She's obsessed with Brooke.

"One man's psycho is another woman's devoted. You're not good enough for her, and now she knows that. So, you might as well ease your broken heart with some meaningless sex."

"Are you in love with her? Is that the issue?"

"Why would I proposition you if I were in love with Brooke?"

"You tell me. It seems like I'm not the person to be answering that question."

"You have groupies wanting to sleep with you all the time. Do they all get the Spanish Inquisition?"

"No, because they didn't just ruin my relationship a few hours ago. They don't throw themselves at me repeatedly, even when I tell them I'm in love with someone else. And they sure as shit aren't venomous bitches who would fuck over their so-called best friend for a celebrity notch on their bedpost."

"She's my best friend, but she always goes for the wrong guy. You have a fake relationship. I don't see what all the fuss is about."

"If you believed that sentence, you wouldn't have dropped a grenade tonight."

Linc appears at my side. "Everything all right over here?" He drapes his arm over our shoulders

"Why the fuck did you tell her we're here? And why the hell do you still have her number?"

"We hooked up a couple of times. No big deal. Why are you so pissed that she's here? I figured she might be able to help you get back in Brooke's good graces."

I can't help but laugh at how ridiculous this whole situation is. "She caused the fight in the first place. She's been trying to get a ride on my disco stick for weeks." It's not until I look at his face, I realize he's the one who gave her the idea in the first place. "You're the one who told her the endorsement was based on a fake relationship."

"I... pillow talk. I didn't think you and Brooke were the real deal at the time. It wasn't supposed to get back to her. Fuck."

"Who needs enemies when I have you for a friend. What the fuck were you thinking? You weren't thinking, of course, not with your brain."

"I'll call her and explain."

"You've done enough. She doesn't believe a word out of my mouth, and fatal attraction over here has her convinced that I'm the bad guy. Shame on her for not believing me. She knows how I feel about her, and if she felt half of what I do, she'd have given me the benefit of the doubt."

"Shit. I can make it right, bro. It's not over."

"Yes, it is. I don't stand a chance as long as your fuck buddy is in the picture. I'm done. You can all go fuck yourselves or each other. I really don't care."

I down what's left of the tequila and stumble toward the exit. Linc starts balling Lacey out, shouting and hollering about what she's done not only to me but to Brooke. Linc may be a lot of things —idiotic and thoughtless for a start—but he would never intentionally sabotage me in any way. I want to march over to Brooke's and tell her what a huge mistake she just made and force her to confront Lacey. Her best friend is dangerous, and even in my inebriated state —especially in my inebriated state—she won't believe a word I say.

I hail a taxi and give him my address as I pull out my phone once more and stare at it, willing her to contact me. Then, the drunk part of my brain takes over, and I'm dialing her number, waiting for her to pick up, but it goes to voicemail.

"Lexington, I swear to God, I don't understand why you couldn't give me the benefit of the doubt. You can think what you like about me, but you need to watch yourself with Lacey. She doesn't have your best interests at heart."

The cab driver comes to a halt outside my place. "Just my opinion, Mr. Verbeck, but a World Series champ shouldn't be drunk dialing some chick and groveling. That'll be twenty bucks."

I hang up the call. "I wanted a ride, not a therapy session." I hand him thirty dollars and stumble my way to the front door. Before I can turn the key in the lock, the tequila decides to make a reappearance. I guess it's only fitting. Brooke and I started on her vomit comet, and we're ending with mine.

Chapter Seventeen

BROOKE

IT'S BEEN a week since I broke up with Anders, although I don't know if it counts when our entire relationship was a lie. I'm annoyed at myself for getting caught up in the idea of my fake boyfriend becoming the love of my life. The only small mercy I can cling to right now is the fact that I didn't say *I love you* when Anders was playing me and saying all the right things. He never needs to know that I feel it and that I hate myself for feeling it.

I had a drunken voicemail from him the night we broke up, but only after Lacey let me know he'd been drunk dialing her, trying to hook-up. How could I have been so wrong about him? Lacey tried to warn me, but I didn't want to hear it. She's always had a sixth sense for assholes, and yet I keep on picking them.

My television is off-limits right now. If I switch it on, I know I'm going to see the advertisement for baseball's new 'power couple.' If people find out it was all a sham, it won't reflect well on the brand, and my name will be mud, not to mention the fact that my family will be horrified.

The contract we signed includes some appearances. Together. I don't want to be in a room with Anders. Not yet. I don't trust myself not to believe his bullshit. This was a bad idea from the start, and all because I needed a stupid date for my parents' vow renewal. My life has gone up in smoke, and all I can do is watch it burn.

I drag my heels getting ready. Anders and I are supposed to be the happy couple at Yankee Stadium today, and nothing could be further from the truth. I've made sure I'm the picture of femininity for this event—no backward ball cap and team jersey. I want him to know what he threw away, and if nothing else, I know his attraction to me wasn't fake. A guy can lie about a lot of things, but a dick doesn't lie, so I'm going to make sure and send him home with a bad case of blue balls tonight.

With my hair and makeup done, I just can't bring myself to wear the heels that go well with my dress. I just about broke my ankle walking from the bedroom to the living room, and I won't make a fool of myself in front of him. I may not want to be a tomboy today, but I can still rock a great pair of Chucks.

I stare at myself in the mirror for a minute, reminding myself that I'm not the kind of woman whose self-worth comes from a guy. I'm a strong, confident, and successful woman in my own right. I've made a few bad decisions over the past few months, but they don't define me, and I certainly don't need to be one-half of a 'power couple' to be fierce.

After a much-needed one-woman pep talk, I jump in my car and head for the Stadium. It's not until I pull up next to Anders' Corvette in the parking lot that I begin to doubt my resolve. Thankfully, he's not in it, but my timing could still have been better. Linc steps out of an Escalade and spies me straight away. He's another smooth talker who needs to give me a wide berth today. I pretend to be looking for something in my purse, but as soon as I look up, he's striding toward my car, and I resign myself to an unwanted encounter.

He opens the door for me. "I guess I lost a bet. I didn't think you were going to show today."

"Bully for you. I'm glad I can still be a source of amusement for you and your dick of a best friend." I slam the car door shut and quickly make my way to the entrance, but he doesn't take the hint.

"Why are you so sure *your* best friend isn't the one in the wrong here?"

"Because she has no reason to lie."

"And we all know people don't lie without good reason, right, Brooke? After all, it was your willingness to lie that started this whole shitshow in the first place."

"Fuck off, Linc. I'm here because I signed a contract. It's business and truly no pleasure. We're not going to flog the dead horse that was my fake relationship with Anders. It's bad enough as it is without picking over the carcass for sport."

"Woe is you. You found a guy who isn't perfect but damn near close, and he had the audacity to fall in love with you. It must be so hard being you. He's right. You're a spoiled little rich girl who has no idea what he's had to do and sacrifice to get to this point in his career. I'm sure you can wipe those crocodile tears with the millions of dollars he secured for you with this endorsement."

"He used me to get this endorsement!"

"You used him to placate your parents. And if you think for a second that this endorsement was about him, you're sorely mistaken. He's already made more money than he could ever spend. Heck, he's worth more than the next generation of little Verbecks in the future could spend. This was all for you, and you don't deserve to shine that man's shoes. You're ungrateful, completely wrong, and totally oblivious to the truth."

"And what's that?" My hands are shaking as I struggle to keep any kind of composure.

"He's in love with you. Stupid, Bugs Bunny, eyes-popping-out-his-head-love hearts-coming-out-his-ears, in love with you."

"Then why was he trying to hook up with Lacey the night we broke up. Doesn't seem like the kind of thing a guy in love would do."

"Is that what she told you?"

I don't have time for this shit. I'm sick of going over and over this. As I'm about to tell him as much, Anders appears at the entrance, and my heart slams into my chest, coming to a grinding halt. He looks as handsome as ever, his hair styled to messy perfection, and dressed to the nines for this photo shoot. Anders does something to a suit that shouldn't be legal. I want to mount him and slap him in the face. I can feel both lust and hate for the man, but the second the other 'L' word comes to mind, I snuff it out before it can take root.

"What's the hold-up? I have places to be. I'm not hanging around all day waiting." He glares at Linc. "Why are you here, Linc? I told you I'd meet you at the batting cages."

"I came to talk some sense into her." He gestures in my direction. "You're miserable. She's miserable."

I cut him off before he says anything else. "I'm just fine, thank you very much." I can't even look Anders in the eye as I end this conversation by brushing past him and into the stadium.

"Great." The scent of his cologne hanging in the air is almost more than I can bear.

"You're both idiots." Linc has no filter. Ever.

"Can you just shut the fuck up? I don't need a chaperone or a relationship guru, so please, for the love of God, leave it alone, and I'll meet you at the cage."

"Fine. You two deserve each other," he mutters as he leaves. "Stubborn. Bullheaded. Idiots. I swear to God, love is wasted on the wrong people."

Anders hangs back, making sure to avoid catching up to me. That would involve some kind of conversing, and let's face it, at this point, we have nothing to say to each other. I'm worried that they're going to make me pose with a Louisville Slugger, and I'm going to use it to bludgeon Anders. I don't know why I assumed they would do the shoot in my current outfit. As soon as the stylist sees me, she looks me up and down, then ushers me to the locker room. I'm grateful to have a minute away from Anders and his delicious cologne.

"They want you to be more casual for the first set of shots. I'm thinking your signature style will work really well."

"What's my signature style?" It's news to me that I have a style. I just wear what's comfortable ninety-nine percent of the time.

"Sort of a tomboy. I have some cute denim shorts, and you're wearing the perfect shoes for this outfit. A cute tee and a Yankees ball cap."

"Shouldn't I be wearing my own team's cap? Not Anders?" It's a little sexist, don't you think?"

"You've been snapped in pictures wearing his jersey. How is this different?"

"Because it is." I can't even tell this random woman that I'd rather shove a needle in my eye than have Anders see me in his team cap.

"Lovers' tiff?"

"Something like that." She tries to seem aloof, but I can tell she wants to probe me for more information. Unfortunately for her, I'm in a foul mood. "I just need you to make me look hot. He's out there in a suit looking edible. Can you do a girl a solid and make sure his jaw drops when he sees me?"

"That I can do. I suspect you'd have that effect on him even if you were wearing a trash bag."

"Can I ask, why is he in a suit, but I'm in booty shorts?"

"The country is captivated by the classic good looks and alpha male vibe of Anders and the fact that he fell for a tomboy. I mean it in a good way. He's the epitome of masculinity, and people naturally assume someone like him would go for a super feminine... bimbo."

"So, I'm not feminine?" This day is getting worse by the minute.

"You are, but you're also a strong athlete in your own right. You're not standing in his shadow, riding his coattails. If I put you in some ballgown to get photographed with him, it won't do you justice. Trust me. I've styled so many sports stars and their girlfriends. You don't want the cookie-cutter shot. This will be more, *I am woman, hear me roar.* I want everyone's eyes on you. Let's spin it on its head. He's going to be the arm candy."

Suddenly, I like this woman a whole lot more. "I like the sound of that."

"Whatever spat you have going on, he'll be begging forgiveness by the time we're done shooting today. I'll make sure of it."

"I wish it were that easy." When she's done pulling me apart and putting me back together, I'm pleasantly surprised when I look in the mirror. This isn't just your average look—although on the surface it is—I'm the sexiest version of a tomboy. It's incredible what the right hair and makeup can do. A lot of effort goes into looking effortlessly beautiful. I know it's an oxymoron, but at this moment, I'm thrilled. Anders can suck my beautiful tomboy ass.

"Okay, here's your final accessory." She hands me a baseball bat, but not just any old kind. It's the one I always choose. Brand-fire new, just out the wrapper. There's nothing better than the new bat smell.

"Awesome. This is my exact make and model."

"Of course, it is. Mr. Verbeck was very specific."

"When did he do that?"

"Two days ago." I'm surprised that he gives a rat's ass about the details, but I'd be lying if I said it didn't make my stomach flutter. *Fuck.*

I sling the bat over my shoulder and head back out onto the field. Anders is standing on the pitcher's mound with a photographer and their entourage telling him where to stand and how to position every muscle in his body. If there's one thing he doesn't need coaching on, it's sex appeal. Holy mother of God. If I had man junk, I think it would be twitching right now, standing at attention for the man before me. Thankfully, I don't, and I'm just stuck with an overwhelming urge to quell the ache and desire pooling between my thighs.

"Wow." It's satisfying to see the wind knocked right out of Anders as his eyes devour me. In my mind, I'm saying, *all this could've been yours… asshole.*

"Stop looking at me like that." My words come out clipped and dripping with venom.

"Brooke, can we talk?"

"No." He's about to reply when I'm saved by the bell—the photographer's assistant.

"If you stand right here." She moves me closer to Anders. "Hold the bat like you're ready to swing. Now back up a little, so you're brushing up against him."

"Is that really necessary?"

"You're the new hot couple. People want to see the chemistry... subtle but oozing sex appeal. You guys have it in spades. Just be yourselves, and it'll shine through on camera."

The irony of the situation isn't lost on me. When she's happy that we're where we need to be, she moves back, leaving us just out of earshot.

"Is it so terrible to be close to me?" His voice is deep and throaty. It takes every ounce of strength to ignore him.

The photographer starts snapping, shouting directions for micro-movements that only serve to make this more difficult. The smell of Anders' cologne is intoxicating, and when they direct him to rest his hands on my waist, I can feel his body react. My breath quickens, but I fight my traitorous desires.

"Tell me you feel nothing for me, Brooke. Tell me you don't want me the way I desperately crave you." My pulse is pounding in my ears.

"I... I don't want you, Anders."

He leans in, his lips brushing against my neck. "Now, say it like you mean it."

"Amazing! Anders, stay there." The photographer gets so excited, moving closer, capturing my torture from every angle. "Brooke, I want you to wrap your free arm up around his neck and look straight into the camera. Show me that raw desire."

I do as he asks, snaking my arm around Anders' neck, gripping a fistful of his hair, and I'm so turned on I can barely breathe.

"This is perfect. Anders, I want you to kiss her neck but look into the lens. Brooke, keep your eyes on the camera. You're giving me exquisite bedroom eyes right now. It's beautiful." I hate this photographer. I want to grab the damn camera and slugger it outfield.

The sensation of his lips on my neck is more than I can take, and when he lets out a low, sexy groan, I snap. I drop the bat, whip around, and slap him in the face. "Stop it. Stop pretending you want me. It's fake. You're fake. I'm fake. We're one big fat fake couple."

There's a collective gasp from everyone on the field, and the photographer's jaw drops. At this moment, I'm really glad I'm wearing Chucks because I take off at a run and head for the tunnel. I can't stand it another minute. I hate my traitorous body. I hate Anders. And I hate that I don't hate him even one little bit when his lips are on my skin.

I can hear him chasing after me, but I don't stop. "Brooke, wait. Just talk to me. Will you just hold up for one minute? Hear me out."

"No!"

He closes the distance between us, stepping in front of me to block my way. "Stop. I love you. Why won't you let me love you?"

"Don't say that to me ever again. It's bullshit, and you know it."

He presses me against the wall, bracing his hands on either side of me. "It's not bullshit. I'm in love with you. Why is that so hard for you to believe?"

"Because if you loved me, you wouldn't have lied about my best friend. You wouldn't have tried to hook up with her. Who does that?"

"I never tried to hook up with her. I told you the truth, but you don't want to hear it. You don't trust me. Yes, this started out as something fake, but I'd never use you, and especially not for some stupid endorsement."

"A stupid four-million-dollar endorsement."

"Why are you so hell-bent on making this about money? We were friends. You and me… we mean something to each other." His mouth is a whisker away from mine, and I can barely contain myself as I watch his tongue dart out to wet his lips.

"Yes. Dollar signs. That's what this means."

"You're afraid to love me, Brooke. I get it. We played the part for your folks' wedding, but you and I both know that we were already dancing around the truth. We have chemistry."

"Chemistry isn't love, Anders. Neither is great sex. It's lust. Nothing more, nothing less."

"If that's the case, then prove it. If we're nothing but a culmination of raging hormones, kiss me. Show me I mean nothing to you."

He pins me with his gaze, biting down on his bottom lip as his eyes set my body on fire, blazing a trail to my mouth.

Damn him!

My lips crash down on his as my emotions wage war inside me. I love him against my will, and yet every fiber of my being wants to feel his hard length inside me, claiming me as his own. Truly. Honestly. And without ulterior motives. He presses his body to mine, deepening our kiss before running his hands up my sides and sliding into my hair.

"Fuck, Brooke, I've missed the taste of you. Come home with me."

His words are like an ice bath to my libido. What the hell am I doing? No matter how much I want Anders, nothing has changed.

"*No!*" I push hard against his chest, forcing some much-needed distance between us.

"Brooke…" When he takes a step back toward me, I recoil.

"No means no, Anders."

"What the fuck? You think I don't know that? So now I'm the villain in your story, is that it? You've gone from being my girlfriend to hating my guts and believing I'm capable of doing anything against your will? Fuck me." He starts pacing in front of me, running his hands through his hair.

"I was never your girlfriend. That's the point!"

"You're frustrating as fuck sometimes, Brooke. For a smart woman, you can be dumb as a box of rocks when it comes to us."

"Insulting me isn't going to make things any better. I just want all of this to be over. We need to get through the ad campaign requirements so we can move on and out of each other's lives."

"I don't want to move on, Brooke. Don't you get it?"

Before I get a chance to answer, the photographer's assistant shouts down the tunnel. "We need you back on set, please. We still have a lot to get through."

"Okay." The trembling in my voice betrays me. "I'm coming." I take a deep breath and put one foot in front of the other.

My pulse is racing in my ears, and as I walk past Anders. He reaches out his hand to brush over mine. "Brooke…"

"Don't. Please, don't." I force myself to keep moving with my eyes cast down and my soul destroyed.

When my stylist appears at the side of the photographer's assistant, her eyes go wide as saucers. "What the heck? You ruined my masterpiece. Couldn't keep your hands to yourselves for an hour?"

"What?" I'm still dazed from our kiss, the taste of Anders fresh on my lips.

"Your makeup. There's lipstick smudged all over your chin. Were you literally trying to devour each other? And your hair looks like a bird's nest. Where did your ball cap go?"

It must have fallen off in the moments that I found myself lost to Anders' touch. I smooth my hair, remembering how he slid his hands into it, holding me in place as he ravished my mouth.

"I'm going to need to fix you before you shoot anything else. You look a hot mess right now, Brooke."

Anders walks up behind me, putting my ball cap on—backward—just the way I like it. "Don't listen to her, Lexington. You look… breathtaking." He runs his thumb over his bottom lip, wiping the remnants of my lipstick from his mouth before shoving his hands in his pockets and striding ahead, back to the field.

My heart aches.

"He's a keeper."

"Sometimes we don't get to keep what we hold most dear."

Chapter Eighteen

ANDERS

TODAY HAS BEEN UNBEARABLE. The photographer tortured us for hours with staged kisses and sultry caresses. Kissing Brooke in the tunnel only made it harder. She's still affected by me. She can't hide that, but she won't give me the time of day to explain what happened, and I can only assume Lacey has been filling her in on a whole bunch of fake shit about me.

I hoped that Linc might be able to talk some sense into her considering they hooked up a few times, but she's ghosting him and filling my girlfriend's—ex-girlfriend's—head with nonsense. I've gone from being desperate to explain myself to being annoyed that she's treating me this way. She knows I'm in love with her, even if she doesn't want to admit it to herself for some reason.

By the time we finish the shoot, I don't even want to look at Brooke. It's too painful.

I grab my wallet and keys from the locker room and head straight to my car. It's easier to assume she wasn't going to hear me out and leave with a shred of dignity. No woman is worth groveling to, especially when I wasn't in the wrong.

Linc text me to change our plans. He wants me to meet him for drinks at Viper tonight instead of going to the batting cages. I'm not exactly the best company and forget about being a useful wingman but drinking sounds better than baseball right now. I shoot him a quick text to let him know I'm on my way.

By the time I get there, I'm ready to turn around and head home. I can still smell the faint scent of Brooke's perfume on my shirt, and I hate that it makes me ache for her. When I spy Linc at the bar, I'm beyond pissed to see him standing, talking to none other than Lacey. Why the fuck would he bring me here for this?

I turn on my heels, but the second he spies me, he comes striding over with his over-confident swagger, and I'm ready to knock him the fuck out.

"Bro, what are you doing? You can't leave."

"Are you shitting me? Why would you bring that bitch with you? I'm not getting within five feet of her."

"Do you trust me?"

"Fuck no! You're thinking with your dick, and she's psycho."

"Au contraire, fuckwad. I'm thinking with my big brain tonight." He slaps something into the palm of my hand, and the second I take a look, I'm confused.

"You're messed up, bro. What the hell do I want with this?"

"Do you see that little mark in the corner? Look closely."

"Fine. So what? A bad decision on a drunken night. What does this have to do with me?"

He nods toward the bar. "I've seen this somewhere. Recently. What are the odds that two people made the same bad call?"

"Shut the fuck up! Are you serious?"

"As a heart attack. I have a plan to fix this. Can you just trust me and go with the flow?"

"I don't think it matters at this point. I just came from the shoot, and I'm done. Brooke wouldn't listen to me for ten seconds. She kissed me, and when I asked her to leave with me, she flipped out. I'm past caring."

"She kissed you?"

"Yeah, but we're not in high school. I'm a grown man who wants a life and a family with her. I guess that's past tense now. *Wanted.*"

"Ugh. You've become one of those limp-dick guys we hate."

"I fucking know that, Linc. You don't have to rub it in."

"If tonight doesn't go as planned, then I'll wave the white flag myself, declare defeat, and help you drown your sorrows in as much pussy as you can handle."

"That's what I love about you, man, you're such a romantic wordsmith."

He throws his head back and laughs. "I'm the one out here trying to salvage your relationship."

"Why is that? You weren't happy that I offered to be her fake boyfriend, then you weren't happy when I thought I became her real boyfriend. Now, she thinks I'm a manwhore who tried to bed her best friend and use her for an endorsement. This is when you choose to get behind it."

"What can I say? It turns out I have a soft spot for your eternal, undying love."

"Fuck off."

"Just remember that when I tell you to roll with it. Let's go."

Lacey's eyes are locked on me, or should I say, my cock. It's creepy and makes me feel dirty as hell. I take a seat and am flabbergasted when she gives me a bright, butter-wouldn't-melt smile.

"Hello, stranger. Can I buy you a drink?"

I'm about to give her a piece of my mind when Linc nudges me in the back. "Sure. Whiskey on ice."

She flags the bartender and barks her order. I'm not surprised she treats everyone like the dirt on her shoe. "So, how have you been?"

"Not that great. You already know that, though, don't you?" She bats her eyelids—actually bats them at me before resting her hand on my thigh.

"You can't stay mad at me, not when I'm more than willing to take you into the back office and suck you off. I know the night manager, so we can have a little privacy."

"Roll with it," Linc whispers in my ear. I turn to face him with fury etched in every line of my face.

"You've got to be kidding me. I'm not letting her anywhere near my junk. She'll bite the damn thing off, and that's before you consider the fact that she's a total skank, and I wouldn't piss on her if she were on fire."

"Trust me, bro. I've got you." He slaps me on the back to send me on my way.

"Come on, slugger. Let me turn that frown upside down."

"Don't call me that."

"Aww, you're still holding out hope for Brooke. Is she the only person who's allowed to call you slugger? You know she's already getting over you. She slept with a guy the other night. Some random we met at a bar. She's always been a firm believer in the philosophy, *the best way to get over someone is to get under someone else.*"

There are so many things I want to say right now. I've never wanted to physically hurt a woman until I met Lacey. "And you want to be that someone else for me?"

"Yes."

"Fine. You win. Let's go to the back office. May as well have your lips wrapped around my cock."

She takes my hand, eager to lead me down the rabbit hole. If I wasn't furious before, I am now.

"I'm going to make you feel so good, Verbeck. You won't even remember her name when I'm done."

"I've got to ask, why aren't *you* thinking about her right now? She's your best friend. You sabotaged her happiness."

"I love Brooke, but she's not the woman for you. I did her a favor, and when it comes down to it, I want you. I wanted you long before she caught your eye."

"You'd never even met me."

"Doesn't mean anything. I knew we'd be great together."

Jesus Christ, this woman has lost her ever-loving mind. Just her holding my hand as she guides me through the crowd makes me want to vomit. My phone buzzes in my pocket, so I pull it out and take a quick glance. It's Linc.

Linc: *When you get in there, you need to ask her, point-blank, about what happened at the wedding.*

He's up to something, and he better pull it off. If he thinks I'm going to try and catch her out with my pants down, he's an idiot.

When we reach the back office, I'm wondering how I'm supposed to stop Lacey from diving right into my boxers.

"I've been dreaming about this for so long."

Linc: *Look up. Top left corner.*

I scan the room, and when my eyes clock what he's talking about, I make a mental note to buy him a great bottle of whiskey for this.

"How long have you been fantasizing about giving me head?" She reaches for my belt, but I take a step back. "Not so quick, Lacey. Anticipation is half the fun. Besides, I want to know how long you've been desperate for my cock."

"The first time I saw you in a Yankees uniform, I knew you'd be amazing in the sack. Then Brooke told me you'd met and were hanging out."

"And you saw me first. That must have grated on you."

"She didn't appreciate you the way I do, so I knew I had to do something."

"Is that why you lied about me? I thought you hated me." She's stalking me with her gaze, following my every move.

"Just the opposite."

"Then why not just tell me?"

"I tried to when I asked you to get freaky with me at the wedding. You shot me down, so I had to fudge the truth a little. It's for the best in the long run."

"So you don't regret lying to your best friend?"

"No. Brooke always gets whatever she wants. She's a rich kid who doesn't understand hard work, but I don't want to talk about her anymore. I have better things to do with my mouth right now."

She takes a step toward me, and although it pains me, I let her get close enough that I can whisper in her ear. "I'd rather fuck a herpes-ridden whore before I let you suck me off. You. Psychotic. Bitch."

I enjoy a deep satisfaction as her face twists and distorts with sheer disbelief.

"I'm going to tell Brooke you…"

I gesture to the top corner. "You'll tell her nothing. Smile for the camera, Lacey. I'll be sure to get a copy of this for Brooke. Then, she'll know exactly what kind of friend you are… a deceitful, two-faced, vapid narcissist."

She's frantic with rage. "She won't believe you."

I reach into my pocket and grab the same photo Linc was waving at me months ago in the locker room. The vajazzled pussy with a distinctive Super Mario tattoo just above her hip. Dropping it in her lap, I turn and head for the door. "That's not the only copy, just in case you were thinking of spinning a new line of bullshit."

"I hate you, Anders Verbeck! I'll make you sorry you ever met me."

"That happened the moment you put yourself before your so-called best friend. She may not give me the time of day, but at least she'll kick you to the curb. Who needs enemies when you have a bunny boiler for a friend?"

"My friend is the manager. He won't give you the footage."

"Sorry to tell you, *my* friend is the owner, and he's sending the footage to Brooke as we speak. Go to hell, Lacey. I'm sure they're waiting on you down there."

I stride out the door with a lackluster sense of relief. I can't undo the damage to my relationship with Brooke, but I can make sure she doesn't continue to have a toxic best friend in her life. I just wish I'd managed it before we were too far gone to repair what Lacey broke.

Linc is waiting for me at the bar with a shit-eating grin on his face.

"Did I deliver or what?"

"Thanks, bro, but I have to know, how the hell you had that photo? I distinctly remember throwing it in the trash with the other fan mail."

"I may have fished it out along with a bunch of others that day after you left."

"Why the fuck would you do that?"

"I was going to make you a Christmas wreath of stalker pics and hang it on your locker."

"Your mind is a truly disturbing place, Linc."

"Come on, you would've found it funny if Lacey hadn't turned out to be a psycho." He's not wrong. We pull pranks on each other all the time, and that would definitely have made me laugh.

Carter is sitting next to him with a more somber look on his face. "Hey, man. Linc has already sent the video to Brooke. I hope it'll help. He wasn't kidding when he said that girl is two cards short of a full deck."

"I appreciate all you did tonight. At least my name and my conscience are clear, and with that, I'm going to head home."

"Are you kidding?" Linc interjects. "We need to celebrate. Ding dong, the witch is gone."

"Maybe another night. It doesn't feel like much of a victory right now. I still lost the only woman I could see a future with."

"When she sees the video, she'll come running back. All is forgiven. Take the win, bro."

"She may forgive me, but I don't forgive her. We're done, and no amount of backtracking will fix it. I'll call you tomorrow. Tonight… I'm out."

Lacey comes barreling out into the bar, but Carter gives the nod to his security guards who quickly usher her toward the exit before she reaches us. She's shouting and hollering like a crazy person, and although I don't want to, I reach into my pocket and grab my phone.

Me: *Whatever you do, if Lacey turns up on your doorstep tonight, don't answer the door. She's dangerous.*

Before I get the chance to watch for the elusive typing dots, or the lack thereof, I shut off my phone and hail a cab. I'm not in the right headspace for anything more. All I want to do is get home and go to sleep. Maybe this will all seem better in the morning. I doubt it, but for a few hours, I can dream.

TODAY IS THE LAST ENDORSEMENT EVENT WITH BROOKE. IT'S BEEN A few weeks since Lacey was exposed as a liar, and it stings because

Brooke hasn't contacted me to apologize or even acknowledge what happened. I'd be lying if I didn't say I'm disappointed. I'm good at putting on a front and telling myself I wouldn't have taken her back if she'd just said sorry. The truth is, if she'd come running back into my arms that night, I'd have forgiven her. Instead, I'm here, dreading seeing her, and I haven't been able to get her out of my mind.

I haven't gotten laid since the last time Brooke and I were together. It's not for the want of willing women. Linc has been coaxing me out every other night, throwing women at me who were eager to bed a World Series champion. My dick didn't get the memo that Brooke and I split up. I can't bring myself to move on with a one-night stand. Something that would've felt so natural just a few months ago, feels wrong—like I'd be cheating on her.

When we arrive at the set of *Good Morning America*, I don't even see Brooke before walking out to greet the hosts on live television. She walks out from the right side of the set, and I know everyone is expecting me to pull her into my arms and greet her with the loving kiss of a boyfriend.

My breath catches at the sight of her. She looks stunning, as she always does. With a forced smile, she presses her lips to mine as if it's the most natural thing in the world. From the outside looking in, I'm sure it seems effortless.

I wrap my arms around her, deepening our kiss for just a fraction of a second, letting myself savor the taste of her. "Brooke."

The live audience claps, breaking the spell. The host gestures for us to take a seat on an oversized sofa.

"Welcome, you guys. We're so thrilled to have you on the show. You two have been lighting up the baseball world, on and off the field this season."

"It's great to be here with you. It's definitely been a season of firsts for me."

I've been on this show before, so they naturally direct their questions to me. "How does it feel to be a World Series champion?"

"Pretty damn good. Obviously, my… I mean *our* personal lives have been at the forefront over the past few months. It's a little over-whelming at times, but we're making it work."

Brooke rests her hand on my thigh, but I can feel how tense she is, so I drape my hand over her shoulder to try and alleviate her discomfort. Unfortunately, I think it has the opposite effect. The moment the host turns her attention to Brooke, her body stiffens, and she looks like a deer caught in the headlights.

"Brooke, how has it been for you? You're a baseball star in your own right, smashing every record in the women's game this year."

"I'm happy to raise the profile of women's baseball. I think a lot of the time we're overlooked for our achievements."

"You make a good point. Do you feel your relationship with Anders helps that cause, or does it bring its own challenges?"

I'm wondering where she's going with this line of question.

"Every relationship comes with challenges. The real question is whether or not those stumbling blocks are too great to overcome. Personally, I think Anders is worth it. What we have is real and beautiful, and he never lets me stand in his shadow. Even before we met, he was an advocate for women in baseball. It's one of the reasons I love him."

My heart stutters to a halt. Did she just admit she loves me? Is she faking it? She squeezes my thigh, and when my eyes meet hers, all I see is genuine contrition.

"Funny you should say that, Brooke. We received an anonymous call before we came on the air today, and this unnamed source claims that you and Anders were never a couple. They said that this relationship is a sham and that you've duped the industry for the very endorsement you're here to promote. Care to comment?"

Brooke's nails dig into my leg as the color drains from her face. I wait for her to say something—anything—but the words don't come. I'd bet my career on who the 'anonymous' caller is, and I'll be damned if I let her win.

"Wow. Isn't it crazy the length some people will go to rain on someone else's parade? I can tell you categorically that I'm in love with her. What's not to love? I'd have to be an idiot to settle for a fake relationship with a woman like Brooke."

"So, you deny the allegation?" Her tone rubs me the wrong way.

"I didn't realize we were here for the Spanish Inquisition today. I've told you how I feel, and what you choose to do with that information is completely up to you, but if you don't want to take me at my word, so be it. Brooke and I can leave right now. If a person doesn't trust me and the things I say, I have no reason to stick around."

I can tell someone in the control booth is screaming down her earpiece by the way her shoulders are twitching. I calmly lean in, kissing Brooke on the cheek. "Breathe. I've got you."

"We're going to go to a quick break, be sure to stay tuned for more from our favorite baseball power couple."

The second they cut to break, the host starts scrambling to backtrack.

I take Brooke by the hand, and it's completely out of character for her to stay silent. She's shaking, and it tugs at my heartstrings, but I quash the feeling as quickly as it comes. "Don't say anything to anyone. Any questions that come at you, you say 'no comment,' okay?"

"It was Lacey."

"Yes."

Everyone on set is begging us not to leave, but it's my only line of defense at this point. There's no way Brooke would get through another segment of scrutiny. "Please, Mr. Verbeck, she was out of line, but any interviewer would've asked the question."

"Bullshit. If you all had a shred of dignity between you, you would've brought the claim to our attention instead of blindsiding us with it on national television. This is a fluff show. People tune in with their morning coffee in hand. Good luck, and don't reach out to my agent about any future interviews. I'll be sure to give any exclusives to your competitors."

Without another word, I head for the door. The place is swarming with people, but I manage to navigate through the crowd and get us to my car. Brooke hasn't said a word, and as I usher her into the car, she looks at me with tears in her eyes, and it's like a gut punch.

All I need to do is get her home, and hopefully, all of this will blow over. I'm annoyed at myself. I should've anticipated Lacey would do something like this. She's the kind of woman who wants to drag everybody down with her. As we pull out of the parking lot, Brooke can't even look at me.

"I'm sorry, Anders. I never meant for any of this to happen. I thought I knew Lacey, but you were right about her."

"It's water under the bridge now."

"Maybe we can..." I know what she's about to say, and it takes every ounce of restraint for me to stop her. I grip the steering wheel until my knuckles are white.

"Don't. Our social obligations for the ad campaign are done. We're done. Let's just leave it at that."

"But you said you're in love with me. Back there, you told her you were being truthful."

"Yep, and before that, I told *you* I was in love with you and that I never tied it on with Lacey. I know Linc sent you the video footage, and I heard nothing from you. You couldn't trust me, and now I can't trust you."

We spend the rest of the drive in uncomfortable silence, and when I pull up outside her building, I realize that this is probably the last time I'll see her. With no more endorsement events, there's no reason for us to be in each other's company. As she opens the door, she turns to me, forcing herself to look me in the eye.

"Goodbye, Anders."

"Goodbye, Brooke." And just like that, it's really over.

Chapter Nineteen

BROOKE

I'VE MADE SUCH a mess of things. For a brief moment, I thought I had it all—the career, boyfriend, and a best friend who was Thelma to my Louise. It turns out I'm the family bunny being boiled in the pot by Glenn Close.

Lacey has been blowing up my phone, begging for forgiveness, but I don't have it in me right now. Even if I find a way to forgive, I can't forget. Anders was right—when trust is lost, you can't click your fingers and take it back. I don't blame him for calling time on our relationship. If it were the other way around, I don't know that I'd stay with him if I couldn't trust him one hundred percent.

Whenever my phone buzzes, I'm hoping it's Anders, but I find myself disappointed every time. This weekend, I'm going to visit my folks in the Hamptons. Bumming around my house week after week isn't good for me. I know my mom will grill me on the rumors about Anders and me, but I could use some of her wisdom at this point. After all, she and my dad have had a long and happy marriage. I know it hasn't always been easy, but they face their challenges together as a team.

The drive seems longer today. Every hour since I stepped out of Anders' car for the last time feels like an eternity. It's been weeks, but I can't shake the ache in the pit of my stomach at the thought of Anders. Yankee Stadium is ruined for me now, and as I pull into the driveway of my parents' house, the memories of our weekend together flood my senses. He rocked my world and left me wanting so much more.

Even at my age, there's a comfort that comes with being at my folks' house—the familiar sights and sounds and the glorious hum of their domesticated bliss. I find my mom baking in the kitchen, and my dad is perched on a barstool at the kitchen island, watching her—entranced even after all these years.

"Hey. Something smells good." My mom smiles brightly, wiping her hands on her apron so she can welcome me with open arms.

"I'm making your favorite, snickerdoodles."

"They're Diana's favorite," I say with a chuckle. "Oatmeal raisin is my favorite."

"Damn. It was a fifty-fifty shot, and I always pick the wrong one. You'd think I'd remember it after all these years."

I grab a hot snickerdoodle fresh from the oven. "I like these too. You can make me oatmeal raisin tomorrow," I jibe.

"I'm making them now. After a breakup, you need your favorite cookie. It won't take me long."

"Mom, it's fine. I just want to hang with you and Dad for a few days. Your epic baking skills are just an added bonus."

She grabs my face with her hands, inspecting my expression. "How are you, darling? I don't want any bullshit."

"Mom!" She never cusses. It's very disconcerting.

"What? I want the truth, not your brave face."

"I'm fine. I messed up, and it cost me my relationship with Anders. There's nothing I can do about it now except learn from my mistakes."

"Sit. Eat." My mom ushers me to take a seat while she pours me a glass of prosecco.

My dad wraps his arm around me, the familiar scent of his cologne a comforting throwback to when I was little, and I snuggled on his lap when I was afraid or sad. At this moment, I'm both. Sad that I lost the man I love and afraid he was my one chance at true happiness.

"He'll come around, baby girl. That boy loves you."

"I don't think he's going to forgive me. Lacey lied to me, and when he asked me to give him the benefit of the doubt, I didn't give him an inch. How could I have been so wrong about Lacey? I feel like I can't trust my own judgment now. I was completely duped by her."

My mom hands me a fuller than usual glass of prosecco. "She had us all fooled, it wasn't just you. You can't keep beating yourself about something you can't control. It's in the past now, and all you can do is move forward."

My dad stands and kisses me on the top of my head like he used to when I was a kid. "I'll leave you ladies to chat. If you need me, I'll be in my office pretending I'm working. This, too, shall pass, sweetheart. I know it doesn't feel like it right now, but life has a way of knowing what we need and when we need it."

"Thanks, Dad."

The second he's gone, my mom pushes the plate of cookies in my direction before coming to sit next to me with a generous glass of pinot. "Start from the beginning. I don't know what's true and what's not. You're going to have to fill me in."

"You're just going to be disappointed in me. I know I am."

"None of that. You're not a girl who feels sorry for herself. It doesn't matter what you did or didn't do, you're my daughter, and I love you more than life itself."

"I didn't want to let you down. You were desperate for me to have a date for the vow renewal, and I wanted to make sure you had the perfect day. You and Dad deserve it."

"Oh, Brooke, I only pushed you on that because I want you to have someone to share your life with. It wasn't about my happiness, and I'm sorry for making you feel like you needed to please me and make yourself miserable in the process."

"If it's any consolation, I didn't hire a gigolo. So that's something."

"Whatever floats your boat. I hear they really know how to satisfy a woman."

"*Mom!* Where the hell do you hear stuff like that?"

"Some of my bridge club friends are widows, and while they aren't spring chickens anymore, they still enjoy a healthy orgasm with a hot young man now and again."

"Jesus, when I think you can't mentally scar me any further, you pull an old-age gigolo out of your bag of disturbing tricks."

"I'm trying to make you feel better. And to be correct, the gigolos aren't old. My friends are old."

"Well, can we just make me feel better without discussing your friends' sex lives?"

"Okay, so tell me about yours. Where does Anders factor into all of this? Were you actually dating? He seemed genuinely smitten, as did you."

"I met him in a club. Lacey likes to go to the VIP lounges around Manhattan that are known as celebrity hangouts. I didn't realize at the time that she was hoping to meet Anders. Apparently, she's obsessed with him."

"So, she introduced you?"

"No. She had gone home, and I stayed behind with the girls from my team. I had too much to drink, and when he came into the bar, he sat down next to me, and I puked all over him."

"Oh, Brooky." I hate to see the pity in her eyes, but I push on, walking her through the events that led to the wedding, and what I thought was my fake boyfriend was becoming my real boyfriend. When I tell her the things Lacey claimed and how I didn't even entertain Anders' version of events, she looks positively murderous.

"You're disappointed."

"No, I'm pissed off. Not at you. At Lacey. You've been nothing but nice to her, and this is how she repays you."

"Yeah, but I should've at least heard Anders out. That blame falls squarely on my shoulders."

"I can't argue with you there. I'm going to give you my words of wisdom, but I need to ask you one simple question first."

"What?"

"Do you love him?"

"Yes."

"Have you told him?"

"I told him in the *Good Morning America* interview."

"Brooke Lexington, I want to shake you right now. No wonder he won't speak to you, he has no idea you're in love with him."

"He knows, Mom."

"He thinks you did it to save face on camera. I'd bet the house on it."

"I tried to speak to him after the interview when he drove me home, but he didn't want to talk to me. We said goodbye, and he hasn't contacted me since. He doesn't care anymore."

My mom rolls her eyes before dropping her head in her hands with exaggerated dismay.

"What am I going to do with you?"

"Buy me ten cats so I can begin my journey on the path to being an eternal spinster."

"I'm going to spoil you this weekend with all the wine you can drink and cookies you can eat. We'll watch some movies, and you can talk baseball with your dad long after midnight. Then, on Monday, you're going to go and get your man back."

"Mom…"

"Don't even think about saying he doesn't love you or doesn't want you. Otherwise, I'll slap you silly."

"I can't force him to talk to me."

"Of course, you can. You're a beautiful, intelligent woman, and he's in love with you."

"Then why hasn't he called me?"

"Because you fucked up. I apologize for the cussing and being so blunt, but sometimes you need tough love. He's mad at you, yes, but that doesn't mean he'll stay mad forever. You were in the wrong, and you need to be the one to extend the olive branch."

"And if he tells me to take a long walk off a short plank?"

"Then you keep showing him how you feel. If, after all that, he still doesn't want to talk to you, then you respect his wishes and move on. The way I see it, you have nothing to lose and everything to gain. At least you'll leave everything on the field. Swing for the fences like you always do. Don't give up before strike three."

"God, Mom, could you shoehorn in any more baseball puns?"

"I'm trying to speak your language. Apparently, I didn't teach you to speak boyfriend, so this is the best I can do. And whenever I try to talk to you about the physical side of intimacy, you shoot me down while covering your ears and singing at the top of your lungs. Honestly, you should be happy that you have parents who love each other and still enjoy the pleasures of the flesh after so many decades together."

"Jesus Christ, you didn't just say that."

"I did and tough luck. You need to hear this because as much as it may gross you out, your dad and I are a shining example of what a loving, caring relationship can be. It takes a lot of work and understanding, but we choose to put in the effort every day."

She's right.

"I know, Mom. I want someone to love me and look at me the way Dad looks at you."

"You have it. A man can mask or fake many things, but true love isn't one of them. The day your dad and I renewed our vows, Anders couldn't take his eyes off you. You were the only person in the room for him, and that, my dear daughter, is the type of man I've always wanted for you. Someone who could keep up with your spitfire personality and love you without being intimidated by your success. Don't let him pass you by."

"I'll try."

"What did we always say when you were in little league?"

"Don't try. Do. Thanks, Mom."

"And if you ever compromise your happiness in an attempt to make me happy again, I'll wring your neck. Got it?"

"You're not an easy woman to say no to."

"Your dad says that all the time." She pours me another glass of wine and lifts her own in toast. "Here's to being fierce and saving your prince charming from his stubborn pride."

We clink glasses, and a small kernel of hope blossoms in my chest. "Wish me luck."

"You don't need luck, Brooky. You have a beautiful heart and a lot of love to give."

"Thanks."

"And you also have a killer rack. It runs in the family, a gift passed down from generation to generation in our DNA. Sometimes you've got to use your assets."

"That was a rousing speech, and then you ruined it talking about my tits and the tits of my foremothers. It's just weird, Mom. Are you ever going to stop sharing wildly inappropriate tidbits about your sex life?"

"Don't you mean *tit*bits?" She throws her head back, laughing so loud my dad reappears to see what all the noise is about.

"Do I want to know why your mother is doing her dirty little minx laugh?"

"Really? Dirty little minx? Do you two have no boundaries? I'm your child."

He stands behind my mom, leaning down to kiss her, and she reciprocates with way too much enthusiasm.

"I was telling her that the women in our family are blessed with amazing breasts. She got all bent out of shape about it."

"Sorry, Brooke, but your mom does have awesome breasts."

"I just threw up in my mouth."

They're both so amused by my horror, but as much as I protest, I envy them. If Anders would give me a second chance, I'd love him every day for the rest of my life. We'd have little league babies, and when they're old enough, we'd embarrass them with how insanely in love we are.

Maybe, just maybe, there's hope for us. One thing's for sure, I'm going to give it my best shot.

I FEEL RE-ENERGIZED AS I DRIVE BACK TO MANHATTAN AFTER A weekend in the Hamptons. My mom and dad were their usual inappropriate selves, and my sister Diana came up today for dinner. We had some laughs, and for some reason, she seemed overly interested in what I know about Linc.

I told her to steer clear of him. He's a well-known player, and I lost count of the number of women I saw him leave bars with when Anders and I were together. A small part of me would pay to see my sister chew him up and spit him out. She's not known for being a lovey-dovey kind of girl. She beats the crap out of other women in a metal cage for a living, she doesn't have a softer side. From the look on her face, she may well have ridden that train already. I hope not.

Pulling into my parking garage, I'm glad to be home, but my mind can't rest. I've been playing a million conversations with Anders in my head. Every single one ends with him slamming his door in my face, but I've got to try.

When I get to my floor and the elevator doors open, my heart sinks, and my shoulders sag. I don't have the energy or the inclination to speak with the monster sitting on the floor, leaning against my door.

"I don't want to talk. I have nothing to say to you, Lacey."

"Come on, Brooke, we're best friends. Hoes before bros. We don't let guys get in the way of our friendship."

"You've lost your damn mind if you think we're still friends."

"Anders is out the picture, now, so we can go back to the way it was." The smile I once found comforting is unrecognizable, disconcerting, and downright weird at this point.

"No, Lacey. We can never go back. You lied to me. You lied about Anders. You tried to seduce him, and I'll bet you were the anonymous source who called *Good Morning America*. Tell me I'm wrong."

"I wanted him first. I wrote him letters. And then you met him five minutes after I left the club. It was supposed to be me. None of this would've happened if I'd been sitting where you were that night."

"Did it ever occur to you that even if you were with me when he came in, he might have still chosen me? Is it that hard to believe?"

"Yes."

"Fuck you, Lacey. He picked me, and I wanted him. I'm in love with him, and because of you, I'll never know if he and I could've made a go of it."

"Woe is you. It's about time you don't get everything you want."

"I thought you knew me and that I knew you, but neither of those assumptions are true. Now, move away from my door, so I can go in and slam it in your face."

"Sure, discard me the same way you did Anders. I'll rest easy knowing that if I can't have him, neither can you." She scrambles to her feet, and it takes every ounce of restraint not to break her nose with a right jab. I may be a baseball player, but I grew up with Diana as a sister. I learned to go toe-to-toe with a cage fighter. One pathetic, deluded ex-friend is nothing.

"Goodbye, Lacey. Don't let the door hit you on the way out. And just so you know, I'll be telling the doorman that you're banned from the building. Try to come up here again, and I'll get a restraining order."

Her face twists with disgust.

"Of course, the pretty princess can be safely locked away in her ivory tower."

"And you had no issues reaping the rewards of being friends with me."

"But somehow, you think a judge would give you a restraining order against me. What would you say? My friend told a white lie. They'll throw you out of court."

"This princess knows that money talks, and I have video footage of you and your psycho bunny-boiler behavior at Viper. You didn't plan on me seeing that, and if you fuck with me or go anywhere near Anders again, I'll post the damn video to every social media platform, and don't forget the tabloids. They'd lap it up."

"You wouldn't."

"Try me, fatal attraction. Now fuck off and don't ever call, text, or show up here ever again."

I unlock my door and go inside with my head held high before enjoying the righteous indignation of slamming the door in her face. That felt so good.

I listen for a while until I know Lacey is gone. I definitely need to warn the staff in the lobby. I don't want her to be able to get back up here. The locks will need to be changed because I'm sure I gave her a key at some point when we had conflicting schedules.

When Lacey and I met, we bonded over breakups. I'd just split up with my high school boyfriend and had arrived at college feeling discarded. Looking back now, he was right to end things. Our respective colleges were thousands of miles apart and trying to keep a long-distance relationship is hard at the best of times, but when you're eighteen and just at the start of it all, it's impossible.

Lacey was my roommate, and she and I were in the same boat. At the end of summer, she said goodbye to her high school sweet-heart—the school's star pitcher—and arrived on campus with a heavy heart.

I should've seen this coming. She had a few unhealthy obsessions with college jocks, but I didn't think much of it. At the time, they seemed like unrelated incidents—always choosing the bad guy. Now, as I sit behind my front door, listening to make sure she doesn't come back, I realize they weren't the bad guys, it was her. So many things make sense, and yet I'm more confused than ever.

There isn't a glass of wine big enough to forget my worries tonight. Worries isn't the right name for it, more like regret. If I could go back, I'd see all the red flags, and when Anders came to me, I would've believed him or at least heard him out before ruining what we had.

I can't change what happened, but maybe I still have time to win Anders back. How? I don't know.

Chapter Twenty

ANDERS

"YOU NEED TO GET LAID, Beck. I can't take any more of you moping around like a lovestruck fool. I have five women I can speed dial right now who would be more than happy to turn your frown upside down. I'm sure at least two of the five would be down for a threesome."

"I'll never indulge in a devil's threesome with you, Linc. I just don't feel that way about you."

"Now you have a smile on your face. You wish you could be there when I rock a woman's world, but I hate to tell you, I'm out of your league."

"Dream on, pretty boy. If I ever ask for a number from your speed dial, I'm going to need you to put me out of my misery and kill me. The thought of dipping my stick where you've dipped yours makes me want to vomit."

He has that sly grin that tells me something I wish I didn't ever have to know. "Remember Clare?"

"No. Before or after?"

"Before. You seemed to like her, so I didn't want to ruin it."

"And yet you're clearly loving this right now. God, I need some

Borax to scrub my dick. Why the fuck would you tell me? Is my current level of misery not enough for you?"

"Sorry, bro. My point is, you need to get laid. You can't just lock your cock away over this chick."

"She's not just a *chick*. I'm in love with her even though I don't want to be."

"Then, what the fuck are you doing? When have you ever shied away from a fight? If you want her, and you let her slip through your fingers, then you deserve to be alone."

"You're right, I'm an idiot." I grab my phone, keys, and wallet from my locker before slamming it shut.

"It's not often, but it does happen. What am I right about?"

"Brooding isn't doing me any good. I'm going to get my girl back."

Without another word, I take off at a jog through the stadium and out to my car. Why the fuck have I been sitting back all this time letting Brooke get away? When the engine roars to life, it dawns on me, I have no idea where she is right now. *Fuck!*

I figure she has to go home sometime, so I'm going to head to her apartment. I can wait. God knows I've waited long enough already. I just hope I'm not too late. In my head, I'd speed through the city streets, running red lights to get to Brooke, but the reality of driving through Manhattan is achingly magnified right now. I'm sitting gridlocked, having moved a grand total of two blocks in the past twenty minutes. I could've walked there quicker.

That's the answer.

I kill the engine and abandon my Corvette. Drivers start honking their horns, shouting obscenities at me, but I don't give a shit. There's a hotel a block up, so I take off at a sprint. When I see a valet, I take care of the car situation.

"I'll give you a thousand dollars if you park my car."

"You're not in a car, sir." Maybe I shouldn't trust this nimrod with my baby.

"Wonder Woman loaned me her invisible jet."

"I…"

"Here." I throw him the keys. "Corvette. Black. A thousand dollars." I don't waste any more time waiting for him to get with the program. I usually love the anonymity that the bustling streets of Manhattan can afford someone like me. All you need is a ball cap and shades, neither of which I have right now. Instead, I'm weaving in and out of the crowd, drawing way too much attention, but now is not the time to walk or even jog.

An entourage seems to be forming in my wake, and I can hear people shouting my name, but I don't have time to slow down. Every fiber of my being is propelling me forward.

"Ver-beck, Ver-beck, Ver-beck!"

"Can I get your autograph?"

"Is it true that you're a male escort?" What? That's a new one. *Fuck it.* Usually, I'd stop and answer questions, even the ridiculous ones, but today they can think what they like. Good or bad, there's only one person whose opinion matters to me.

"For Brooke Lexington, I'll be whatever she wants me to be… male gigolo, boyfriend, escort, colleague, or husband," I shout more for myself rather than the throng of people now invested at this moment, trailing behind me.

I push myself, trying to outrun them, but apparently, I have the Olympic track team chasing me down. Either that, or I'm in piss-poor shape, and I know that's not the case. When Brooke's building comes into view, a wave of relief washes over me. I quickly duck inside, yelling at the doorman to lock it down.

"I'm here for Brooke. You've got to stop anyone from coming in." I race for the elevator button but hitting it four million times won't make it come any faster. "Stairs?"

"Left." The doorman hollers as he locks the lobby doors. I really hope a resident doesn't need in anytime soon. By the time I reach Brooke's floor, I'm pumped and ready to win her back. Rapping my knuckles on the door, I wait impatiently, listening for any sign that she's going to let me in.

"Brooke! It's Anders, please open the door. I need to talk to you." I pause for a minute but get no reply. "I'm going to wait here until you let me in." When she still doesn't answer, I settle in for the long haul. "I live in your hallway now."

A door opens, but it's not Brooke's. The old lady next door peeks her head out with a sympathetic smile. "You're that Yankees boy."

"Yes, ma'am. My name is Anders." I push myself off the wall and hold out my hand. "Nice to meet you."

"I'm Doris, but you can call me Dory."

"Thank you, Dory. I don't suppose you know if Brooke is home right now?"

"I heard her leave this morning, but I haven't heard her door since then. It could be my old lady hearing. I need to change out the batteries in my hearing aids."

"You're a spring chicken, Dory. None of this old lady nonsense." She cracks a smile.

"I can see why she likes you. You're very charming."

"Can I let you in on a little secret, Dory? She doesn't like me right now."

"Take it from an old lady who's courted many a suitor in her day, that girl loves you."

"You think?" Why am I pinning my hopes on an elderly woman who doesn't know me from Adam?

"The walls are thin, and if I need to listen to any more of those sad love songs, I'm going to have to switch my hearing aids off."

"We can't have that. I'll be sure to try and win her back. Only happy music from now on."

She looks at me, searching my eyes for—something.

"You're a good man, I can tell. It's all in the eyes. There's a reason people call them the window to the soul. Stay the course, Anders. She'll come around."

"I will. I'm just going to sit here and wait for her."

"Do you want to come inside and wait?"

"No thanks, I want to make sure I don't miss her. Thank you for the offer, though. It's very kind of you."

"I'll bring you some coffee."

"Thanks, Dory."

I get comfortable on the floor, my back propped against Brooke's front door. Dory is true to her word, bringing me a large cup of coffee and some kind of pastry. It's delicious, and as minutes turn to hours, I close my eyes while I wait for Brooke to return. After my dash through the streets of Manhattan, this feels rather anticlimactic, but no one said the path of true love has to be all fireworks and grand gestures.

As it gets later, the coffee buzz wears off, but I'm not leaving until Brooke talks to me. After a while, my mind starts ticking over with a million different scenarios of why she's not home yet. She could've been in an accident, or she's out on a date. What if Lacey went full-on psycho and has her locked up in a basement?

I must nod off at some point because all kinds of strange dreams take over—in every one, I can't get to her. She's right there. I can see her, I can catch a hint of her perfume in the air, but she's just out of reach. I shout her name, but she doesn't look back, and no matter how hard I try, I can't touch her. God, I hope this is all just a bad dream because even in slumber, my heart aches for her.

―――――――――

Thud!

I'm jarred awake as I fall backward, my head hitting the floor as the door opens, and Brooke stands over me.

"What's with you people camping outside my door? What don't you understand? I don't want to see you, or talk to you, or have to shove you out the way to get in my apartment."

"Brooke, I know things have been weird between us, but…"

"I tried to apologize, Anders, but you wouldn't let me. I don't know what more you want from me. I was wrong. Lacey is cuckoo's nest crazy. I believed her without question. You didn't want to forgive me, and I moved on. This is me moving on, so kindly get the hell out of my doorway so I can slam the door in your face too."

"Brooke…"

"Go away, Anders. I don't want to talk to you." Now I'm just pissed.

I jump to my feet, making sure to position myself so as not to get a door right in the kisser. "Well, I want to talk, and you're going to listen. This has gone on long enough." I loom over her, loving the way her breath catches at my proximity.

"Don't kiss me, Anders, because if you do, I'll kiss you back, and you'll break my heart all over again."

"Even though it kills me, I won't kiss you without your consent, but I need you to listen and listen good."

"Okay." Her voice quivers, and it gives me a glimmer of hope.

"I've been in love with you since the moment we met. I knew when I lifted you into my arms that first night and lay you in your bed that you were going to wreck me."

"But you kept talking about us as only friends."

"No, that was you, Brooke. Somewhere along the line, you decided that the way we met meant we couldn't move forward in a relationship. I was waiting for you to realize that we became more than friends, more than a fake relationship, and a hell of a lot more than fuck buddies."

"I was the one who asked if we could be more. Get your facts straight."

"Yeah, but you never really believed it. You questioned it at every turn. I gave you no reason to think my feelings for you were disingenuous. I told you I love you. I don't go around saying that to women, Brooke. It wasn't easy for me, and you..."

"And then I ruined it by believing the understudy for *Fatal Attraction*, the reboot."

"Yeah, you did." She drops her gaze to the floor. "Look at me, Brooke."

"I can't. I'm ashamed of myself."

"Stop. Look at me and listen." She still can't lift her gaze all the way to mine. With my heart hammering in my chest, my pulse racing so hard I can barely hear over the cacophony of blood rushing through my veins, I gently coax her chin with my finger. Just this smallest touch sets every fiber of my being ablaze.

"Anders."

"I'm in love with you, Brooke. It's not fake, I didn't say it for an endorsement. I want you in every possible way… your friendship, your sexual desire, and most importantly, your love. I need you to love me back, and if you're not there yet, I can wait. I'm not a patient man, but when it comes to you, I'd wait a lifetime to bask in the glow of being a man worthy of your love."

She thrusts herself forward, her lips crashing down on mine, begging entrance which I freely give. Her taste is all-consuming, even more so than I remember. I've been craving her kiss for weeks, but now that I'm here, I'm greedy. I want it all.

"Door. Keys." It's all I can manage. I'm ready to rip her clothes off, and I'm not sure I can hold back the surge of desire coursing through me at this moment.

She quickly fumbles with the lock before dragging me inside. I kick the door shut behind us as we begin divesting each other of our clothes. I need to feel her skin on mine, warm and oh so inviting. There's no way we're making it to the bedroom. We kiss and stumble our way to the couch, and when the only fabric between us in the lace of her panties, I tear them off and sink inside her. A primal roar escapes me, and for the first time in my life, I feel complete.

"Anders." My name slips from her lips like velvet. "I love you." Those three little words I've been longing to hear. It's the sexiest thing I've ever heard.

"Say it again." I thrust in long, slow, measured movements, letting her feel every hard inch of me.

"I love you, Anders."

"Brooke…" My lips crash down on hers, my hands roaming her body, pulling her tight against me as I rock back and forth, her warmth surrounding me as I claim her pleasure as my own. "You're mine, Brooke."

Her breasts are full and heavy in my palm, her nipples tightening as she climbs toward her release. Every line and curve of her body is mesmerizing—glorious Technicolor, paling in comparison to the memory of her that tormented me over the past few weeks.

"God, Anders, I've missed you." Her words fade with every kiss, turning to moans of pleasure as I continue to drive into her, letting her take as much as she wants, and as I sink to the hilt, I can't hold back.

"I want to hear you, Brooke. The way you scream my name when you come has plagued my dreams for weeks."

She pulls me in for a kiss, her tongue darting out to meet mine in the same rhythm as our hips.

"I love you, Anders. I love you."

"Jesus, Brooke, I'm close. You have to stop. I need to slow it down."

"I love you. *Oh God!* Harder... faster... I'm..." She crashes over the edge, screaming my name, catapulting both of us into the stratosphere. I thrust harder, a sheen of sweat covering our skin as we ride our release. It's so intense, and I can't seem to catch my breath. Wave after wave of ecstasy washes over me, keeping me on that high, my release holding tight, unwilling to let me go.

Brooke spirals out of control over and over again, her walls contracting around my cock.

"*Fuck!*"

When I can't hold my weight above her any longer, I pull out, loving the way she gasps at the loss of my cock filling her, loving her. I slump onto the couch beside her, struggling to fill my lungs.

"Anders, that was..." She runs her hand down my chest. "Earth-shattering."

"I can't breathe."

"I know, right. Mind-blowing."

"No, I'm serious, and I can't breathe." I gasp. I'm having a head-rush or something.

"Shit. Please don't have a heart attack. I can't be the girl who kills you with sex."

"I'm not having a heart attack. I think all my blood rushed to my cock."

"I have very much missed your cock."

"It missed you, too," I say with a wry smile. Leaning over, I brush her hair off her face. "*I* missed you."

"I'm so sorry. If I'd just believed you in the first place, none of this would've happened."

"Let's not ruin the moment talking about *her*." I press a gentle kiss to her lips. "There's plenty of time to talk later. Right now, I'm taking you to bed. I'm nowhere close to being done watching you come. I've been dreaming about kissing every square inch of your body for weeks, imagining the moment I'd be able to nestle my face between your thighs again and make you come so hard you forget everything else."

"Talking's overrated."

"Glad you agree. I have much better things to do with my tongue."

I take a few minutes to let my breathing go back to normal, and then I scoop Brooke into my arms and head down the hallway to her bedroom. Having her close again and her naked flesh pressed to mine, all seems right in the world.

I'm true to my word, kissing and tracing every curve of her body for hours, listening to her come again and again. She rides me like a prize bull, and it's not until we collapse, exhausted, that I notice Brooke's voice is hoarse.

I throw my arm up over my eyes and laugh. "Shit."

"What's wrong?"

"We just gave Dory an earful."

"Who?"

"Your neighbor. The walls are thin."

Her cheeks flush at the thought. "I'm sure they're thick enough to keep our dirty little secrets."

"Afraid not. How loud do you play your music?"

"Not too loud. Why?"

"Because your sweet old neighbor came out to talk to me while I was waiting on you to come home. She said you listened to a lot of sad love songs over the past few weeks."

"Shit. My volume is on a permanent five. I was at least an eight right now. My throat hurts from screaming so loud."

"I hate to tell you, but that wasn't an eight. You're a fifteen at your quietest."

"Oh God. I'm going to have to move. I'll never be able to look her in the eye again."

"She's a feisty old broad. I bet she was a minx back in the day."

"Are you crushing on my octogenarian neighbor?"

"Lexington! Just… no! But you better believe we'll still be going at it when we're that old. I'm always going to want you… wrinkles, gray hair, toothless, and senile."

"Why am I aging so badly? I brush my teeth after every meal, and I've never had a cavity. I floss. Also, I plan on dying my hair, and there's no way in hell I'm chopping it all off for one of those old lady hairdos. Maybe the wrinkles because I'm terrified that Botox would freeze my face. And senile, really? That's a bleak picture you paint. Why don't we just go ahead and call it for the saggy tits that'll be coming my way. They'll look like a couple of oranges in tube socks, swinging low enough for me to tuck them in the waistband of my ludicrously high granny panties."

"I draw the line at tube sock breasts. I can deal with all the rest."

She shoves my arm. "Very funny."

"As always, you completely miss my point. I just told you I want to grow old and gray with you. Are you purposely ignoring that fact, or do you not realize how devastatingly overwhelming and all-consuming my love is for you?"

"I hurt you. I know that. I don't want to take anything for granted. I've been miserable without you. I shouldn't have doubted you, and now you don't trust me."

"I was angry and hurt, yes, but I never stopped loving you. Life without you just isn't enough for me. I'm here, in your bed, after camping outside your door. I forgive you for not letting me explain, and I hope you can forgive me for being too proud to come back before now."

"I love you, Anders Verbeck, and I always will."

"I'm going to need some more convincing."

"And what do you have in mind?" she asks with a sly grin. "I have a few ideas."

"I'd like to hear yours."

"It involves the shower, soapy and still very pert breasts, and me on my knees with your cock in my mouth."

"Definitely better than my idea."

We spend the rest of the night making love in every room of her apartment—wet, dry, naked, half-dressed. I can't get enough of her, and I never will.

Chapter Twenty-One

BROOKE

I'M SO EXCITED TODAY. We're playing a charity game at Yankee Stadium, and that means I get to step up to the plate and stare down the barrel of my sexy boyfriend's pitching arm again. Anders and I are heavily involved in raising money for youth baseball for underprivileged kids. We were talking over drinks about a month ago, and we decided it would be fun to bring in the extremely talented women from my team and play with Anders and his buddies.

Tickets sold out within a few days, and if this game goes well, we're going to schedule another one for later in the year. This game was thrown together in a really short space of time, but it could become a regular thing, and that only means more money for the charities we support, and we get to have fun in the process. Plus, we can have time to plan next time around. Now that Anders and I are dating for real, we've had a couple of nights out with friends and teammates, and I'm almost certain some of my teammates have made sketchy decisions when met with the charms of the rock stars of Major League Baseball.

"Are you ready to get your ass handed to you, Lexington?" Linc has that look in his eye—mischief and seven ways of sexy. If it weren't for the fact that he's a total manwhore, and I'm deeply in love with his best friend, I'd shamelessly flirt with him.

"You wish, Nash. I'm taking you and your boy down today." I give Anders a sly wink as I say it, knowing he's going to lord it over me for years if I don't deliver.

"She talks a big game, but there's no way we'll lose. They really shouldn't have put Beck and me on the same team, it's unfair to the rest of you. The Nash-Beck combo is too electric."

"Did he just refer to you as the Nash-Beck combo?"

Anders rolls his eyes. "Yeah, he did. I can only apologize."

I slide my arms around his waist and plant a kiss on his lips. "You ready to be on the losing team?"

"It's cute that you think you can beat me, baby, but I'm afraid I can't let that happen. The guys would never let me live it down."

"You don't have a choice in the matter," Linc interjects. "There's no way you can beat us."

If I wasn't hellbent on showing him up today, I certainly am now.

"I'll be sure to tell my sister you don't think a woman can beat you. I'm not sure why having XY chromosomes seems inferior to you."

"I love the vagina monologues, and don't get me wrong, you're the best female baseball player I've ever seen, but when it comes down to the best male player versus the best female player, you can't hit as hard or pitch as fast."

"You're a colossal dick, Linc."

"And why would I care if you told your sister? What are you going to do, tell her to come beat me up?"

"Don't make out like you wouldn't try to mount her if I was dumb enough to introduce you."

"Can we focus on the task at hand? I don't mount random women anymore, not after your lunatic friend. I learned my lesson, although I could be tempted. Your sister is hot."

I punch him full force, giving him a dead arm. "Bad dog. No spreading your rabies to my sister. I mean it."

"You brought it up!"

"Let's do this." I'm fired up now. I'm going to be picturing Linc's face when I knock the ball out of the park.

Anders slips his hands into my hair, pulling me toward him, his lips a whisker away from mine. "Good luck, baby." He teases me with a kiss. "Just remember, whatever happens, we leave it on the field. Tonight's celebration will happen regardless of who wins."

"And how are we celebrating my impending victory?" My pulse quickens as he darts his tongue out to lick the seam of my lips.

"Naked. I plan to bury my face between your thighs. If you win, it's a treat for *you*. If I win, it's a treat for *me*."

"Teamwork makes the dream work."

"What? A sixty-nine? I'm down for that."

"Not what I meant, but sure." I press one last kiss to his lips before taking my place with the rest of my team, ready to run out onto the field.

The stadium is packed, and as we take in our surroundings, a rush of adrenaline courses through me. I'm determined to win today if only to wipe the smug grin off Linc's face. He bested me the last time we were on this field, and I don't want a repeat performance.

Anders steps up to a microphone. "Welcome to our first coed charity game here at Yankee Stadium." A collective roar echoes all around. "We appreciate you coming out and supporting such a worthy cause." Everyone applauds. "I'm not going to lie, folks, I am a little worried that my girlfriend is going to whoop my ass tonight." He looks at me with a beaming smile.

"You know it!"

"You all know my girlfriend, right? Brooke Lexington, greatest female batter of all time. Give her some love." Screams come from every seat, my name being chanted by thousands. It's one thing when a crowd cheers for you when you hit a home run, but being applauded because of who I'm dating makes me feel oddly shy.

He sees that I'm out of my comfort zone and leaves the microphone to come and give me a quick hug and a kiss that gets another roar. "Can you stop drawing attention to me right now? I feel weird."

"Why? You've been playing in front of crowds your whole career."

"I'm fine with that, and I'm going to do my best to show you up out here, but they're all cheering for your girlfriend, not Brooke Lexington, pro baseball player."

"Hang on." He runs back over to the microphone. "Hey, everyone. I need you all to repeat after me. Can you do that?"

"Yes!" Holy shit, these people are loud.

"Okay, here we go. *Anders Verbeck is Brooke Lexington's arm candy.* Yell it loud so I can hear you all the way in the back."

On cue, they shout at the top of their lungs. "Anders Verbeck is Brooke Lexington's arm candy!"

"Say it again, so this time she believes it." They chant it again and again until I'm laughing so hard my face hurts. "Good job. Look at that beautiful smile of hers. I'm one lucky SOB. Now, let's play ball!"

They're first up to bat, and as I take my place on the field, the rest of my team takes to their positions. I can hear Linc smack talking as he steps up to bat, but I can't help focusing in on Anders. I find him impossibly sexy when he's in uniform, and he knows it. Even from this distance, I know he's got that look in his eye—the promise of our celebration later tonight—dark and seductive.

I try to shake off the desire unfurling deep in my core, but Linc's first hit flies past me, snapping me back to the task at hand. My mixed bag of teammates—half my girls and a handful of Yankees —are shouting at me to get my head in the game.

Linc rounds two bases, and when he's safe, he yells in my direction. "Thanks, Brooke. Your lame mooning over Anders really helped me out."

"Just wait until you have to take the walk of shame back to the locker room after the game."

"Never going to happen."

"Bite me."

"You love me. Admit it."

"Nope."

"We're basically family now, so you have to love me."

"Okay. I like you fine. Now, can you shut up so I can win this thing?"

"You won't beat us."

"Watch me." From my lips to God's ears, I watch as a ball goes soaring into the air and Linc takes off running. This time, I don't take my eyes off the ball, adjusting my position and lifting my mitt. The sweet sound and feel of the baseball as I close my hand around it is glorious.

As the crowd goes wild, Linc glances over his shoulder and watches the biggest grin spread across my face. He starts cussing like a sailor, but one voice catches on the wind, my ears honing in on his dulcet tones. I can hear Anders, and it makes me laugh when I realize he's cheering for me, even though I'm on the opposing side. "That's my girl! Show them how it's done, baby!"

Anders jumping up and down is up on the Jumbotron, and there's a mix of laughter from the men in the crowd and a collective sigh from the women. He's getting so lucky when we get back to his place tonight.

By the time we get to the bottom of the ninth inning, the crowd is having the time of their lives shouting and supporting both teams. We're tied, and it all comes down to this last hit. If I strike out, we're toast. There's only one outcome where my team comes out victorious.

The bases are loaded.

The crowd goes silent.

Anders is focused on pitching.

Strike one.

I can do this. I can win.

Strike two.

Fuck. I don't want to lose this on a strikeout. It's been too good a game on both sides. This would be a lame way to end the night. There might be a little ego resting on this. I told them I came out here to win, and Anders was true to his word. He's pitching his very best to the men and women alike.

I take a moment to steady myself, swinging the bat a few times to loosen my arms. My whole body is tight right now, and as I look up into the eyes of the man I love, I know what he's going to do. He's going to give me a do-over.

That first time we stood out on this field, Anders beat me with a screwball. He's about to give me a chance to redeem myself. I just know it. So, it's time to put my money where my mouth is. I steady myself, blocking out everything and everyone around me, except for Anders and his throwing arm. I track the ball with every twitch of his muscles, readying myself as much as I can.

I've watched every YouTube video that shows his screwball. They're rare, but I think I can hit it today. The second the ball leaves his hand, time seems to slow down. I feel like I'm in the *Matrix* or something. I track the ball and adjust my bat to give myself the best chance of connecting. It doesn't need to be pretty, it just has to hit far enough for my teammate on third base to slide into home.

I don't hear a dead ball, and I'm stunned, frozen to the spot. The Jumbotron cuts to the stand where a fan caught the ball. *I just won the game!* I stand, staring up at the screen, my bat dragging on the ground beside me. All three of my teammates hit home plate and are shouting at me to take my victory lap.

It's not until Anders sweeps me up into his arms that I snap back to the roaring crowd. He runs the bases with me cradled against his chest. "That was fucking amazing."

"Oh my God. We're on the big screen." He jogs through the bases with such a huge, loving grin on his face.

"Let them look. I'm so fucking proud of you right now. I've never been so happy for a batter to hit one of my pitches. You're incredible, Brooke Lexington." The second we hit home plate, he plants a kiss on me—one of those mind-altering, soul-shattering kisses that makes me weak at the knees. If he weren't already carrying me, I'd need him to now.

"Be honest, did you go easy on me."

"Hand on heart, I gave you my very best. That was all you, baby. Listen to the crowd, that's for you, and it's well deserved."

The second he sets me down on my feet, I grab his face with my hands and kiss him so hard our teeth knock together. "I love you, Anders."

"I'm going to take my time with you tonight. Long, hard, and all night."

"Now, that's something to celebrate." I lose myself in his kiss until the rest of my team rushes us and hoists me up onto their shoulders, cheering and laughing as we all enjoy this moment.

More than the win, I'm thrilled to sit back and see what we accomplished today. Anders and I brought all of these people together for charity, and looking around, I feel so proud.

When I finally find my way back to Anders, I wrap my arms around his neck. "We should make this an annual thing. Look at all the good we've done. Isn't it amazing?"

"You're amazing." I melt into his kiss, forgetting everything around us. After the mayhem dies down, we find ourselves alone on the field, still wrapped in each other's arms.

"Wow, that was like a good old-fashioned make-out session. How long have we been out here?"

"No idea. Can we skip out on the afterparty? I want to take you home and start celebrating."

"You're the one who organized it. We have to go."

"Fine, but we're staying the minimum amount of time, and then I'm throwing you over my shoulder and taking you home. I want you all to myself."

"Maybe we can find a dark corner at the party."

"Do I have a little exhibitionist on my hands?"

"I still have some secrets up my sleeve. You'll have to wait and see."

"I bet you do, and I look forward to finding out all your little quirks and kinks over the years." He's so cute when he shows his softer side.

"Years? You plan on sticking around that long?"

"You don't?"

"I'm in it to win it, slugger."

"Good. I know you refuse to accept defeat. I guess you're stuck with me."

"I'm okay with that. You'll be a total silver fox when you're older."

"True. I'm pretty dashing."

"Ego much?"

"You said it. I'm just agreeing. And, if you'd let me finish that thought, I was going to say that young or old, I'm always going to be hot for you."

"Nice save."

"Okay, smooth-talker. We better get ready and head to Viper."

"Why the hell did I think we needed an afterparty?"

"Because you're a big softy." Anders booked out the whole VIP lounge at Viper for the night.

"You're privy to that secret. Don't let it get out. I don't want my hardcore image dashed."

"I hate to tell you, slugger, but everyone knows you're like a fluffy Labrador under those washboard abs and that chiseled jaw of yours."

"Hush your mouth, woman, I'm fierce like a lion or a bear. Something manly."

"Teddy bear."

"I'm going to show you just how animal I can be." He chases me toward the tunnel, laughing and roaring like a lion.

"You're such a cutie pie." I duck into the women's locker room and hear him giving me a last little growl before heading to his locker room. I don't know why it takes me by surprise, but my heart skips a beat, and butterflies take flight in the pit of my stomach. I fall more and more in love with him every day, and I don't think that will ever change.

***

"You made it." Linc clearly started drinking without us. "Finally. You two lovebirds are all anyone is talking about." He throws his arm over my shoulder.

"How many shots have you had, Linc?"

"Drowning my sorrows."

"I warned you I was going to beat you this time around."

"Yeah, and you didn't pay up last time, so don't be expecting congratulations tonight."

"Never. Winning is its own reward."

"I want to dislike you right now, but seriously, that last hit was fucking awesome. I don't think I could've hit that, and let's face it, that's high praise."

He makes me laugh, unable to give a compliment without complimenting himself in the process.

"It is high praise. Why don't you let me buy you a drink?"

"I'd settle for your sister's number."

"I'm going to use one of your favorite phrases right now, just so you understand. Never. Going. To. Happen."

"Fine. Then, I'll take a whiskey sour. You realize it's a free bar, though, right? Your boy here is covering the tab, so you're basically just asking the bartender for a drink on my behalf."

"It's the thought that counts." I follow Linc to the bar while every person who crosses Anders' path stops him to talk future events.

The music is blaring, so Linc leans in to speak to me. "I'm glad you guys sorted things out. He was unbearable without you."

"And I have you to thank. I should've said it sooner, and I apologize that you got tangled up with the whole Lacey situation."

"I manage to find the psycho girls all on my own. One more added to the list isn't a big deal. Just don't leave my boy again, or I'll be the one going psycho."

"You're a good friend. You didn't need to help expose Lacey. I messed up big time, and without your intervention, not only would I have lost the love of my life, I'd still be hanging out with a total nutbar."

"Yep, I'm basically a superhero. You're welcome."

"I'm not going to argue with you. You have an uncanny power to enlarge the size of your head."

"You're spicy, Brooke. I dig it." We order our drinks and one for Anders. When he finally makes his way through the crowd to join us at the bar, he raises his glass for a toast.

"Here's to my two favorite people. You helped make today possible, and I think we kicked ass."

"Cheers to that," Linc and I say in unison. Anders snakes his arm around my waist, and Linc is ready to make a sharp exit.

"Okay, amigos, I'm off to flirt shamelessly with Brooke's teammates and rock one or more of their worlds." He gives me a sly wink.

"Just this once, I'll give you a heads-up. The blonde and brunette slinging back margaritas at the end of the bar... they're into bed-sharing."

"You're quickly becoming one of my favorite people. I bid you adieu. I'm off to get laid."

The second Linc disappears, Anders sets his drink on the bar and slides his hands into my hair, his lips caressing mine in a tender kiss. "You're definitely my favorite person."

"The feeling's mutual."

"Do you realize where we're standing right now?"

"In a bar."

"Very funny. I'm not surprised that you don't remember, you were too busy puking on me. This is the exact spot we met."

"Oh my God. You're right. This is where I lost the contents of my stomach all over your designer shirt."

"You may have lost the contents of your stomach, but you stole my heart. I couldn't explain it, but now I see it clearly."

"What?"

"I knew that night you were going to change my life. I didn't know how or why, but your pukey little face just set my world on fire."

"I love you, Anders. Thanks for taking a chance on the grossest version of me, even if I don't remember most of it."

"Move in with me." The words tumble out my mouth before I have a chance to think it through. "I'm sorry, I don't know where that came from."

"No takebacks."

"I... is that a yes? I mean, we wouldn't live in my apartment, obviously. Yours is way nicer and bigger. Wait. If we live at your apartment, does that mean I just invited myself to move in with you? I don't know how this stuff works. Shit. I'm rambling again."

"You're cute when you ramble. It's a hell, yes, and I don't care where we live as long as you're there." He lifts me into his arms, spinning me around.

"Stop! I don't want to blow chunks on you tonight."

"I second that thought. This is my favorite shirt." His lips crash down on mine, and my stomach does somersaults, every lick and flick of his tongue making me weak at the knees. "Are we really going to do this?"

A self-assured calm settles over me, and I know without a shadow of a doubt that this is what I want—a life with Anders, and I can't wait for it to start. I found real and honest love in the unlikeliest of situations. My fake boyfriend turned out to be the love of my life. The relationship gods pitched us a screwball, and we most definitely knocked it out of the park.

"I'm game if you are."

"Batter up."

Epilogue

ANDERS

"TELL me this is the last of it." Brooke drags another box from her bedroom into the living room.

"Not quite."

"We're going to need a bigger apartment. It would seem fifteen thousand square feet won't be enough for your sneaker collection."

"I make no apologies for my love of Chucks. They just keep bringing out new ones." She gives me her puppy dog eyes—the ones I can't resist. "You wouldn't deny me the joy of opening a new shoebox and slipping on a fresh pair of sneaks, would you?"

"This is going to be our life together, isn't it? You make that face, and I melt, agreeing to anything you want."

"Yes, but remember how well that turned out the night you gave me carte blanche in the bedroom." She wiggles her eyebrows at me as she shoves another packing box in my direction.

"Damn, now I'm rocking a semi. Remind me again why we're not letting the movers take your shoe collection?"

"They're too precious. I like to keep what's near and dear to me close." I drop the box and pull her into my arms.

"I like the sound of that."

"You won't like it when I'm close enough to knee you in the nuts if you manhandle my sneaks."

"Do you want to share a bed with me at the new place, or are you going to sleep with your Chucks?"

"I haven't decided yet."

I slap her ass before kissing her hard. "Your shoes aren't going to give you a screaming orgasm."

"You underestimate their power, young padawan."

"Challenge accepted. Tonight, I'll be fucking you in our new bedroom, and you'll be wearing nothing but a pair of sneakers." I watch in awe as her stunning smile spreads across her face.

"Isn't the sexy thing to fuck in a pair of heels? The mental image you just conjured in my mind was far from sexy."

"Trust me, anything that involves you naked is a turn-on."

"Tell me more, roomie."

"There might also be food and me eating it off your body."

"Yummy."

"And then you'll be a mess, so we'll need to take a bath, and I'll make love to you, slow and sensual."

"That takes care of the kitchen and the bathroom. What about all the other rooms?"

"I'm sure we'll figure it out."

She throws her arms around my neck, pushing up onto her tiptoes. "Have I told you lately how much I love you, slugger?" Then, she plants a chaste kiss on my lips.

"Maybe once or twice."

"Get used to it because I'm going to be saying it every day until I get bored with you." She scrunches up her nose the way she always does when she's being playful.

"Here I thought I was getting a proposal or at least a profession of eternal love, and you give me *until I get bored with you*."

"Awe, poor baby. Your ego is just fine without me. I need you to be able to make it through the doorway with the last of my sneaks."

"I'm going to take these down to your car. Shove the last of them out to the living room, and I'll be back in a few minutes for them. You're going to have to ride on the roof rack because your shoes have taken over every inch of space in the car."

"Fine by me."

Today marks the beginning of a new chapter in our lives. We closed on our new place two days ago, and the movers have been working around the clock to get my stuff into our first home together. I make two more journeys before we're ready to close the door on her apartment and hand the keys over to the landlord.

This is the last of it from Brooke's apartment, and as she walks through the empty rooms, tears form in her eyes.

"Are you okay? Realization setting in that you're going to be living with me?" I jibe, hoping to lift her spirits.

"I have a lot of good memories here. I'm excited for you and me to have our first home together, but it's still sad to close this chapter."

"I know. I have fond memories of holding your hair back the first night we met. The sweet smell of vomit in the air, followed by a night of zero sleep on what can only be described as the most uncomfortable couch ever made."

She shoves me before wiping the tears from her eyes. "I love that couch."

"It can go in the guest room at the new place."

"I'm offended."

"It's still going in the guest room."

"Maybe I'll make *you* sleep in the guest room."

"Good luck with that. You'd miss me too much. You know you love me, Lexington, just admit it. You need me."

"Fine, I need you. Happy now?"

"Yes. Delirious actually. You're smiling rather than crying. That's always going to be my goal. I never want to make you cry, Brooke. Our home is going to be filled with laughter, love, and a lot of really dirty sex."

"What every *Disney* princess dreams of." She takes one last look around and slides her arms around my waist. "Take me home, Anders."

"Your wish is my command."

It's a short drive to our new place, and when we get to the front door, I lift Brooke into my arms.

"What are you doing? Put me down."

"It's customary to carry you over the threshold of a new home."

"No, it's not. That's for brides, like a hundred years ago."

"I'm trying to be chivalrous, woman. Can you just let me?"

"Fine." I fumble with the lock, realizing I should've opened it before I picked her up.

"Do you need help? Give me the key, and I'll do it."

"I've got it." A sudden pang of nerves courses through me as we walk over the threshold for the first time, stepping into our new life together. "Welcome home, Brooke."

"Welcome home, slugger."

I set up three boxes on our bed this morning—gifts for Brooke. "I have something to show you." I'm excited for her to see the modifications I had made to her closet. All the shoe space a girl could ever want. "Come with me." I take her by the hand and lead her to our room. Her face lights up when she sees the gifts.

"Are those for me? I didn't get you anything."

"I don't need anything. I have you, and I just wanted to mark the occasion. You need to open them from left to right. There's an order."

She gives me a puzzled gaze before picking up the first box and unwrapping it. Inside, there's a set of keys on a little baseball bat keychain. "Eek! My new house keys. Do you have a baseball keychain? We could be totally corny, and you can be the ball to my bat."

I reach into my pocket and pull out my keys. Sure enough, she called it. "It's cute, not corny."

She kisses me and ruffles my hair. "You're so stinking cute, Anders."

"Yeah, yeah. It seemed better in theory. Open the next one."

"I know the shape of this box."

"Clearly, from all the boxes I've been carting around today."

Tearing off the wrapping, she uncovers a Converse shoebox. "You know the way to my heart. Chuck Taylors!"

"Yeah, but before you open them, bring the box and follow me."
I grab the third box off the bed and usher her into her new closet.

"Holy crap!" She starts jumping up and down, giddy at the sight
of her custom shoe space." This is amazing. Where are you going to
put your stuff?" she jokes.

"I have my own closet. This is just for you."

"I was kidding. Are you serious?"

"Yes, and just as well. You have a ridiculous number of shoes,
baseball caps, and clothes."

"Can I open the sneaks now?"

"Yes." She's got the biggest grin on her face as she opens the box
and sets eyes on her new customized Converse—the Yankees
pinstripe with baseball tongues and the heel stripe is red with her
name in white.

"These are awesome. I want to put them on right now." I take
them out of her hand and drop to my knees. She quickly kicks off
her shoes and slides her foot into one and then the other.

"Open the last box while I tie your laces."

"I can tie them."

"Don't you like me on my knees? I'm at the perfect height for
you to ride my face."

"Tie them and do it quickly because I concur and agree that you
should be nestled between my thighs."

"Okay, Cinderella, your shoes are done."

She unwraps the third gift with giddy excitement, but it's not
until she opens the box that her expression sobers. Her eyes flit
between mine and the little velvet box in her hand.

"Shut up! Shut up!"

"I haven't said anything yet."

Tears well in her eyes. "This is fake, right?"

"It would be poetic, wouldn't it, but no, it's very real." I take the
box from her hand and pull out the ring that's been nestled safe and
sound inside for three weeks.

"Anders."

"Let me get through this." I clasp her hand, holding the
diamond ring at the tip of her ring finger. "Brooke, I've been in love

with you from day one. There hasn't been a moment of our time together that was fake for me. You make me feel the most *real* love I've ever experienced. I've been quoted saying that baseball is the love of my life, and that was true until you came into my life. I love you more than throwing the perfect screwball, and the fact that you know exactly what I mean only makes me love you more. Brooke, will you marry me?"

Tears stream down her face as I push the ring onto her finger. My heart is hammering in my chest, waiting for her to answer.

"I don't know about a screwball, I think you're a goofball."

"Yeah, but I'm your goofball if you'll have me. Are you going to leave me hanging?"

"Of course, my answer is yes!" She launches herself at me, knocking us both onto the floor. "You're about to hit a home run, slugger."

It's amazing how one split-second decision can change your life. I never imaged for one moment that a fake relationship would lead me to my happily ever after, and I, for one, can't wait to see where our journey takes us next. As long as Brooke is by my side, we can take whatever screwballs life throws our way and get through them... together... until death do us part.

THE END

PREORDER LINC'S BOOK, STRIKE ZONE Now
SIGN UP FOR EVA'S NEWSLETTER
FOLLOW ON AMAZON
REVIEW SCREWBALL
If you haven't read any of the other Hall of Fame titles, check them out today!
BUY ROMANTIC COMEDY *FUMBLE*
BUY ROMANTIC COMEDY *INTERCEPTION*
BUY *A VERY FUMBLING MERRY CHRISTMAS*

Social Media

www.instagram.com/evahainingauthor
www.facebook.com/evahainingauthor
www.twitter.com/evahaining
www.amazon.com/author/evahaining
www.bookbub.com/profile/eva-haining
https://www.goodreads.com/author/show/20271110.Eva_Haining
https://tiktok.com/@evahainingauthor
http://www.evahaining.com/newsletter
www.evahaining.com

Acknowledgments

As always, my first thanks has to go to the guy who makes it possible for me to pursue my dreams, my wonderful husband, Simon. Your support means everything to me. I feel so lucky to get to do life with you!

Ria, I appreciate you reading the roughest versions of my work and always finding the positives. It definitely makes the red pen easier to swallow. Your friendship and support are so near and dear to my heart. Thank you for believing in me.

Nicki, I know I keep making the same mistakes over and over again, but my brain is mush and I'm so thankful you understand the madness. You take my work and elevate it to the next level, and I appreciate your hard work. I can't wait to get started on the next book!

To everyone who works to help me get my books out there, and keep me sane in the process, I can't thank you enough. I hope that the finished product makes you proud.

To my readers I want to say a huge thank you. Without your support I wouldn't get to wake up every morning and do my dream job. I knew I wanted to fly on the pages of the written word, but you gave me wings.

Made in the USA
Coppell, TX
27 September 2024

37799235R00134